Sacrifice, Toil and Tears

China and the World in the Fight against the Pandemic

— A compilation of China Daily's commentaries on the novel coronavirus outbreak and its impacts

 China Intercontinental Press

Foreword

The winter may not have been severe and the mercury across China may not have dipped below alarming levels in late 2019 and early 2020. Yet the Chinese people were eagerly awaiting the warmth of spring. What they encountered instead was one of the worst "cold waves" in the form of the novel coronavirus outbreak.

The outbreak in Wuhan, capital of Hubei province, changed the festive mood of the city, the province and its people before the Spring Festival holiday. Dire and tragic reports of people losing their nearest and dearest emerged. But Wuhan residents, in true Chinese spirit, displayed exemplary courage and resilience in combating the disease.

Their heroic fight was ably, and gallantly, supported by the more than 40,000 medical personnel from across the country who began arriving in Wuhan on Jan 24, Lunar New Year Eve, to join the fight against the novel coronavirus epidemic, first identified in Wuhan and later named COVID-19 by the World Health Organization.

With the central authorities' swift and decisive response, China not only showed its determination to fight against the pandemic, but also coordinated its policies and decisions, and cooperated with the WHO and other countries to combat the common enemy threatening the whole of humankind. By making the courageous decision to lock down the whole province of Hubei, and mobilize natural resources to contain the epidemic, China once again demonstrated its commitment to protect its people.

The pandemic has taken a heavy toll on China's economy, as it has done on the global economy. Now that the epidemic has been largely controlled in China, Chinese governments at different levels have to strike a subtle balance between containing the outbreak and encouraging resumption of production. The central government has taken a series of measures aimed at supporting the small and medium-sized enterprises to overcome the impact of the health emergency and keep the job market stable.

Apart from challenges, the outbreak, however, has also created opportunities for the digital economy. For instance, online work and education have gained strength.

China has weathered many a storm, economically, socially and politically. And it has always emerged stronger from each crisis. This time, too, China's economy is exhibiting its resilience.

But despite China's huge sacrifices and painstaking efforts to fight the virus, many in the West have raised questions on China's governance, and stories of discrimination, even violence, against Chinese nationals and people of Chinese origin have been reported from many parts of the world. Though there is still no scientific evidence to prove the virus originated in Wuhan, some foreign politicians and media outlets have blamed China, using racist and other derogatory terms, for the global health crisis. Which has put Chinese, even other Asians, at risk.

By demonizing Wuhan's sacrifice, Hubei's suffering, and China's fight against the virus, some Western politicians and media outlets are doing a great disservice to global public health governance. Fortunately, across the globe many people, who can tell right from wrong and good from bad, have strongly opposed such racist anti-China campaign.

A virus respects no borders, favors no ethnic group and is loyal to no political dispensation.

This is a big test for the international community. And the worst of times brings out the best in the people. Many countries and their people have lent a hand to China in this time of distress.

China, on its part, has shared its experiences in dealing with the health emergency with the WHO and other governments since the beginning of the outbreak, in order to help them strengthen the global fight against the virus. And after largely containing the outbreak in the country, it has sent medical supplies and medical teams to many countries to help them contain the pandemic.

The world has to understand that we are in this together, and no one is safe until everyone is safe. The COVID-19 outbreak is a threat to not only global public health but also the global economy. Only with cooperation and coordination, rather than indulging in a blame game, can the world win the fight against the virus and overcome the global economic and social risks.

This book, Sacrifice, Toil and Tears, is a compilation of the commentaries published in China Daily and on its website since the outbreak. We hope they provide some food for thought, offer solutions to problems faced by the Chinese and global economies, and help promote global coordination and cooperation.

Winter always makes way for spring. And with better coordination, deeper cooperation and greater confidence, we can make sure this crisis will eventually make way for a brighter future.

Contents

I. Pains and Gains in China's Handling of the Outbreak   1

Hope for the best, prepare for the worst to control pandemic coronavirus   2

Pioneering efforts to contain virus outbreak   4

No sinister hand, but nation needs to be prepared for biochemical risks   8

Time to strengthen health governance   11

Institutional advantages instill confidence that fight against coronavirus will be won   14

Health and production both vital concerns of the people   17

Change in frontline commanders sign defense has turned to attack   19

Proposed delay of key meetings pragmatic move   22

Only a China solution can combat coronavirus   24

Preventive measures should never go too far   28

Clarity of communication   30

Decisive stage in fight against COVID-19   34

The world needs to follow China methods to combat epidemic   39

Fight against epidemic should be strategic   42

Prevention is always better than cure 45

Crisis won't disrupt China's renaissance 48

II. China's Economy Resilient 51

No reason for undue pessimism 52

Securing certainty amid uncertainties 56

Efforts needed for minimizing serious shock to production 60

Watchful eye on the middle-income trap 63

Rational estimation to the impact of coronavirus 67

The coronavirus will not debilitate China's economy 71

Virus' economic impact manageable 74

Orchestrated response required 78

Economic fight against epidemic must be won 82

Fundamental strengths 86

Outbreak to have limited impact on economy 89

More govt funds needed to fight epidemic 92

Fiscal support to weather the storm 95

Integrity as nexus must be maintained 99

Outbreak also offers opportunities 103

Online emergency help 106

China will emerge stronger after outbreak 110

No serious impact of virus on BRI projects 114

It's still too early to gauge broad economic impact 118

Joint efforts needed to reduce global economic shocks 121

III. Panorama of Emerging Social Phenomena — 125

TCM can help control spread of coronavirus	126
Standardizing TCM will help it go global	129
Wildlife trade ban will protect health	133
Better protecting wildlife good for all	135
The vulnerable need more support	139
Discarded masks must be properly disposed of	143
AI can make big difference in fighting virus	146
Working from home, distant dream for Chinese	149
Online classes can't replace classrooms	152
Therapy key to ease outbreak-induced stress	155
We-media shouldn't be a plague of false news	158
People's health knowledge requires a boost	161

IV. Anti-Prejudice Best Prescription for Joint Fight — 163

World must give China support against virus	164
Racist reports symptom of West's Sinophobia	167
Discrimination against Chinese a virus	170
Opportunistic racists find a golden opportunity within the outbreak	173
Racism behind coronavirus paranoia	176
Something's not right when they criticize China	179

Racist reports infect the truth with prejudice	184
A sincere letter to friends of China	186
"Yellow peril" virus more contagious and condemnable	188
Novel coronavirus outbreak puts fresh spotlight on media's racism	191
Bias undermines solidarity in virus fight	194
China should be praised not insulted	196
Epidemic exposes West's colonial mentality	199
Epidemical discrimination violates spirit of human rights	202
Coronavirus and world responsibility	205
Coronavirus not China's Chernobyl	208
Headlines in New York Times are misleading	211
This is not the time to play the blame game	215
Neither "Wuhan virus" nor "Los Angeles virus"	218

V. International Coordination Essential to Deal with Global Risks — 221

Global solidarity essential to defeat outbreak	222
Region shows solidarity in anti-virus fight	225
Sino-Mongolian true friendship endures amid outbreak	228
Show of solidarity	231
Russia supports China's fight against outbreak	235
Hardships more bearable with help of friends	238
Future of China-Japan ties lies in peaceful coexistence	241
Three neighbors must stand together	244

Our role in the coronavirus outbreak	248
Biosafety challenge calls for greater cooperation	251
Adversity reveals true friends	253
UAE stands resolutely with China during coronavirus challenge	257
Responsibility, support, confidence and tolerance	260
Victory will be won	264
United in solidarity	267
Two or three words about my China	270
Old friend stands firm	273
Peru is far away, but its friendship with China is close	277
Global cooperation more vital in fighting viruses	280
Strong public health response key to containing virus	284
Fight against virus will be uncertain without cooperation of China, US	288
China-US relations during coronavirus outbreak	291
Global cooperation vital to fight against COVID-19	294
Only coordinated response can control outbreak	297
Preventing global food security crisis	301
Outbreak to impact EU-US-China ties	306
We will get through the pandemic together	310
Policy action for a healthy global economy	313
Protect workers from economic pandemic	316
Afterword	319

Pains and Gains in China's Handling of the Outbreak

Sacrifice, Toil and Tears — China and the World in the Fight against the Pandemic

Hope for the best, prepare for the worst to control pandemic coronavirus

Li Min/China Daily

That the number of people infected with the new coronavirus nationwide rose to 440 on Wednesday from 291 the previous day speaks volumes about how serious the situation is. With the death toll having increased from six to nine, it is imperative that the country bring the epidemic under control.

No matter how transparent the daily reports of the central government department are about the number of cases, there will likely be those who have been infected but are yet to be identified. This makes it very probable that more people have been infected than are yet known.

And there is no knowing about whether the new virus will mutate during transmission, which will likely make it acuter and more infectious.

As a result, the country is facing a critical challenge to effectively bring the spread of the new virus under control.

It is therefore exigent that the National Health Commission and its local counterparts spare no efforts in mobilizing as many resources as possible to contain the spread of the virus. They should always err on the side of caution and not take any chances.

First of all, as it is clear that Wuhan, the capital city of Central China's Hubei province, is where there is the largest cluster of infected people, it is vital to strictly screen people traveling from the city to the rest of the country and elsewhere. Compulsory quarantine measures must be adopted to ensure those who have had close contact with those infected in the city and elsewhere spread the virus to as few people as possible. If necessary, travel from the city should be prohibited.

The travel rush for Spring Festival poses a serious threat to the efforts to control the spread of the virus. With hundreds of millions of people on the move, governments and departments at all levels must remain vigilant. Public transport must be disinfected at least on a daily basis, since this proved to be effective during the fight against the transmission of the coronavirus responsible for the outbreak of severe acute respiratory syndrome in 2003.

The screening of travelers for high-speed trains and airlines should also be strictly carried out. Those who have a fever should not be allowed to travel.

Those who travel should wear masks. The more people who wear masks, the less opportunities there are for the virus to be transmitted from one person to another. This also proved to be effective in the 2003 fight against SARS. If possible, masks should be provided to those travelers who do not have one.

Preventive measures work, which has been verified in the fight against SARS in 2003. While hoping for the best, we need to ensure we are making every effort to prevent the worst.

January 22, 2020

China Daily Editorial

Pioneering efforts to contain virus outbreak

By Dan Steinbock

Security personnel stand guard at the Dashilan commercial zone in Beijing on Feb 7, 2020.

Feng Yongbin / China Daily

After the outbreak of a new coronavirus in China and evidence of rapid human-to-human transmission, the central government has urged people to stay at home, restricted travel and cancelled major public events. These moves have led to a big fall in the number of trips during this Lunar New Year, but probably saved lives.

China also extended the Lunar New Year holiday by three days to keep people at home to help curb the transmission of the virus, and extend several billion dollars to help contain the virus.

Pains and Gains in China's Handling of the Outbreak

While the full effect of the outbreak on the Chinese economy is too early to assess, the probable impacts can be tentatively assessed.

Despite enhanced capabilities, there are new risks

Internationally, markets have responded to the virus outbreak with sharp but temporary reactions until the spread of the virus can be halted. Recently, analysts have been using the outbreak of the coronavirus responsible for the severe acute respiratory syndrome of 2002-03 as a guideline to these projections. But that's premature.

China's efforts to control SARS were criticized as the disease spread internationally before the outbreak was subdued. A decade later, China's response to the avian influenza (H7N9) outbreak was significantly faster, broadly praised and the disease did not spread widely.

In recent years, China has significantly strengthened its national and local systems to prevent and control diseases, and laboratory and hospital capacity have been significantly reinforced.

But the emergency management record is varied at the local level.

However, despite improved Chinese capabilities, and the Chinese authorities alerting outside bodies, including the World Health Organization, to the novel coronavirus relatively quickly, there are new risks, due to greater global integration.

In 2003, China's air, rail and road travel was only a fraction of what it is now and most Chinese lived in the countryside. Today, China has the world's largest logistical hubs and 60 percent of the population reside in densely populated cities. That's the reason the government has sought to insulate Wuhan, capital of Hubei province, where the virus were first detected, and other urban centers in its proximity, altogether 51 million people — which is comparable to the total population of South Korea.

The timing also differs. Unlike SARS, the current outbreak took place before the Chinese Lunar New Year, which is accompanied by the world's largest human migration. That's why the government took extraordinary measures to reduce the risk of accelerated spread, which may set a new norm for the struggle against epidemics in megacities.

Early human and economic costs

During the SARS outbreak, 8,100 people worldwide were infected, while 774 died, mainly in the Chinese mainland and the Hong Kong Special Administrative Region. It was determined a newly-infected person was likely to pass the SARS virus to about 2 to 5 people. With the new coronavirus, there are currently more than 9,000 confirmed cases in China, while more than 200 people died. According to early research, the number of people that a newly-infected person was likely to pass the virus to is between 2 to 3. Despite similar transmissibility, so far the mortality rate of the new coronavirus seems to be less fatal; one-fourth that of SARS but infection rates will increase through the escalation phase.

However, health authorities suggest that symptoms may not show during the two to 14-day incubation period for the new coronavirus, which would undermine traditional containment practices. That means that there may be worse economic damage to come as the Chinese authorities have suggested.

The current outbreak has already hit transportation, tourism and travel, restaurants and retail, which will impair near-term consumption data, while harming stocks most exposed to consumer markets. Globally, the damage was first felt in commodities, which react fast to outbreaks, until global health experts called for calm and reason.

What analysts are now monitoring is the milestone when the number of new infections begins to decelerate because that tends to signal the turning point for sentiment as well. But that may still be some way ahead.

Impact on economic growth

Before the outbreak, China was moving toward a mild recovery. Despite the trade war with the United States, GDP growth amounted to 6.1 percent in 2019. Given progressive deceleration, which is normal after intensive industrialization, China was expected to grow by 5.8 to 6.2 percent in 2020.

After the outbreak, three possible scenarios prevail. In the SARS-like impact scenario, a sharp quarterly effect — down to or below 5 percent — would be followed by a rebound in short order. The broader impact would be relatively low and regional.

In the accelerated impact scenario, the adverse impact would be significantly steeper in terms of growth, and a rebound would only follow later. The broader impact would prove more significant and affect global prospects.

In the disruptive impact scenario, the adverse impacts are harder to assess. The new strain occurred at the worst time, before the Spring Festival travel rush, and in the worst place, a huge regional transport hub, which was expected to record 7.8 percent growth in 2020.

Compounding the difficulty in assessing the economic impacts of the outbreak, coincidentally — or not, the timing of the two outbreaks has led some to suggest a sinister hand is at work — African swine fever, which appeared during the trade war with the US, decimated half of China's pigs, doubling pork prices.

For now, the central government is focused on containing the outbreak of the novel coronavirus. But over time, it is likely to further strengthen the national and local systems to monitor public health events, improve the emergency management in megacities, and make greater efforts to protect China against potential bio-threats that have destabilizing potential.

January 31, 2020

The author is the founder of Difference Group who has served at the India, China and America Institute (USA), Shanghai Institutes for International Studies (China) and the EU Center (Singapore).

No sinister hand, but nation needs to be prepared for biochemical risks

By Li Daguang

A truck sprays chemicals to disinfect a street in Jianghan district in Wuhan, Hubei province, on Feb 10, 2020.

Zhu Xingxin/China Daily

The novel coronavirus that emerged in Wuhan, capital of Hubei province, has caused nationwide alarm and prompted some people to claim it is a biochemical attack.

Although the source of the pathogen remains unclear; a seafood market where wild animals were butchered and sold is suspected. However, the possibility of another source earlier than the market cannot be ruled out. Yet that does not mean the virus outbreak is a biochemical attack on China.

Conspiracy theories always have a market during a crisis. But without any evidence to support them, they don't hold water.

But the fact that the possibility is being debated reflects people's growing awareness of modern biological warfare and fear of it. Any government, including Chinese government, should be alert to such risks and ready to counter any such attack. For this, it is necessary for people to have a basic understanding of biochemical warfare and epidemics.

Biochemical warfare is when biochemical toxins and germs are used as weapons to kill or incapacitate and cause panic. The United States, the United Kingdom and the former Union of Soviet Socialist Republics began research into biochemical weapons following Germany and Japan using biochemical weapons and programs during wartime.

Biochemical weapons have been severely condemned by the international community and gradually banned. For instance, the 1925 Geneva Protocol prohibits the use of chemical and biological weapons in war. The Biological Weapons Convention (BWC) was opened for signatures in 1972 and came into force in 1975 to ban the development, production and stockpiling of an entire category of weapons of mass destruction. Eight review conferences of the BWC were held until 2016 and the Ninth BWC Review Conference will be held in 2021.

However, the threat of biochemical warfare remains. Because biochemical weapons can cause mass casualties in a large area at a lower cost than conventional weapons, they have been taken as an approach for terrorism.

Because of their potential wide dissemination and impacts on public health and morale, as well as public stability, the high risk to national security of anthrax, botulism, plague, smallpox, tularemia, and viral hemorrhagic fevers such as Ebola and Lassa are listed Category A bioterrorism agents/diseases by the US Centers for Disease Control and Prevention. And people still lack effective measures to combat viruses such as Nipah, Zika, and the coronaviruses that caused severe acute respiratory syndrome and Middle East respiratory syndrome, and Ebola. Emerging infectious diseases such as Nipah virus are listed by the US CDC as Category C bioterrorism.

Therefore, improving the ability to prevent and cope with biochemical warfare is necessary for national security. Not only the government but the public should be alert to the risk of biological and chemical agents and diseases.

By establishing biological defense security in the new era, people can increase their awareness of precautions. Industries and fields that play a significant role in national security, national economy, people's livelihood and public health should be strictly managed. In addition, more importance should be attached to biotechnology to enhance the scientific and technological reserves of national defense and the capacity for coping with biological warfare.

The novel coronavirus has brought back the memory of the panic and hard fight against SARS in 2002-03. Great attention is being paid to the new coronavirus and the cure for it, raising groundless doubts of a biochemical attack will neither help control nor reduce the public panic of the epidemic.

The Central Committee of the Communist Party of China and the State Council, China's Cabinet, have paid close attention to the coronavirus outbreak, launching a nationwide deployment and mobilization for disease control, virus research and supply security. With strong determination and concrete efforts, China will win the fight against the new virus again.

And the debate that has been sparked by the public health incident has highlighted the importance of being vigilant against any biochemical risks.

February 3, 2020

The author is a researcher at the National Defense University of the People's Liberation Army.

Time to strengthen health governance

By Lai Xianjin

Shi Yu/China Daily

The sudden outbreak of the novel coronavirus ahead of this year's Spring Festival holiday has turned into a nationwide epidemic that poses severe challenges to China's public health and epidemic prevention management system. The Communist Party of China Central Committee and the State Council, China's Cabinet, are paying the greatest attention to the epidemic prevention and control work, and a joint battle against the virus has been launched by the Party committees and governments at various levels.

One of the advantages of China's national governance system is its ability to concentrate efforts and resources as needed, which is not only manifest in major projects and significant events, but also in coping with national emergencies. China's successful governance and social management during the severe acute respiratory syndrome (SARS) outbreak in 2002-03 and the Wenchuan earthquake in 2008 demonstrated its ability to effectively deal with significant emergencies. Based on its national governance system advantages, China is confident in and capable of winning the battle against the novel coronavirus.

To this end, China has established a unified, high-level leadership mechanism to further leverage its governance system advantages. On Jan 25, the Standing Committee of the Political Bureau of the CPC Central Committee decided to establish a leading group to guide the battle against the epidemic. And President Xi Jinping has deployed military medical teams to assist the novel coronavirus prevention and control work in Wuhan.

China's capabilities are also evidenced by the newly built Huoshenshan hospital in Wuhan. More than 4,700 workers participated in the construction of the hospital that covers 25,000 square meters and has 1,000 beds, and which was completed in only 10 days. Behind this incredible "Chinese speed" is China's excellent governance system, which is also the guarantee that the country will win the battle against the novel coronavirus.

Learning from the lessons of SARS outbreak, China has improved and modernized its modern emergency management system as well as public health management. Nevertheless, the sudden outbreak of the novel coronavirus has exposed some loopholes in local public health emergency management.

First is the slow response of public health emergency sector in the epidemic outbreak region. After the novel coronavirus broke out in Wuhan, Zhejiang province immediately launched a top level public health emergency response, but despite being the epicenter of the outbreak in China, Hubei province, did not initiate a top level public health emergency response until Jan 24.

Second, the reserves and supply of emergency medical equipment such as face masks and hazmat suits have proved to be insufficient in many local areas. In the early stage of the outbreak, many local areas, Wuhan in particular, have faced severe shortages of essential epidemic prevention and control items such as masks and protective clothing as well as necessary medical materials.

Third, the public health emergency management capacity of local officials in epidemic outbreak regions needs to be improved. At the early stage of the outbreak, many local officials lacked sufficient risk-prevention consciousness and exposed insufficient resource planning capacity and information communication capacity. In addition, the public's widespread panic reminds us the public's awareness of what to do in a public health crisis needs to be enhanced.

The novel coronavirus epidemic should hammer home the point that the public health emergency management is an indispensable part of national and local governance. The government should pay more attention to the public health emergency management to promote its modernization.

To further improve the public health emergency management system, the government should first learn from the experiences and lessons of coping with epidemic situations, and optimize the public health emergency plan mechanism and emergency response mechanism.

Second, the authorities should improve the cross-regional and cross-department emergency response mechanism. A unified and highly efficient public health emergency frontline command mechanism should be built to integrate emergency resources to the maximum.

Third, local officials' public health emergency management capacity, in particular their executive capacity, should be strengthened through training.

Fourth, the authorities should enhance research and development of public health technology to improve the country's public health management capabilities, and enforce the ban on the trade of wild animals to cut the disease transmission at the root. They should also emphasize development of the relevant basic sciences to fight against epidemics with scientific weapons.

Last but not the least, the public should strengthen its capacity to cope with a public health emergency so they can better play their part in epidemic management.

February 7, 2020

The author is a researcher with the Chinese Academy of Governance.

Institutional advantages instill confidence that fight against coronavirus will be won

Hao Yanpeng /For China Daily

Some Western epidemic experts' remarks in the wake of the outbreak of the novel coronavirus have provided some food for thought, as they said to some extent it is good that the virus was first detected in China, not in any other country, because China has a unique system that can help it effectively control the epidemic.

They are right in that regard, but even as China has efficiently used the advantages of its system to the full in the fight against the virus, it is by no means a good thing that the outbreak has occurred, for itself, or the world.

As of Tuesday afternoon, the virus had infected 42,717 people in

China, and killed 1,017 of them, among which 31,728 of the infections and 974 of the deaths have been in Hubei province, which has been at the heart of the outbreak.

These numbers have already been hard-earned results, as not only have 13 cities in Hubei, home to nearly 50 million people, been locked down, but also the rest of the nation has come to a virtual standstill for nearly one month as the central authorities seek to cut the transmission of the virus.

To help those infected in the province, about 12,000 doctors and nurses, including military medical personnel, from the rest of the country have been sent to Hubei to swell the ranks of those combating the epidemic on the front line, where two large field hospitals have been built within 10 days from scratch, and workshops producing medical care materials are running at full speed to support the "war of the people".

It is the resolute leadership of the Communist Party of China that has activated the mobilization of these forces in this life-and-death struggle and targeted the virus in Hubei to prevent it rampaging throughout the nation and beyond.

Thanks to the central authorities' swift and decisive response when it was clear a new virus had emerged, China was not only able to isolate the virus, sequence the genome and share it with the World Health Organization and the world in record time, it was also able to implement the unprecedented quarantine measures aimed at containing the outbreak in Hubei.

To more effectively provide assistance to the affected cities in Hubei, the central authorities on Friday instructed 16 provincial-level regions to assist the anti-epidemic fight in the 13 locked down cities and three others on a one-to-one basis, a mechanism that proved effective in relief and restoration work after the 2008 Wenchuan Earthquake.

No wonder WHO chief Tedros Adhanom Ghebreyesus and world leaders have hailed the speed and scale of China's response to the outbreak. Hopefully, the advantages of its system which have so remarkably been demonstrated will start to increasingly show the desired results.

Rather than trying to portray China's system as a weakness that allowed the outbreak to happen, the world should recognize that it is the strengths of its system that have enabled the remarkable response to the virus. They should not take China's system as a reason to desert the fight.

February 12, 2020

China Daily Editorial

Pains and Gains in China's Handling of the Outbreak   I

Health and production both vital concerns of the people

Li Min/China Daily

That all departments related to the economy, industry, trade and employment have urged factories, other than those in Hubei province, to resume production, is actually a call for the public health department and local governments to give the nod to it.

Such an open call for inter-departmental coordination is rare, and it can only be explained by each side thinking its work serves the fundamental interests of the people.

Those responsible to curb the transmission of the novel coronavirus, mainly by reducing the mobility of the population, are reluctant to see gatherings of the people and large numbers of migrant workers moving around the country, as it might render their previous efforts in vain.

While those who want to reduce the impact on the economy and safeguard people's jobs and livelihoods — not to mention the need to prevent domino effects on international supply chains in which China is an indispensable link — want people to get back to work.

To overcome the prisoner's dilemma they find themselves in entails striking a delicate balance between the needs of disease control and production. Bearing in mind that the resumption of production cannot be carried out in a particular area if it is likely to worsen the situation.

So the reopening of production plants must be implemented prudently in a phased manner to ensure sufficient anti-epidemic measures are in place to protect workers and their families, whichever industries they are in. Producing badly needed materials is not an excuse to compromise the safety of employees.

According to data of the 22 provincial-level regions responsible for most of the country's industrial output, 94.6 percent of the total capacity in grain production and processing and 57.8 percent of their total coal mining production capacity had recovered by Monday, while nearly 80 percent of the plants producing protective masks and overalls have resumed production.

Meanwhile, the operation of these regions' transport and energy industries are almost undisturbed, which explains how the daily needs of 1.4 billion people can be satisfied even though the country has appeared to be at a virtual standstill for nearly a month.

With the number of infections in the country, aside from in Hubei, having dropped eight days in a row as of Wednesday, it means as long as the balance between epidemic control and production can be maintained, the concerns of both sides can be eased as the situation continues to ameliorate.

But with 160 million people due to leave — mainly Henan, Anhui, Hunan and Jiangxi provinces, the major sources of migrant workers — for Guangdong, Zhejiang and Jiangsu provinces over the following week, a close eye needs to be kept on the situation in these areas in particular to ensure the health production balance is maintained.

February 12, 2020

China Daily Editorial

Pains and Gains in China's Handling of the Outbreak

I

Change in frontline commanders sign defense has turned to attack

Medical workers from East China's Fujian province arrive at Wuhan Tianhe International Airport on Feb 13, 2020, to help control the outbreak.

Zhu Xingxin/China Daily

Having seemingly successfully contained the novel coronavirus epidemic in Hubei province, the Communist Party of China Central Committee demonstrated its firm intent to bring the epidemic to an end in the province by changing the leaders on the front line of the fight against the virus on Thursday.

The Party chiefs of Hubei province and its capital Wuhan, the epicenter of the outbreak, were replaced respectively by the Shanghai mayor and the Party chief of Jinan, Shandong province.

With the full support of the central leading team, the new

frontline commanders, together with some newly appointed officials to head the local disease control and prevention systems, have been entrusted with the urgent mission of getting to grips with the situation in the hardest-hit region.

One day before the change of local leaders, the province announced an alarming jump in the number of people confirmed infected with the virus. The daily increase of 14,840 — 13,436 in Wuhan — was more than seven times that of the day before, and accounted for nearly one-third of the overall amount of infected cases the province has reported since the onset of the epidemic earlier last month.

However, this heralds the new front line commanders will take a more proactive approach to defeating the virus, as the hike was due to the province, without any forewarning, confirming infections by replacing the comparatively complicated genetic analysis with quicker CT scans.

The change in diagnostic procedure will make a big difference to the situation in Hubei, as it will help patients get treatment more quickly, which has been shown to improve the chances of recovery.

Also on Thursday, showing that the central authorities are now eager to get on the front foot, another 2,600 military medical professionals, and 3,170 non-military doctors and nurses in 21 teams from elsewhere in the country were sent to the province, which has already received about 21,500 medical staff in total, swelling the ranks responding to the statistical growth in the number of infected cases in the province and increasing the number of sick beds available.

Thanks to the central authorities' powerful and resolute support, the fast increase of sick beds in Hubei — nearly double in Wuhan for instance within half a month — gives the belated diagnostic procedure reform real significance.

At this critical time, when the fight against the epidemic in Hubei requires effective and responsive execution capabilities, the personnel change, will not only boost the public confidence in the measures being taken but also improve the efficiency of the local prevention and control work by addressing the evident shortcomings, such as poor logistics, which have been criticized by the central government guiding team.

Which dyes Wuhan with a solemn yet noble color, as it is the city's lockdown that has been crucial to largely restraining the "devil epidemic" where it appeared.

February 13, 2020

China Daily Editorial

Proposed delay of key meetings pragmatic move

Municipal workers disinfect a pavement outside SOHO complex in Sanlitun in Beijing on Feb 13, 2020.

Zhang Wei/China Daily

That the National People's Congress Standing Committee, China's top legislature, and the Chinese People's Political Consultative Conference National Committee, the country's top political advisory body, are considering postponing their annual sessions that are usually held in March is a pragmatic move at a time when the country is still battling the novel coronavirus, about which more still needs to be known.

Although the number of people in the country outside of Hubei province that have been infected by the virus had dropped for 13 days in a row as of Monday, it is still too early to claim that the situation has been brought under control, and the nation cannot relax its vigilance.

Not to mention that the fight against the virus in Hubei — particularly its capital Wuhan where the death toll accounts for more than 70 percent of the national total — remains an uphill battle.

Given that the two sessions would see thousands of lawmakers and political advisers from across the country descend on Beijing, not to mention the reporters and meeting service staff that would also be in attendance, it is natural that the NPC Standing Committee and the CPPCC National Committee should deliberate on whether they should delay their annual sessions since the country is still discouraging gatherings in a bid to stop person-to-person transmission of the virus.

Since one-third of the 3,000 NPC delegates are provincial and municipal-level cadres with important leadership roles on the front line of the battle against the virus, their work is directly related to the epidemic control and prevention work.

The fight to contain the epidemic is in a critical stage, but China is also fighting another battle to revive the momentum of its economy, which is obviously also of great importance to the world economy. How to steer the world's second-largest economy through the choppy waters of the epidemic is a severe test for China's decision-makers.

With China's ongoing cooperation with the WHO, the resumption of industries and business, and the understanding and support of the whole nation, the country's efforts to end the epidemic will pay off.

But there are many lessons that need to be learned from the outbreak of the novel coronavirus and China's response to the epidemic. The NPC delegates and CPPCC National Committee members must reflect on how and why the people's war needed to be fought, and the shortcomings in the governance system that have revealed, so that they can contribute to improving and further modernizing the country's governance capacities.

February 18, 2020

China Daily Editorial

Sacrifice, Toil and Tears
China and the World in the Fight against the Pandemic

Only a China solution can combat coronavirus

By Laurence Brahm

Luo Jie/China Daily

Not too long ago, I wrote a column for China Daily, "China Shall Overcome," observing that the Chinese people and nation have overcome one crisis after another in the past, and have the wherewithal and determination to do this again facing the coronavirus crisis. I wrote this column, even while the infections in Hubei province were climbing. Why?

I have both observed and participated in many of the reforms and policies of China to overcome challenges over the four decades living here. I have seen a consistent pattern of unity and cooperation among the Chinese people, and meticulous coordination of government policies when faced with a crisis or challenge. Experience has shown me, time and again, when a crisis occurs, China's leadership faces it with a rational clear-headedness. Something seems to kick into the subconscious of the people and they work together in synergy with the organizational institutions of government to overcome these moments of crisis.

This pattern has been reoccurring throughout my life living in China and I believe that it is an innate aspect of the Chinese collective consciousness that has roots in Confucian tradition. Philosophical influences that are both Taoist and Buddhist embedded in the national cultural psyche allow for adept flexibility in response to crisis and a vision of positive hope when faced with negative adversity. This ability to see positive through negative and to use that perception to turn even the most difficult situations into advantages is a deeply rooted part of Chinese culture and the collective unconscious of the Chinese people.

At times of prosperity, when things are going well, everybody is out there doing their own thing. But in those moments of crisis everybody comes together. This is unique to the Chinese culture that allows them to respond and work together. This is what we see happening during this incredible coronavirus crisis. Where on earth could you have 100 million plus people stay at home and self-quarantine as part of a coordinated government policy? This represents a collective response to an unprecedented epidemic. There are very few places in the world where everyone can come together in a patient collective force. This is unique to China and its people.

China has cordoned and locked down Hubei province. We are all aware now of the deathly potency of this coronavirus and the unexplainable occurrence of its rapid airborne spread. The ability to lock down and isolate is the first step to be able to contain any virus. This is a true act of humanitarian responsibility. Even at China's own economic and social costs.

When you talk about humanitarianism this is an act in the global interest. This ability of the Chinese culture, social fabric of its people and the organizational capability of the institutions that have been established in the country are what allow China to respond quickly, decisively and collectively to a crisis of unbelievable and unforeseeable proportion.

Under such circumstances where the threat of this coronavirus is a threat to anybody, we can see everybody is collectively and patiently staying at home. Self-isolation and working at home remotely, working around the dangers in order to meet this challenge. I don't think one would see this response in any of the Western countries whose politicians and mainstream media are so quick to criticize China for everything it does. This is a distinctive, collective response among people to work and bond together in order to get through this crisis together.

One of the reasons why China is able to respond so effectively is the system of macro-management that evolved to address economic reform but is now being used to address a health and humanitarian crisis. Throughout the 1980s to 1990s, a system evolved of state guidance of the economy, together with checks and balances to prevent economic crisis, and the ability to tighten and loosen valves to allow the market to function in free flow, or to use administrative means to guide the market toward more stable conditions to prevent volatility. This is in the interest of everyone collectively rather than the self-interest of a few.

Of course this coronavirus is having an impact on China's economy. Shops are closed, movement of goods restricted. This will have implications throughout the entire chain of production, transport and supplies not only in China but globally.

It's interesting to observe that despite the slowdown in China that the US stock market has continued rocketing to the highest levels historically. This is very strange at a time when the fundamentals of that economy are not good, and social divisions also at their greatest. It calls for even more questioning given the chain of product supplies in the US coming from China. Even the high-tech service companies that dominate accumulated capital market wealth are totally dependent upon China's supply chain for their product parts.

So why is the market so high?

We could see this as a projection of a perception of economic decoupling or fragmentation of the globalization system that has existed. We see America's isolationist policies causing alienation of other nations such as China. So it is foreseeable that we could see more collaborative arrangements in Asia, not only in economic policy and business, but also in combatting disease and crisis. This may be just a natural evolution of the times we live in now.

Once we get through this stage of containment and control of the coronavirus and its spread, then China will enter a new stage of its own economic growth, a reboot period. The same types of reforms applied to business and enterprise and economy now need to be applied to the healthcare sector. These are areas that now offer opportunity for more state investment and private investment and there will be a new growth era with breakthroughs.

In science, technology and AI for healthcare. I believe these are areas where China will lead in bringing together other countries of the region, such as India, where there are similar challenges with population concentrations, water and food security, and healthcare. We could see a new regional growth and economic revitalization. It is a question of using negative to create positive. That is core to Chinese philosophy and culture.

February 18, 2020

The author is a senior international fellow at the Center for China and Globalization, founding director of the Himalayan Consensus and co-chair of the Silk-Spice Road Dialogues.

Preventive measures should never go too far

Community workers check on senior citizens and bring them supplies at Shili Jinxiu community in Hanyang district of Wuhan on Feb 21, 2020.

Zhu Xingxin/China Daily

Staying at home, no socializing, wearing a face mask if going anywhere have proved to be the most effective ways to prevent the spread of the novel coronavirus. It is therefore indeed necessary for communities to ensure residents adhere to these practices.

For individuals, they must be aware that they have to sacrifice a lot in order to make sure as few people as possible get infected so that the spread of the virus will finally be brought under total control.

However, what security guards or volunteers are doing to seal residential areas or neighborhoods should never go too far. They need to bear in mind the principle that what they are doing is meant to prevent the spread of the virus, not prohibit people's freedom, or harm their legitimate rights.

It was reported that a family of three were playing mahjong in a city of Hubei province, which has been hit the hardest by the virus, when a group of security guards broke in at the report of neighbors and smashed the mahjong table. The son of the family was slapped across his face when he questioned what the security guards did.

In another instance, a teacher jogging without wearing a face mask in an empty residential area was stopped and forced to be quarantined for 14 days. The teacher's argument that it is not necessary to wear a face mask in an empty open field according to experts fell on deaf ears.

What the security guards did in both these instances, and others, has seriously infringed upon the legitimate rights of other people.

Despite being rare and extreme, such abuses of power by some security guards to deal with this emergency of the current coronavirus outbreak will only do a disservice to the campaign against the virus. Not the least because such overreactions are directed not at preventing the spread of the virus but directly restricting the freedom of individuals.

It is important for security guards to be instructed that they need to show enough respect to other people when doing their job. They must toe the line between what should and what should not be done and strive to reduce to the minimum the sacrifices that people are making to fight against the novel coronavirus.

Details make the difference. The more attention community leaders pay to the details in preventive efforts, the better the results they will achieve. This should be what local leaders learn from this public campaign.

The shortfalls and deficiencies this public campaign has exposed should serve as lessons to consolidate the governing capability of this country.

February 18, 2020

China Daily Editorial

Clarity of communication

By Zhao Deyu

Workers secure the roof of Leishenshan Hospital, a makeshift hospital built in less than two weeks, with waterproof material in Wuhan on Feb 5, 2020.

Zhu Xingxin / China Daily

With the passing of time and geographical spread, an epidemic entails increasingly large socioeconomic costs. Therefore, those responsible for policymaking and its implementation need to have firm resolve and agile responsiveness. In the case of the novel coronavirus, the role of the government, indeed policymaking in general, boils down to minimizing the gaps and inaccuracies in all kinds of information about the virus, with the goal of limiting the number of infections, reducing the negative socioeconomic impacts of its spread and preventing public panic.

The biggest information gaps are found in specialized information on the nature and origin of the novel coronavirus and effective treatments. From the Ministry of Science and Technology to the Hubei provincial government and the governments of other regions across China, research efforts are being stepped up to find a vaccine for the novel coronavirus epidemic. Some have teamed up with the World Health Organization and research institutions in countries such as the United States, India and Europe. However, it will take time to develop an effective vaccine.

The Chinese government has employed rigorous screening methods to gather information on infected patients, patients whose infection is in incubation period and those who have been in close contact with the former. Before a vaccine is developed, the focus of policy intervention is to isolate the source of the virus and to reduce interpersonal contacts. To contain the novel coronavirus epidemic, the authorities "sealed off" Wuhan, canceling transportation via train, plane and car into and out of the city. This was a necessary measure.

Additionally, strengthening awareness campaigns can help individuals take better precautions. Thanks to the prevalence of multimedia, the vast majority of the population know how to best protect themselves from the virus and they are actively avoiding occasions on which they might come into contact with carriers. They are also likely to report those at risk of carrying the virus. In turn, people returning from infected areas or those who are at risk of carrying the virus are more likely to agree to take quarantine measures.

How can we make the most of these measures and behaviors? In other words, how should we look at intervention measures taken across China up until now?

The most important intervention thus far has been beefing up medical resources, namely doctors, nurses, health screening staff and facilities. Unless diagnosed quickly, people who are incubating the virus or are susceptible to infection remain the biggest risk to the healthy population and pose the greatest challenge to controlling the spread of the epidemic. Information gaps not only exist among the general public about each other's health status. Even medical staff, the government and the public at large do not have the full picture of the epidemic or the health status of given individuals.

Sacrifice, Toil and Tears — China and the World in the Fight against the Pandemic

Big data has proven to be an effective tool for intervention, through the timely release of the geographic information of the residential communities where new cases are confirmed and areas in which they frequent. For example, cities such as Shenzhen and Guangzhou in Guangdong province have the capacity to release highly specific geographic and spatial information of the spread of the epidemic in a timely manner, which will go a long way toward reducing the public's information gaps about the epidemic and helping populations in at-risk areas to increase awareness of prevention. With clarity of information, the government can significantly reduce the number and types of people subject to quarantine, relax quarantine measures in relatively safe areas, and thus use a separating equilibrium strategy more effectively.

China's experience of disclosure of information in the fight against the novel coronavirus can also serve as a valuable lesson for the international community.

First of all, China has strengthened cooperation with the international community, especially the World Health Organization when it comes to epidemiology and vaccine research and development. As epidemic response is the shared responsibility of all countries, the diagnosis and treatment of the novel coronavirus also calls for joint efforts by all parties. Shortly after the discovery of the first confirmed case of the coronavirus infection, Chinese scientists released the genetic sequence of the virus. The sharing of such information on a global level can help catalyze international cooperation on this new and mysterious pathogen.

Second, sharing all kinds of information on the epidemic that has been released in a timely manner with the international community can support global efforts in preventing and managing the spread of the epidemic. Information on the epidemic across different regions in China, as well as aggregate data on confirmed cases, suspected cases, deaths and cured cases are updated every day and released in a timely manner. The transparency and efficiency with which epidemic-related information has been disclosed are extremely valuable for other countries that want to know how China is doing in terms of epidemic control and prevention.

Last, but absolutely not the least, as a responsible stakeholder,

China has undertaken strict health screenings for all entries into and exits out of the country, so as to control the cross-border spread of the virus. In all major cities across China, all residents and visitors who enter and exit the city (or the country through the city) go through temperature checks and health screening. This is an example of responsible behavior that can help to minimize the spread of the virus from carriers to other cities and countries and can contribute to the protection of health and safety in other countries.

February 18, 2020

The author is professor in the School of Social Development and Public Policy at Fudan University. The author contributed this article to China Watch, a think tank powered by China Daily.

Sacrifice, Toil and Tears — China and the World in the Fight against the Pandemic

Decisive stage in fight against COVID-19

By Chen Dongxiao/Liu Kan/Liu Chuanying/Zhou Yiqi

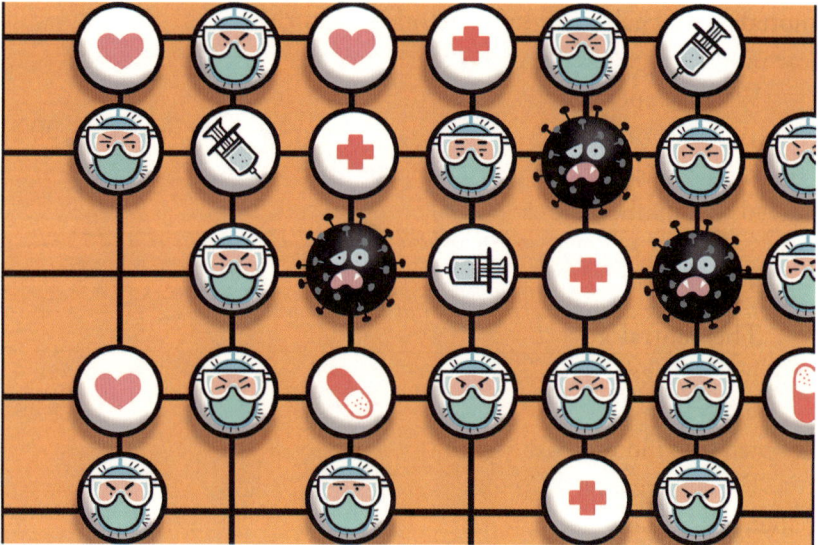

Li Min/China Daily

The people's war against the novel coronavirus (COVID-19) epidemic is entering a decisive stage in China. Statistics show that the epidemic has been kept in check. Nationwide, except for Hubei province, the growth rates of confirmed infections, suspected cases, and patients under medical observation are all showing a steady decline.

More positive signs

The epicenter of the epidemic has essentially been confined to Hubei province, the cities of Wuhan, Xiaogan and Huanggang in particular. The confirmed cases in other regions in China are relatively few and mainly imported ones from Hubei. On the whole, Hubei has witnessed the majority of confirmed cases, severe cases and deaths.

The increase in the number of severe cases around China is slowing down and the rehabilitation rate has surpassed the death rate. As a key indicator to the severity and fatality of the epidemic, severe cases received the most meticulous treatment and care.

The mortality rate of COVID-19 is on a steady decline. As shown by the daily ratio between accumulated deaths and severe cases. The mortality rate has been decreasing significantly in Hubei and remains low in other regions of China.

With deeper understanding of the coronavirus and enhanced effectiveness of medical treatment, the number of cured patients continues to rise. Besides, the number of cured patients has begun to exceed the number of deaths.

Top priority

The central government is mobilizing and coordinating steady supplies of medical equipment and materials for the frontline areas such as Wuhan where tailored and targeted measures have already been adopted to build up local capacity in patient admissions and treatment.

First, a precisely tailored system has been established to leave no patient unattended or under-attended.

Second, a three-level quarantine model has been put in place to improve the allocation of medical resources, which allows patients to receive the most appropriate treatment depending on their condition.

Third, the central government is mobilizing more resources from all over China to reinforce Wuhan in the war against the epidemic. Moreover, 19 provinces and municipalities have each been assigned to help a specified area in Hubei.

China's whole-of-government approach and efficient social mobilization system are the basic guarantee for victory in the battle against the novel coronavirus.

TCM's advantages

Although there is still no one-size-fits-all cure for COVID-19, China's government department in charge of epidemic prevention, medical institutions and medical researchers have joined hands in optimizing the epidemic control strategy and patient treatment plans. These have been continually refined and have proven increasingly effective in detecting, confirming and treating infected people at the earliest opportunity, as well as helping severely ill patients recover and reducing mortality rates.

Apart from Western medicine and medical treatment, medical institutions in China are also exploring what role traditional Chinese medicine can play in the fight against the virus. Eight patients, including six severe cases, were cured and discharged from Jinyintan Hospital in Wuhan on Feb 3 after receiving TCM and traditional Chinese-Western hybrid treatment by experts from Guang'anmen Hospital and Xiyuan Hospital, two preeminent hospitals affiliated to the China Academy of Chinese Medical Sciences.

Thus, the 5th edition of China's Guidelines for COVID-19 Treatment advises medical institutions to "give full play to TCM treatment, enhance traditional Chinese-Western hybrid approaches, and set up joint traditional Chinese-Western diagnosis and treatment mechanisms".

Turning point

In general, strong epidemic control, effective medical treatment for patients and enhancing the rehabilitation rate are three interrelated key missions of China's war against the novel coronavirus. Only when all of them are achieved, can China win the war at the earliest time.

Above all, a decrease in the number of new confirmed and suspected cases will be the most direct indicator of the turning point having been reached and clear proof of the effectiveness of the prevention and control measures.

Next, as the biggest threat to public health, severe cases and virus-caused deaths are people's main fears. A decreasing number of severe cases and deaths will indicate that medical treatment is effective and that the severity of the epidemic is in check.

Finally, the ultimate victory will be achieved when all infected COVID-19 patients are cured.

The situation in Hubei and other regions is expected to be further improved with enhanced national strategy and measures. Nevertheless, the turning point of the epidemic will depend on the effectiveness of the current prevention and control measures, as well as the cooperation of the general public.

But as Professor Chen Wei, academician of Chinese Academy of Engineering and researcher at the Institute of Military Medical Sciences of the People's Liberation Army Academy of Military Sciences, warns, although the turning point may be coming, the possibility of the epidemic recurring will remain, and thus it is necessary to plan for the worst and make the fullest preparations for a long-term fight against it.

Lessons ring true

Although the epidemic continues, China is well-positioned to win the ultimate victory against it. The seriousness of the epidemic and the unknowns surrounding the virus offer China and the world a number of important lessons regarding international cooperation on global public health emergencies.

First, a globalized world featuring more densely-populated metropolitan areas with higher population mobility poses unique challenges for epidemic prevention and control. Although megacities have generally established full-fledged public health emergency response mechanisms, economic, political, social, and security concerns all magnify the sensitivity of decision-makers and the public to the outbreak of infectious diseases. Therefore, emergency response mechanisms, social mobilization systems and reserve systems for strategic assets must be institutionalized in mega-cities.

Besides, the competence of community-level officials and individuals' public health awareness need to be improved through more training courses and public education programs.

Second, China's cross-regional medical supply systems and coordinating networks for medical experts are playing a decisive role in the current war against COVID-19 epidemic. Rallying more than 20,000 medical professionals and coordinating huge amounts of medical materials to reinforce Wuhan's public health system at short notice is not only a result of the full functioning of the central and local governments, but also thanks to efficient logistics and appropriate resources allocation, including human resources. China should share its challenges and good practices with the international community.

Last but not least, international cooperation proves increasingly important in the war against the novel coronavirus. In partnership with China, the World Health Organization has been closely monitoring the epidemic and coordinating a concerted international response. National governments across the world have also extended a helping hand.

More than 30 countries, including developing countries with medical supply shortages such as Pakistan and Myanmar, have donated medical materials to China. Such acts of international humanitarianism indicate that in times of global emergency, international solidarity and coordination, rather than extreme rhetoric and excessive reaction, is what is needed for the well-being of the international community. As the Chinese saying goes, "Saving him to whom you're tied from the river is saving yourself."

February 18, 2020

The authors are researchers at the Shanghai Institutes for International Studies. This is an excerpt of their report "China's Fight Against COVID-19 Epidemic".

The world needs to follow China methods to combat epidemic

By Colin Speakman

Workers and security personnel transfer medical supplies at Wuhan Railway Station on Jan 31, 2020.

Zhu Xingxin/China Daily

Many countries and the World Health Organisation have praised China for extensive and prolonged action to control the outbreak of the novel coronavirus hitting China this year. Just how contagious Covid-19 can be has been illustrated by the over 64,000 cases and 2,495 deaths as of Feb 24 in the epicenter, Central China's Hubei province, and in confined spaces, such as a cruise ship, giving Japan 838 cases with four deaths. There are rising cases in many other countries, with South Korea suddenly seeing 763 cases and seven deaths and Italy 157 cases and three deaths. (Source: Shanghai Daily) These numbers will surely

Sacrifice, Toil and Tears

China and the World in the Fight against the Pandemic

rise with 28 countries outside China identifying cases.

Dr. Anthony Fauci, director of the National Institute of Allergy and Infectious Diseases in the US, has stated that "we are nearly at the brink of a pandemic" and the WHO has said that further spread of the virus is likely. It seems that many other countries will have to follow the strict and rigorous actions that China has taken and it is worth summarising them. To be clear the battle is not yet won, as President Xi Jinping has warned, especially in Hubei province. Yet the number of new cases in the rest of China was only 18 on Sunday, and Shanghai as a mega city has only recorded 1 new case in the last few days and just 3 deaths in a city approaching 25 million. The lockdown and isolation of Hubei province on a scale never before witnessed and the effective control, screening and self-isolation at home in the rest of China have notably controlled the spread.

In many cases across China, authorities have placed restrictions on communities that only one family member may go out every 2 or 3 days to get some of the food supplies or that essential food be delivered at a safe distance to homes. Museums and galleries, schools and universities, concerts, conferences and sports events have all been suspended, and parties and family gatherings in restaurants banned. The people of China have responded and made a great contribution to these needs as have foreigners who chose to remain in China. Strong guidance on minimising the chances of catching the virus, including wearing suitable masks, coughing and sneezing into a tissue that is quickly and carefully disposed of, frequently washing hands and keeping a safe distance from others have supported the effort. The frequent health screenings on public transport and at workplaces and eateries has been an essential element. All of this is proving effective and there is now some loosening of restrictions as new cases slow.

In Hubei province we have the example of what needs to be done in an epidemic concentration with 30,000 medical staff sent into the province, new hospitals built in record time and, of necessity, tightened restrictions on locals to ensure transmission is contained. Even patients that show as recovered are now to be quarantined for 14 days in case they can still spread the virus. Movement in and out is extremely limited. Medical staff has seen 3,000 of their colleagues infected as frontline heroes and some high-profile deaths in this battle. Now all these strategies may need to be applied in other parts of the world as clusters of the outbreak emerge.

The lockdown of such areas, be it in Italy, Japan, Singapore or South Korea, and any future areas where concentrations of the virus occur, will be essential to contain the spread. We have just seen that the Venice Carnival has ended early and some Italian Serie-A soccer matches are cancelled now. Churches in Singapore and South Korea, where recently congregations hugged each other, are now worshiping online. South Korean President Moon Jae-in has stated he will take "unprecedented powerful measures". The screening of travelers will now have to be extended to many more countries, illustrated by Austria halting a train from Italy at its border, and more people will have to think whether the common cold is just that or they too have symptoms of the virus.

Lessons can be learned from China's experience to help all countries defeat this common enemy through awareness, responsibility and prompt action. We are all in this together.

February 24, 2020

The author is an economist and an international educator with CAPA: The Global Education Network.

Sacrifice, Toil and Tears

China and the World in the Fight against the Pandemic

Fight against epidemic should be strategic

By Dong Chuan

Sun Shaobo /For China Daily

The battle against the COVID-19 outbreak, which has affected almost every Chinese citizen's life, should forge forward strategically without sparing any efforts.

The Communist Party of China Central Committee with General Secretary Xi Jinping as the core has been leading the fight against the COVID-19 epidemic. It has been taking measures to control the epidemic, as well as maintain healthy economic development. So, from the highest authorities to the grassroots departments, all should strictly implement the CPC Central Committee's decisions, and society should unite under the strong leadership of the Party to win the fight against the epidemic.

The aim of the fight is to contain the spread of the novel

Pains and Gains in China's Handling of the Outbreak   I

coronavirus, safeguard people's health, promote scientific research to identify the origin of the disease and develop a vaccine, and help resume production to stabilize socioeconomic order. To make sure it wins the fight against the epidemic, China has mobilized officials, publicity departments and the military to control the virus.

Since economic adjustment measures play a vital role in preventing and controlling any epidemic, it is necessary to take steps to resume full production. Or else, social problems such as unemployment and loss of livelihoods will worsen, and the impact of the epidemic on different industries and industrial chains such as hospitality, catering, tourism and agriculture will increase.

Five departments including the Finance Ministry jointly issued a document in early February vowing to increase funding for enterprises that play a critical role in fighting disease outbreaks, such as pharmaceutical and medical supply companies.

For instance, to support the enterprises that are vital to epidemic prevention and control, the People's Bank of China, the country's central bank, has carried out hundreds of billions of yuan worth of reverse purchases to ease the liquidity strain and encourage prime-based loans totaling 300 billion yuan ($42.75 billion).

And the State Taxation Administration has implemented 18 measures to support the epidemic fight, including preferential tax policies to help enterprises resume production, improved on-site tax payment services to prevent disease transmission, and adjusted tax administration measures to reduce the pressure on enterprises. Accordingly, the local governments have also issued measures to help enterprises resume production.

Also, the international community's understanding and support will help us win the fight against the epidemic. Ever since the outbreak emerged in Wuhan, Hubei province, China has regularly shared information on the measures it has taken to contain the disease with the people in China and abroad, winning the praise of the international community, including the United Nations. And it has constantly maintained that the fight against the epidemic is part of its efforts to build a community with a shared future for mankind.

More important, with the COVID-19 spreading to more countries, including the Republic of Korea, Japan, Italy and Iran, international cooperation has become increasingly important to win the battle against the epidemic. As part of international cooperation, China has already donated 250,000 face masks to Iran.

Since it is important to scotch rumors in order to prevent social unrest and win the fight against disease outbreaks, more than 300 journalists are at the epicenter of the outbreak, Hubei province and its capital Wuhan, to report from the front line about the effectiveness of the measures China has taken to contain the disease.

China has also taken action against non-performing officials and law-breaching individuals to boost epidemic control measures. And the military has made great contributions to the fight against the epidemic, particularly with its medical assistance to the frontline medical staff.

China should learn a lesson from the coronavirus outbreak, and intensify reform, especially in the medical and related fields, so as to better deal with such emergencies in the future. Especially, it needs to strengthen its emergency response system, strategic reserve and production, and urban governance. Also, it should more actively promote the modernization of the national governance system and governance capacity.

Moreover, the authorities should make greater efforts to heal the psychological trauma of people, especially those people in Hubei. Under the strong leadership of the Party, China will win the battle against the epidemic and realize national rejuvenation.

March 5, 2020

The author is a deputy director of International Exchanges Office at Beijing Language and Culture University, and PhD candidate at the Party School of the Central Committee of CPC.

Prevention is always better than cure

By Asit K. Biswas/Cecilia Tortajada

Zhang Xueshi /For China Daily

On different occasions, Chinese top leader Xi Jinping has asked Party officials to be on the "highest alert to 'black swan' incidents and take steps to prevent 'gray rhino'" events. He has emphasised the importance to fight well with preemptive warfare so as to prevent and withstand risks, and at the same time fight well the war of strategic initiatives to convert danger into safety and turn crises into opportunities.

A black swan incident is one that occurs even though it had been thought impossible and which could have extreme consequences. A gray rhino event is a highly probable, high-impact yet neglected threat. The president wanted to "prevent and defuse major risks" in order to maintain the country's economic health and social stability.

Xi's perceptive early warning about black swans became a reality when the novel coronavirus epidemic broke out in December.

Since the Lunar New Year fell on Jan 23, State media asked all

Sacrifice, Toil and Tears — China and the World in the Fight against the Pandemic

Chinese families to cancel gatherings and the government imposed strict quarantine measures on Wuhan. On Jan 30, the World Health Organization declared the novel coronavirus a public emergency of international concern.

While there is still much to learn about the novel coronavirus, compared with the 2002-03 severe acute respiratory syndrome (SARS) epidemic, which was transmitted from civet cats to humans, its transmission rate is much faster. But while the mortality rate for SARS was about 10 percent, preliminary estimates for the novel coronavirus, based on Chinese data, appear to be 1 to 2 percent.

This means the novel coronavirus's mortality rate is higher than seasonal influenza but much lower than SARS, because by the time the SARS outbreak was officially declared to be over, in 2004, there were 8,098 reported cases of infection and 774 deaths.

In fact, China shared with the WHO the genetic sequence of the new coronavirus soon after the start of the outbreak, which facilitated global efforts to understand and contain the virus. This, in turn, will accelerate the development of a vaccine.

There is another important difference between the SARS epidemic and the current one which most analysts seem to have missed. China was a very different country during the SARS epidemic in 2002. Its per capita GDP then was only $1,148, whereas in 2019, it was $10,263. Medical facilities, scientific knowledge, research and development capabilities, and the quality of medical care in China have improved significantly since 2002. China is significantly better prepared to contain the epidemic now than it was in 2002-03 to tackle SARS.

The unprecedented quarantine measures, suspension of public transport in many places, closure of entertainment venues and banning of public gatherings appear to have limited the spread of the virus.

Now, China is gradually easing restrictions in lower-risk areas, and many factories are reopening.

The policies China has used have several advantages. It has built new hospitals in an incredibly short time, increased the number of beds in existing hospitals and greatly improved medical facilities. It has also trained a large number of healthcare workers to treat those infected with the novel coronavirus, and developed commercial test kits for the virus, and distributed them in the most vulnerable areas. And it has made people aware of the hygiene requirements to protect themselves against the novel coronavirus.

China's strict measures to contain the epidemic has given the world more time to make necessary preparations for dealing with novel coronavirus cases. Actually, China's measures to contain the spread of the virus have been quite effective. For instance, they have helped Japan handle passengers and crew on the cruise ship Diamond Princess.

Based on SARS and current experiences, some aspects of China's policies needed improvement. And the Chinese authorities have already taken a big step in that direction by banning the illegal trade and consumption of wildlife.

Live animal markets can be found in most Chinese cities. After the SARS outbreak, these shops were closed. This time, the Chinese authorities have banned the consumption of animals under the Wild Animals Protection Law and other laws and all terrestrial wildlife, including those artificially bred and farmed, across the country.

More important, Xi said on Feb 3 that "it is necessary to strengthen market supervision, resolutely ban and severely crack down on illegal wildlife markets and trade, and control major public health risks" at source. Which means the Chinese government believes in the old Chinese proverb, fáng huàn yú wèi rán (prevention is better than cure).

March 4, 2020

Asit K. Biswas is a distinguished visiting professor at the University of Glasgow and chairman, Water Management International Pte Ltd., Singapore. And Cecilia Tortajada is a senior research fellow at the Lee Kuan Yew School of Public Policy, National University of Singapore.

Sacrifice, Toil and Tears — China and the World in the Fight against the Pandemic

Crisis won't disrupt China's renaissance

By David Gosset

Liu Xiaoliang /For China Daily

In the age of artificial intelligence, which is supposed to better anticipate, or of smart cities, which are intended to better protect, the novel coronavirus outbreak is obviously a major public health crisis having global implications.

While they test people, institutions or nations, extraordinary situations, especially when they are unexpected and life-threatening, are also deeply revealing. China and the world are currently having to cope with such a scenario.

Confronted with such a complex and rapidly evolving situation, analysts have to remain prudent. In a paper published in The Lancet, a medical journal, on Jan 31, the authors said: "On the present trajectory,

2019-nCoV could be about to become a global epidemic in the absence of mitigation. Nevertheless, it might still be possible to secure containment of the spread of infection."

When the severe acute respiratory syndrome, or SARS, epidemic affected China 17 years ago, authorities were not only criticized for the lack of transparency around the disease, but also for the lack of appropriate communication with the World Health Organization.

While the exact conditions for the emergence of 2019-nCoV are not yet completely understood, mistakes have certainly been made at the very early stage of the outbreak.

It is widely recognized that the communication around the current crisis and the coordination with the international community are this time much more satisfactory.

On Jan 30, the WHO declared the outbreak a global health emergency. The evolution of the crisis into a pandemic should not be ruled out. The rapid propagation of the virus is a reminder of the intensity of the links between China and the world.

The level of integration between China and the world is also reflected by the prominent role the WHO is playing. The immediate priority is to save lives and control the outbreak. It is a phase in which medical experts should be at center stage. International cooperation among scientists can hasten the win over the epidemic.

The economic loss inflicted by SARS was substantial but relatively limited to the Chinese market. China's weight in today's world of interdependence is much more significant. As a consequence, 2019-nCoV is already having an impact on worldwide trade and supply chains.

With the rapid propagation of the virus, some of the shortcomings of the Chinese healthcare system became evident. In the eyes of public opinion, the dedication of the medical staff and the commitment of the People's Liberation Army are able to offset, to some extent, these deficiencies.

The outbreak has sadly exacerbated Sinophobia, be it in Asia or in some Western countries. When United States Secretary of Commerce Wilbur Ross declared on Fox Business News that the health crisis "will help to accelerate the return of jobs to North America", he demonstrated a shocking insensitivity.

While Twitter and WeChat are platforms through which factual information can be presented to a wider public at an unprecedented speed, social media also circulate rumors and conspiracy theories that are not conducive to management of critical situations.

Diverging narratives based upon at least two different underlying assumptions structure the discourses of those going beyond purely factual reports.

Some may believe that many fragilities almost incapacitating the country can be interpreted as a serious blow to the Chinese government.

Another postulate is arguably much closer to reality. It first takes into account the truly unique resilience of the Chinese people.

Moreover, following its own path, China has been accumulating for decades the resources of a truly great power. Therefore, the country has enough assets to manage this crisis. Through what is indeed a highly painful process, Beijing will keep learning precious lessons and, by doing so, strengthen itself.

In that sense, this outbreak won't disrupt the Chinese renaissance nor fundamentally alter the long-term global changes it involves.

At this moment, if they are unable to remain focused on the long-term trends, governments, businesses and other organizations would be making a serious strategic miscalculation.

February 6, 2020

The author is a Sinologist and founder of the Europe-China Forum.

China's Economy Resilient

Sacrifice, Toil and Tears — China and the World in the Fight against the Pandemic

No reason for undue pessimism

By Zhang Ming

Ma Xuejing/China Daily

There is ample policy space to respond to the adverse impacts of the novel coronavirus outbreak on economic growth.

While one should not overlook the potential shock to economic growth caused by the outbreak of the novel coronavirus, it would not be wise to predict doom and gloom either. What we need instead is a comprehensive view of the extent of the impact on growth.

A first takeaway of the coronavirus epidemic is that the most heavily affected sector over the short term is the service sector, especially transportation, tourism, hospitality, catering and the entertainment industries, given the fact that the outbreak took place during the Spring Festival holiday.

A second takeaway is that the Spring Festival holiday has been extended on a national basis because of the outbreak, which will dampen investment and export growth in February. Manufacturing, real estate and infrastructure construction will see slower investment growth as a result, which will hold back export-oriented industries as well.

A third takeaway is that the consumer price index may continue to grow at an accelerated rate on a year-on-year basis for longer than the year before, or take longer to fall back to its normal level as a result of the outbreak, which has impacted more than just economic growth. Additionally, the labor market may also suffer as a result of the outbreak, something that we must also take into account.

Undeniably, there are many similarities between this current outbreak and the severe acute respiratory syndrome (SARS) outbreak in 2002-03. This is the reason why many analysts have cautioned against excessive pessimism regarding the current situation given what happened in 2003. However, we must not turn a blind eye to the structural changes that have taken place at home and abroad between then and now.

The first change has been in the most important variable underlying China's long-term economic growth: its demography, which has undergone significant changes. For China, the demographic turning point happened around 2010, before which the labor force had been growing as a share of the population, generating demographic dividends. After 2010, the trend has reversed as the population has aged rapidly, and the potential growth rate has continued to decline as a result of shrinking demographic dividends.

The second change has been in external demand, which has become much more ineffective at driving growth at home. The high export growth in China we saw between 2002 and 2003 was the result of the rapid recovery as the global economy after the busting of the internet bubble, from which China was able to benefit as a member of the World Trade Organization, which it joined in late 2001. Exports currently contribute a much smaller share of growth as the Chinese economy has grown significantly in size since then. China's exports are also growing at a much slower pace than before as the global economy declines and the China-US trade conflict escalates. There is yet another factor worth mentioning: China can expect to see its trade surplus playing a reduced role in driving overall growth over the short term, as China commits to increasing its imports of US goods by $200 billion between 2020 and 2021 in light of the signing of the recent trade deal.

Third, the Chinese economy now faces completely different systemic financial risks. When the Chinese banking sector struggled with bad loans around 1998, the government was able to shore up the balance sheets of the commercial banks and bring systemic financial risks under control by 2003 by issuing special government bonds, injecting capital into asset management companies in charge of non-performing assets, and taking over bad loans from commercial banks at book value, which were possible because the government entities were not highly leveraged back then. Currently, the country is still wrestling with systemic financial risks, as local governments are now highly indebted, small and medium-sized commercial banks are struggling with potentially significant default risks, and the real estate sector is going through a critical period on its path toward stabilization.

In other words, given the current state of the economy, we are currently facing higher downward pressures in growth as well as risk control and prevention compared to the SARS outbreak. This is the reason why we cannot simply copy and paste the lessons from 17 years ago, and we must steer clear of excessive optimism on the impacts of the coronavirus outbreak on the Chinese economy.

Having said that, there is no reason to go to the other extreme either. The Chinese government has robust governance capacity, and ample policy space to respond to the adverse impacts of the epidemic on economic growth.

First, with the SARS lessons in mind, the government took timely and correct measures this time around, a fact recognized globally. This means that the negative impact of the outbreak will be limited as the government will bring the outbreak under control.

Second, there is high likelihood that the Chinese government will respond with even more expansive countercyclical macroeconomic policies. On the fiscal front, the central government still has ample policy space and can be expected to counter downward pressures on the economy by committing more fiscal resources to public health, worker reskilling and easing the tax burden on companies.

Additionally, there is little risk of the Chinese government overreacting, as it must keep systemic financial risks under control. For example, it is extremely unlikely that the measures aimed at financial institutions such as deleveraging, risk management, and robust regulatory measures will be dialed back completely, nor are there likely to be major reversals in the adjustment measures in the real estate sector (especially those undertaken in major cities). When it comes to macro policies, another enormous stimulus package is also unlikely.

In conclusion, growth in China this year is unlikely to fall off a cliff even in the face of the adverse impacts of the novel coronavirus.

February 6, 2020

The author is director of the International Investment Department of the Institute of World Economics and Politics at the Chinese Academy of Social Sciences. The author contributed this article to China Watch, a think tank powered by China Daily.

Sacrifice, Toil and Tears — China and the World in the Fight against the Pandemic

Securing certainty amid uncertainties

By Jia Kang

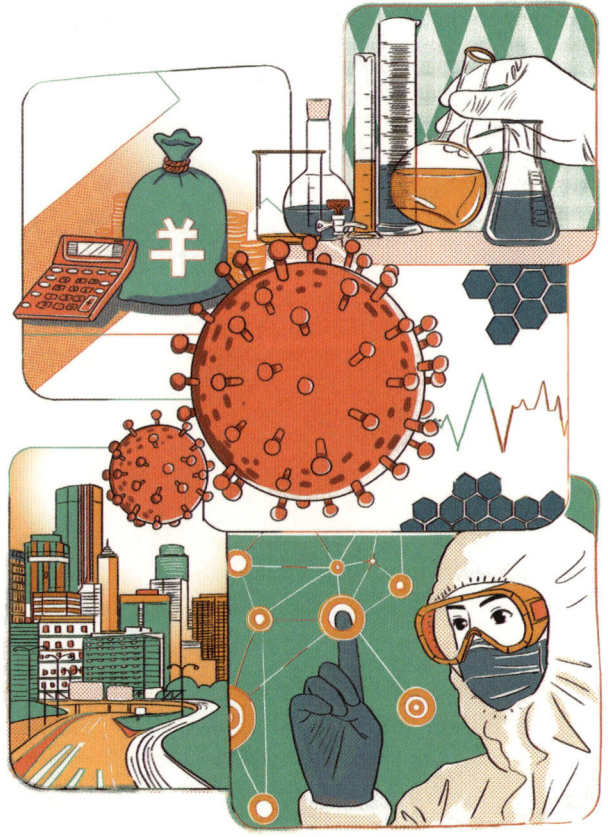

Shi Yu/China Daily

The novel coronavirus outbreak has added to the downward pressure on the Chinese economy, but further potential can be tapped by pushing forward reform and opening-up.

The novel coronavirus that broke out in China prior to the Spring Festival holiday, a peak season for consumption, has had a considerable impact on the consumer market. Complicated by the delay in opening businesses in many parts of the country because of the extending of the holiday, the epidemic is expected to drive the growth rate of China's GDP in the first quarter to below 6 percent. The downward pressure on the economy is increasingly being felt.

The ultimate influence of the epidemic on the Chinese economy remains to be seen. Based on previous experiences, the economic vitality that has been depressed in the early period of a crisis will be released after it ends, with recovered investment and consumption.

For instance, after the SARS outbreak was contained in 2003, the Chinese economy rallied quickly. When it is clear that the fight against the novel coronavirus has been won, we should ramp up reform efforts and expand effective financing and investment to release consumption potential, so as to offset the negative influence caused by the epidemic. If the epidemic can be controlled in the second quarter, we should strive to ensure the smooth transition of the economy from the second quarter to the second half of the year.

In response to the novel coronavirus outbreak, we need to keep the macroeconomic policy consistent, and adhere to a more active fiscal policy and a monetary policy that aims for reasonably abundant liquidity.

It is estimated that hundreds of billions of yuan will be spent in the fight against the virus. But it is not a big sum compared with China's total fiscal expenditure of more than 20 trillion yuan ($2.8 trillion) a year. So the fiscal deficit ratio will not rise significantly due to the epidemic.

Downward pressure on the economy will persist after the outbreak ends. In the long term, the Chinese economy will still be pushed forward by reform, of which the focus should be innovation. People will only spend more and save less when the economic fundamentals are stronger.

But there is undoubtedly still huge development potential for the Chinese economy to tap.

Many scholars, based on the experiences of Western countries, believe that China has reached the later stage of industrialization. In fact, although many coastal areas of China have reached the later stage of industrialization, many areas in the central and western parts of the country are still in the middle, or even early, stage of industrialization. China still has an arduous journey to undertake to upgrade its manufacturing industry from "made in China" to "created in China" and "intelligent manufacturing". The urbanization process, which unfolds along with industrialization, also has a long way to go. Only with further industrialization and urbanization can China realize its growth potential in the modernization drive.

Besides, there is a wide gap between urban and rural areas in China. We can narrow this gap through effective investment.

According to the guideline of modernizing governance and improving governance ability established at the fourth plenary session of the 19th Communist Party of China Central Committee, it is a pressing task to stimulate consumption and improve the country's economic prospects by expanding effective investment and financing and improving the innovation mechanism.

The China-US trade frictions, which are probably going to last for a long time, mean the Chinese economy still faces a lot of uncertainties. But given the resilient performance of the macroeconomy and the ongoing efforts to improve the economic structure, China still has some leeway in its march toward industrialization, urbanization, marketization and globalization. The country will strive to stabilize its economic growth rate at around 6 percent after absorbing the uncertainties in the economic downturn, and realize the transition to the L-shaped growth pattern.

After this year, the Chinese government should seek for certainties amid uncertainties. It should expand domestic demand through effective investment. To overcome the middle income trap, it should upgrade the economy by combining an efficient market with a limited and effective government and supply-side structural reform, and unleash the potential of scientific innovation and management innovation through institutional innovation so as to realize high-quality and sustainable development.

As long as China keeps on the path of reform and opening-up

and focuses on developing its economy in a high-quality manner, time will prove to be the best friend of China in its journey.

February 6, 2020

The author is head of the China Academy of New Supply-side Economics. The author contributed this article to China Watch, a think tank powered by China Daily.

Efforts needed for minimizing serious shock to production

By Xu Qiyuan

Cai Meng/China Daily

Measures should be taken in advance to reduce the impact of coronavirus outbreak on manufacturers.

The fight against the novel coronavirus remains the top priority for the country at the moment. Nevertheless, how to restore production after the battle is won and minimize the impacts on the economy should not be neglected.

Since the seriousness of the situation became evident, it is the offline service industry that has borne the brunt of the outbreak, especially the hospitality industry and education. Given that the service industry accounts for a larger share of the economy than during the outbreak of severe acute respiratory syndrome (SARS) in 2002 and 2003, it is estimated that the impact on the economy will be much greater this time.

However, the impact on the service industry is primarily being felt on the demand side, which is likely to rebound. The overall impact of the epidemic on the offline business of the service industry is limited, and it is expected to gradually weaken. The online service industry may even prosper.

The manufacturing industry has also felt the effects of the outbreak. According to my research into the effects of the epidemic on the apparel, steel, machinery and petrochemical industries in places such as Guangdong, Hubei, and Zhejiang provinces, many industries have felt the pinch in different aspects such as recruitment, production and transportation. Different from the service industry, which is affected on the demand side, manufacturing is feeling pressure on both the supply and demand sides.

Due to people postponing their return to work, and the shortage of protective equipment such as face masks and hazmat suits, industrial production is likely to be delayed. The quarantine measures imposed by the government in a bid to contain the spread of the virus pose severe challenges to the transportation and logistics industries, and enterprises will incur losses due to the delayed delivery of manufacturing orders.

It is noteworthy that the impact of the epidemic on industrial production may extend beyond the first quarter.

First, export orders for manufacturers will decrease temporarily.

Based on statistics since January 2005, the number of export orders usually reaches its peak in March and April. As foreign purchasers are worried about the virus outbreak in China, the delivery time of orders already placed remains uncertain, and there is a high probability of delay. If production cannot be resumed in March, the orders might decrease, extending the impact on industrial production into the second quarter.

For enterprises with global competitiveness, the problem is less worrying. But for apparel companies, which face competition from companies in other countries, the orders from foreign purchasers might be reduced if the recovery of production in China is slow.

Second, fixed expenses and other difficulties put pressure on the capital chains of enterprises.

During the downtime caused by the delayed return to work and quarantining of employees, enterprises still have to pay fixed expenditures such as rent and interest. Moreover, some enterprises need to pay employees' wages during the downtime. As a result, many private companies are struggling under the financial strain. Coupled with the extra costs incurred by the protective measures taken against the virus, these enterprises will suffer a big shock from the outbreak.

To mitigate the shock caused by the epidemic on production, it is suggested that the following measures be taken.

First, targeted tax exemptions and temporary short-term financing should be introduced to ease the capital shortage of enterprises in need, especially private companies. On Feb 1, the People's Bank of China, along with four other central government departments, issued a circular, promising to ramp up financial measures such as credit easing to provide adequate liquidity to the market to tackle the virus outbreak.

Second, logistics should be resumed soon. As imbalanced supply and demand still plague the market and overcapacity and shortage coexist, the government should not roll out stimulus policies. Rather, it should focus on rebalancing demand and supply, to which the key is to ensure smooth flows of materials. Transport should be kept in smooth operation, and normal logistics transportation should be resumed as early as possible.

Third, to resume the flow of people and industrial production. The government should communicate with enterprises to determine the time before they expect to resume production based on their actual situations. As the epidemic has not ended, the specific time when normal production can be resumed cannot be determined yet in many places. But based on information such as the number of confirmed cases, migrant population and enterprises' measures against the virus, measurable requirements for production resumption should be given for enterprises as reference.

The government should also provide guidance to enterprises in the protective measures they can take against the virus, and ensure abundant supplies of protective gear.

February 11, 2020

The author is director of the International Development Department of the Institute of World Economics and Politics at the Chinese Academy of Social Sciences. The author contributed this article to China Watch, a think tank powered by China Daily.

Watchful eye on the middle-income trap

By Zhou Weisheng

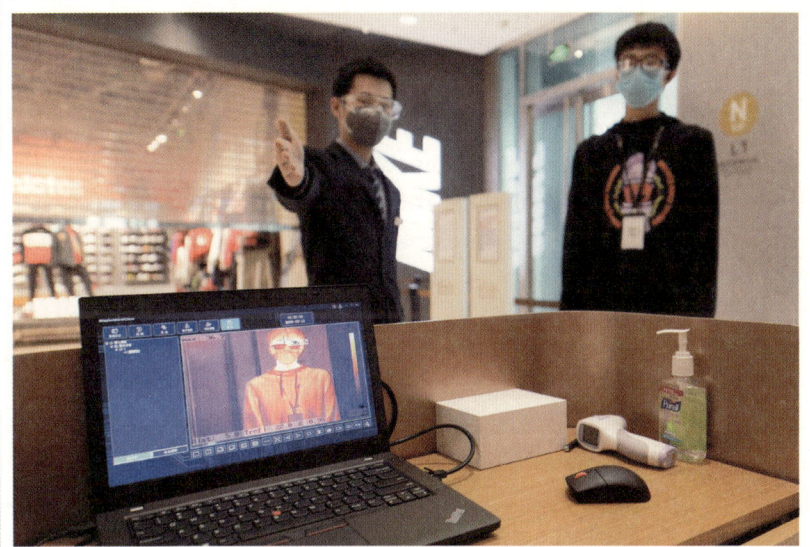

An employee guides another to take an infrared temperature test at the entrance of China World Trade Center in Beijing on Feb 12, 2020.

Wei Xiaohao /China Daily

Policymakers need to bear in mind a number of challenges when drawing up long-term plans for the country's economic and social development.

As consumption is determined by income, rising incomes in China mean there is much growth potential for spending on consumption. As people acquire more disposable income, they are willing to spend more on more sophisticated goods and services. At the same time, the growing economy also means more opportunities for foreign companies to expand their businesses, and the enhancing of comprehensive national power, which provides robust support for focusing efforts on important tasks.

Once per capita GDP exceeds $10,000, there will be growing demand for education, healthcare, security and other intangible needs while demand for goods decline. This is something we should bear in mind as we draft long-term development plans to promote evidence-based and orderly national governance.

Having said that, there is also something else that needs to be considered. Many developing countries, such as Argentina, Brazil, Chile, Malaysia, Mexico and Thailand, have found their economies stuck in a rut for years after achieving per capita middle-income status, as a result of their inability to change their mode of development. This is known as the middle-income trap. Based on the World Bank 2015 benchmark, China is now considered an upper-middle income country, and many are concerned that the middle-income trap may be a real possibility for China.

In 2001, per capita income in China exceeded $1,000 for the first time, and it took China another 18 years for per capita income to rise from $1,000 to $10,000. It took Japan 17 years to make the leap, around the same as China, whereas it took the United States and Brazil 36 years each and Russia 41 years. While a simple comparison of numbers means little given the different national circumstances and the time periods, the high speed of China's development is no doubt an accomplishment. However, there are also challenges lurking in the following aspects.

The first is in land and real estate. In the past few decades, local governments in China have profited from selling state-owned land to developers and they have amassed large amounts of construction capital. With the rapid development of cities, the living standards of urban residents have risen, which in turn has driven the transformation and development of rural economies in surrounding areas, attracting rural workers from other parts of China to find better-paid work in the cities. Nowadays, a large part of GDP growth is driven by land-based finance and the real estate sector. When there is no more land to sell, or if the real estate bubble busts, GDP growth will suffer as a result.

The second challenge is in the transformation of economic growth drivers. Economic development during the past four decades since the beginning of reform and opening-up happened largely thanks to concentrating capital and labor in labor-intensive industries that produce low-priced goods. Going forward, if we do not raise productivity through technological innovation, we may see our economic development lose steam, and with it, we may lose the momentum and the ability to overcome challenges at home and abroad.

The third challenge is in product upgrading. According to a study conducted by the Asian Development Bank, the countries that have fallen into the middle-income trap are those whose exports are limited to primary products and labor-intensive products and where little efforts have been made at diversification and sophistication of the above mentioned products.

The fourth risk is in unbalanced development. The Gini coefficient is an indicator of the fairness of wealth distribution in a given country, with 0.4 usually considered the warning level in terms of income gap. In 2017, the Gini coefficient for China was 0.47. Aside from the wealth gap, the gaps between urban and rural areas, between the more developed eastern and less-developed western areas, as well in education and healthcare in China are all risks that may push China into the middle-income trap.

According to estimates by the Research Institute of Global 3E, if the Chinese economy grew at a rate of 6 percent between 2016 and 2020, 5 percent between 2021 and 2030, 3 percent between 2031 and 2050, then its GDP per capita would be $30,600 in 2049 on the 100-year anniversary of People's Republic of China's founding.

But that forecast is based on smooth sailing over the next 30 years. However, the world is going through changes unseen in the last 100 years, on top of which there are uncertainties both at home and abroad, such as the US-China trade conflict and the novel coronavirus outbreak in Hubei province, among others, all of which are putting downward pressure on the economy. This means that we must push for coordinated development in economic, social, environmental sectors in our pursuit of sustainable development.

To do that, the first thing is to improve the efficiency and quality of investment, given the high investment levels China currently has. It is necessary to make the transition from an investment-led growth model to one led by technological progress, and promote the sophistication and diversification of our industrial and export structure.

This calls for skilled workers and highly trained human capital to undertake technological innovation, which means better training and improvements to the education system. It is also necessary to expand the Chinese middle-income group through urbanization. This is because the upgrading of the industrial sector and export depend on growing market recognition and the consumption of high value added-goods and services, which in turn lead to sustainable growth. To keep this positive cycle going, it is essential to continue to increase the middle-income group.

Additionally, due attention must be given to ramp up production and employment to galvanize the domestic market. China should also drive reform efforts that focus on expanding domestic demand to fully capitalize on the economy of scale.

February 11, 2020

The author is a professor at the College of Policy Science at Ritsumeikan University and the director of the Research Institute of Global 3E in Japan. The author contributed this article to China Watch, a think tank powered by China Daily.

Rational estimation to the impact of coronavirus

By Lu Ting

Ma Xuejing/China Daily

Epidemic should serve as a catalyst for reforms to drive social development, improve the country's institutions and boost its economic efficiency.

While it would be misguided to underestimate the short-term impact of the novel coronavirus epidemic on the Chinese economy, it would be equally unwise to overestimate the long-term impact, which is likely to be marginal.

For the government, aside from managing the epidemic and ensuring people's basic livelihoods, the goals of policymaking should be supporting small and medium-sized enterprises instead of launching a new round of macroeconomic stimulus. As it is the evolution of the epidemic that will ultimately determine when the economy gets back on track, the government should have plans in place for different scenarios.

The epidemic has highlighted some of the advantages of the system in China, while throwing into sharp relief issues and deficits in its development thus far. If the country can reflect honestly and address the problems that have appeared, the epidemic could prove to be a catalyst for reforms to drive social development, improve the country's institutions and boost its economic efficiency.

The extent of the economic impact of the epidemic beyond the first quarter will largely depend on the evolution of the outbreak itself, which has proven to be highly uncertain. Given the fact that China is fully committed to bringing the epidemic under control no matter what, it is extremely unlikely that the novel coronavirus will continue to wreak havoc over an extended period of time. Having said that, it is not the time to let down our guard, since the peak in the flow of people returning from their hometowns to work after an extended Spring Festival holiday is still to come.

But based on the evolution of the SARS epidemic in 2002 and 2003, it is reasonable to assume that the spread of the virus will be reined in within months, concluding with close to zero new cases by the end of that timeframe.

For an optimistic scenario, we can assume that the virus will be thoroughly contained within a month. For a pessimistic scenario, we can assume that it will take three months to bring the epidemic under control.

Regardless of the scenario that ultimately plays out, a reasonable policy response should, besides meeting the urgent needs of managing the epidemic and ensuring the production and transportation of emergency supplies, also focus on being the helper of last resort to small and medium-sized enterprises to prevent them going out of business en masse.

When the entire country is doing all it can to control the epidemic and prevent it from spreading further, local measures to shut down the main transportation routes can lead to a classic case of the prisoner's dilemma. Therefore, it is a good idea for the central government to consider banning local governments from such attempts aside from areas under lockdown, so as to ensure the smooth circulation of goods.

In terms of trade, based on the past international experience, the WHO's announcement of PHEIC has limited impact on the overall trade in the related countries, while this year, due to the 2019-nCov, manufacturing companies cannot resume work on time after the holiday, goods delivering and payment collection will be significantly impacted.

With several major countries having issued varying degrees of travel restrictions, their airlines have successively canceled flights to China, which will have a greater impact on Chinese companies engaged in service trade in the short term.

The central bank and State Administration of Foreign Exchange can give care to these enterprises in terms of liquidity supply and foreign exchange management. While the central government is keeping the production of critical medical supplies, the prices of everyday products can rely more on the invisible hand of the market to bring supply and demand back into balance. The government can spare energy to focus on ensuring production, prohibiting local roads from being excessively closed, and improving logistics.

Under the pessimistic scenario in which the epidemic lasts three months or more, the government should ensure access to key supplies such as masks, protective coveralls and disinfectant. The government can also take a localized approach in prioritizing the reopening of factories in places with significant improvement in epidemic management.

In key manufacturing hubs, factories with good isolation practices can reopen depending on their individual circumstances. An old adage tells us to repair the roof when the sun is shining, and indeed, the outbreak has served to expose glaring deficits in basic facilities and capacities in epidemic prevention in many major cities. If the epidemic lasts longer than expected, the central government can consider subsidizing local governments for them to build permanent health establishments that can serve as centers for the prevention and control of infectious diseases in cities of a certain population size and above.

A case in point is the Nanjing Public Health Medical Center, established five years ago. The experience of Nanjing and other cities can be quickly replicated in areas in need, and as it does so, the central government can stimulate demand while beefing up prevention.

Sacrifice, Toil and Tears
China and the World in the Fight against the Pandemic

Barring extreme, unforeseen circumstances, the impact of the novel coronavirus on the economy should be limited to the near term. We can expect to see poor growth in the first quarter, with revenue losses in sectors such as hospitality and transportation. Therefore, a slowdown in the first quarter will inevitably drag down annual growth figures.

Should something be done to stimulate the economy to recover the GDP lost in the first quarter during the rest of the year? Not necessarily. Once the epidemic comes to an end, there will be a rebound in demand. As the demand that has been delayed or constrained is released, the economy will bounce back and quarterly growth will bottom out, offsetting to a certain extent demand depressed during the outbreak. When that happens, accommodative policies should be rolled back in an orderly manner, so as to avoid going overboard and resulting in unnecessary inflation, over-indebtedness and a possible rise in defaults.

Expansionary policies and potential stimulus packages in response to the epidemic must be disciplined, manageable, targeted, and focus on helping those in dire need over the short term.

As long as the impact is handled properly, market players can outlive the outbreak with government support, and the long-term impact on the Chinese economy should be negligible.

And, as long as this epidemic is taken as an opportunity for soul-searching and learning hard lessons, this misfortune may end up being a catalyst for needed reforms in many areas including the public health system, emergency response system, social governance and government administration.

February 13, 2020

The author is chief China economist at Nomura Securities.

The coronavirus will not debilitate China's economy

By Zhang Jun

A worker disinfects an installation on a pavement around a mall at the Big Wild Goose Pagoda Scenic Area in Xi'an, capital city of Northwest China's Shaanxi province on March 6.

Huo Yan/China Daily

Five days before the Chinese New Year, the authorities in Beijing declared the novel coronavirus outbreak that was first reported in Wuhan to be a major public health emergency.

Unsurprisingly, China's economy is slowing down. The service sector, which includes retail, tourism, hotels and transportation, and accounts for more than half of the country's GDP, is suffering severely. Disruption in this sector will in turn affect manufacturing. And growing international concern at the continued spread of the virus might further strain trade and limit the movement of people. The key question is whether the epidemic will last much longer.

My answer is no. The novel coronavirus epidemic is very unlikely to last long in China. Despite all the problems, China undoubtedly still has an unparalleled ability to mobilize resources in response to a large-scale emergency. During the last two weeks, for example, official efforts aimed at controlling panic have been first-rate. In addition to ordering a nationwide mobilization of medical personnel and resources (including from the military), the authorities have been assessing major hospitals' capabilities to diagnose and treat coronavirus patients. More important, as part of a national disease-control campaign announced on Jan 20, officials are identifying and observing any citizen who traveled to and from Wuhan since the outbreak began.

Meanwhile, urban communities and rural villages alike have tightened access restrictions in order to reduce unnecessary movements and aggregations of people, even establishing temporary rationing systems to distribute face masks to families and individuals. In addition, holidays have been extended and schools remain closed. By helping to minimize the public's exposure to the peak of the epidemic, these steps are playing an effective role in curbing the spread of infection. There is a higher probability that the increase in the number of infections will slow down in the coming weeks.

It is still too early to assess the full economic impact of the coronavirus outbreak. However, the key factor will not be the epidemic's range or severity, but rather its duration. The sooner the epidemic is over, the quicker China's economy will recover, given its growth trend. Although severe control measures will weaken immediate economic performance, they should help to end the outbreak earlier and so enable the economy to pick up steam again.

The epidemic will only create a short-term economic slowdown, it will not significantly alter the Chinese economy's medium- and long-term growth trend. Once the coronavirus crisis passes, therefore, the economy will bounce back and return to its previous course.

Back in 2003, for example, most economists and researchers estimated that the severe acute respiratory syndrome (SARS) outbreak would lower China's second-quarter GDP growth by about one-fifth, but shave less than 0.5 percentage points off the full-year figure. These forecasts reflected the limited number of regions and sectors affected by SARS, as well as the expectation that the outbreak would last no more than three months.

In the event, second-quarter GDP growth fell by two percentage points, much as expected. At the time, China's economy was expanding by about 10 percent annually, and the SARS-induced slowdown was quickly offset by subsequent strong growth. So, on a graph of Chinese growth from 2002 to 2007, the impact of the SARS outbreak is not even visible.

Although the scope of the coronavirus outbreak now exceeds that of SARS, its duration will be the key factor for assessing the extent of its impact on the economy. Current data suggest that the epidemic will likely reach a turning point in the coming weeks. That would mean China might conquer the virus in the first quarter, which is essential to mitigate the epidemic's impact on overall growth in 2020.

True, China's annual GDP growth of just over 6 percent in the last several years is much slower than at the time of the SARS outbreak. But the Chinese authorities can still ensure a robust recovery through targeted fiscal and monetary policy adjustments that support small and medium-sized enterprises and service-sector businesses affected by the coronavirus epidemic.

According to my preliminary estimates, the worst-case scenario is that the epidemic lowers GDP growth in the first quarter by one-third or half, leaving the figure 2-3 percentage points lower than in the first quarter of 2019. But if things start to look up in the second quarter, the ensuing rebound will partly offset that drop. And with the necessary macroeconomic policy adjustments in place, economic growth will accelerate again during the second half of the year.

Provided there are no further external shocks, continued policy loosening should limit the full-year decline in GDP growth to 0.5-1 percentage point. That would imply a 5-5.5 percent full-year economic expansion in 2020, which is still largely in line with China's current growth trend. But it is not yet clear whether the Chinese government, currently preoccupied with tackling the epidemic, will cut its GDP growth target for this year accordingly.

February 15, 2020

The author is dean of the School of Economics at Fudan University and director of the China Center for Economic Studies, a Shanghai-based think tank./Project Syndicate

Virus' economic impact manageable

By Yu Ze

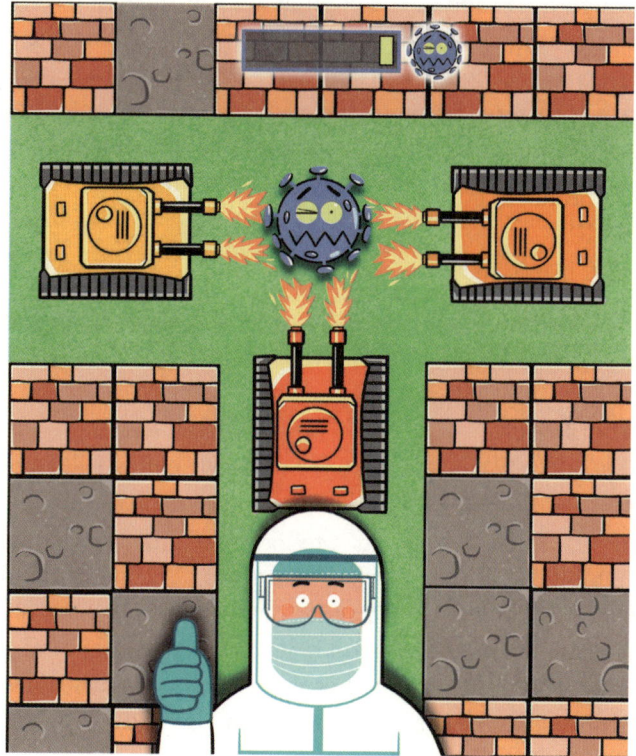

Li Min/China Daily

To fight against the novel coronavirus outbreak, Wuhan, the capital of Hubei province, and some other cities in the province have consecutively suspended all public transportation and closed all outbound transportation channels from Jan 23, in a bid to curb the spread of the virus.

Many provinces and cities have since launched a top-level significant public health emergency response. The country's Spring

II China's Economy Resilient

Festival holiday was extended to Feb 2 after the approval of the State Council, China's Cabinet, and some regions even further extended the time of returning to work according to local situations. Many people are concerned about whether the novel coronavirus outbreak will seriously undermine China's economic development.

In 2002-03 the severe acute respiratory syndrome (SARS) broke out in China, which offers some historical data for us to evaluate China's current economic situation. But China's economic demand structure, industrial structure and macroeconomic regulation system have drastically changed compared with 17 years ago, which means the impact of the novel coronavirus on China's economy will not be the same as SARS.

First, China's demand structure has changed from investment driven to consumption driven. At the time of SARS, investment played the biggest role in driving the economy. Because SARS' impact on investment was limited, in 2003 China's GDP growth rate rapidly rebounded after the decline in the second quarter.

Since 2019, infrastructure construction and manufacturing investment have slowed while consumption has become the major driving force for economic stability. Consumption's contribution to GDP growth has increased from 35.4 percent in 2003 to 57.8 percent in 2019. As the novel coronavirus outbreak has greatly curbed people's daily consumption including catering, shopping, entertainment and tourism during the Spring Festival holiday, it has had a greater impact on China's economy than SARS.

Second, China's industrial structure has changed from secondary industry-dominated to being tertiary industry-dominated. The service sector's proportion in China's economic structure has increased from 42.03 percent in 2003 to 53.9 percent in 2019. As the novel coronavirus outbreak has seriously impacted industries including transportation, tourism, wholesale and retail, as well as film and television, its impact on China's economy will be greater than SARS.

Third, the World Health Organization declared on Friday that the outbreak of the novel coronavirus constitutes a public health emergency of international concern, which will probably have a negative impact on China's exports of goods, although it will not reduce its trade surplus to a large scale. Although WHO opposed countries imposing a travel ban or trade ban on China, the international public health emergency will unavoidably impede personnel exchange and custom clearance for goods between China and overseas regions. One of the major trade deficits of China's trade in services is overseas tourism, which will stop until the epidemic is known to be over. However, in general, China's total trade balance will not be greatly impacted by this public health emergency.

Fourth, after 17 years China's macroeconomic regulation system, fiscal policy, monetary policy, industrial policy and employment policy are much improved, which will play a crucial role in preventing the outbreak having a serious long-term impact on the economy.

China's central bank pumped 1.2 trillion yuan (about $173.3 billion) into the financial system via reverse repos on Monday to keep liquidity in the banking system at a reasonably sufficient level during the epidemic control period.

But with consumption and the tertiary industry the most affected by the novel coronavirus outbreak, China's economic downturn pressure will further increase this year. Based on the statistics of 2003 and 2019, in the first quarter of 2020 China's GDP may decline by up to 800 billion yuan ($113.92 billion), and the actual GDP growth of the first quarter may be about 5 percent. As the first quarter is always the off season for production, if the novel coronavirus outbreak can be effectively curbed by the end of February, its impact on China's GDP will be 0.5 to 1 percentage point considering the economic recovery after the epidemic situation.

Under such circumstances, China could achieve the goal of the 13th Five Year Plan (2016-20) to double 2010's GDP by 2020. That means the novel coronavirus outbreak's negative impact on China's economy is controllable if the epidemic can be curbed within the following two months.

To reduce the negative impact of the severe novel coronavirus outbreak, top priority must be given to effectively curb epidemic. If the population migration to other regions, especially the regions with poor medical treatment conditions leads to a further spread of the novel coronavirus, there will be great impact on enterprises' production.

Moreover, the authorities should strengthen social policy to guarantee people's basic livelihoods. Many migrants need to return to urban areas to work for living, which face great economic pressure due to the epidemic. And the authorities should reduce enterprises' economic burden and cost during the lockdown, in order to help them overcome operational difficulties during the epidemic period. Most important, we should guarantee smooth economic circulation as much as possible. For instance, it is difficult to deliver fodder for livestock and manufacturing enterprises to get raw materials, which will interrupt enterprises' operation and reduce capital turnover efficiency. Hence we should improve economic circulation to guarantee agricultural and industrial production.

February 5, 2020

The author is a researcher at the School of Economics, Renmin University of China. The views don't necessarily represent those of China Daily.

Sacrifice, Toil and Tears — China and the World in the Fight against the Pandemic

Orchestrated response required

By Yang Panpan

Song Chen/China Daily

Three events in the past two decades had notable impacts on the Chinese economy, including one epidemic (the 2003 severe acute respiratory syndrome outbreak) and two natural disasters (the 1998 floods and the 2008 Wenchuan earthquake). On these three occasions, China accounted for 6.8 percent (1998), 8.7 percent (2003) and 12 percent (2008) of the global economy respectively in terms of purchasing power parity, but now its share is nearly 20 percent. So the current novel coronavirus outbreak may affect not only the Chinese economy but also the world economy.

After the outbreak of the virus, major research and financial institutions share the view that the Chinese economy will slow by 0.3 to 0.6 percentage points against previous expectations. Since China has become an engine for the world economy, in this scenario the global economy will slow by 0.06 to 0.12 percentage points against previous forecasts, so long as nothing big happens in other economies.

The impact of the current epidemic on the world economy is being largely felt in such aspects:

Since China is a major global consumption market, the consumption demand for other countries is reduced. The sector that will bear the brunt is cross-border tourism, other tradable consumer products industries will likely to be impacted too. Take Thailand for example, China, as its largest source of tourists, contributes 30 percent to its inbound tourists. The National Tourism Bureau of Thailand estimates its loss in the tourist sector at $3 billion. So Thailand has already cut its 2020 growth forecast and its central bank has lowered its policy interest rate to 1 percent, a record low.

The effects of the slowing Chinese economy will cascade through global value chains. As the time to resume work in China after Spring Festival has been delayed, production industries will be affected, so will investments in the manufacturing sector. As a result, China's import demands for overseas commodities and intermediate products will drop. At the same time, production, assembly and the manufacturing of intermediate and final products in China will all be delayed due to the epidemic, so consumption in both Chinese and other markets will all feel the blow.

The automobile and electronic industries are the first to feel the pain in the value chains. Take the auto industry as an example. Hyundai announced on Feb 4 that due to broken supply chains, its South Korean factory, the largest among all its factories, will halt production, making it the first automobile company outside China to do so. Considering the fact that the auto and electronic industries are key categories for the economy to recover, their slowdown and weak demand will make a dent in global manufacturing.

The impact of the epidemic on key regions should be closely followed. The Association of Southeast Asian Nations and Latin America are two such regions. The ASEAN countries are suffering a direct negative impact because of the close value chains and personnel exchanges in East Asia. Although, from a longer-term perspective, the outbreak may speed up the industrial chain transfer and thus benefit regional growth and investment. But in this process, the interaction and connectivity between China and the ASEAN countries are essential.

As for the Latin American countries, the spillover effects are mainly negative. China accounts for one-fourth of the exports of Peru and Brazil and one-third of Chile's. What's more, countries in this region are relatively reliant on bulk commodity exports. So if commodity prices remain low due to the epidemic, these countries' exports and growth will be stressed.

To deal with the effects, China's economic policies are the main ones to rely on.

The central tasks of China in addition to epidemic prevention and control, are resuming production and ensuring people's livelihoods. Governments at various levels have issued policies to support production industries and companies. In terms of monetary policy, on Feb 3 and Feb 4 the central bank of China, the People's Bank of China, conducted open market operations beyond expectations, accumulatively putting 1.7 trillion yuan ($242.7 billion) of liquidity into the economy to stabilize it. In terms of fiscal policy, as of Feb 8, a total of 71.85 billion yuan of earmarked funds for epidemic prevention and control have been arranged through public finance, a package of policies have been rolled out, and the Ministry of Finance and the central bank have joined hands in "special refinancing and interest discount" policy, the first of its kind.

Such policies can all help China enhance resilience against the shocks produced by the epidemic, and thus provide basic support to reduce to the minimum the epidemic's negative impacts on the global economy.

However, since the global economy is experiencing a weak recovery, international policy coordination is both necessary and urgent.

To be specific, study or work groups on the epidemic should be established within the G20 or other frameworks for international cooperation to fully evaluate its impact on the world economy and work with international organizations to assess the fragility of each economy and financial market. By so doing, macroeconomic policy coordination and collaboration could be enhanced, and the black swan event could also be prevented from escalating into a local or even systematic crisis.

At the same time, international mechanisms for emergency materials distribution, transportation and customs clearance should be put in place. Countries should not take excessive or beggar-thy-neighbor measures. Instead, they should all work together to ensure reasonable flows of personnel, materials and funds and strengthen cooperation on vaccine R&D.

In the long run, global economic policy coordination mechanisms should include responses against public health emergencies and other black swan events. Such responses should have a package of recognition strategies, specific measures, work tools, relevant planning and source of funds in order to help global economic development in such scenarios.

February 20, 2020

The author is a researcher at the Institute of World Economics and Politics at the Chinese Academy of Social Sciences.

Sacrifice, Toil and Tears
China and the World in the Fight against the Pandemic

Economic fight against epidemic must be won

By Yu Yongding

Ma Xuejing/China Daily

The novel coronavirus outbreak that was first reported in Wuhan, Hubei province, has spread across the country and beyond its borders, leaving governments at all levels in China scrambling to limit further person-to-person transmission of the virus, now known as COVID-19.

Wuhan, with a population of 11 million, is under lockdown. Many provinces have postponed the resumption of work at non-essential enterprises following the Chinese New Year holiday, with residents staying indoors. Inter-city and inter-provincial transportation have been reduced. And some local governments have established special checkpoints to prevent vehicles carrying industrial products and materials from entering areas under their jurisdiction that contain factories.

The epidemic and the extraordinary measures to contain it have hit China's economy hard. No one knows when the epidemic will be contained and what the eventual cost to the economy will be. But the Chinese people have, once again, shown courage and solidarity in the face of a national emergency. And there is no doubt that China will win the battle against the virus.

When the severe acute respiratory syndrome (SARS) outbreak hit the Chinese economy in 2002-03, everyone initially was pessimistic about the outbreak's likely economic impact. But as soon as the epidemic was contained, the economy rebounded strongly, and ultimately grew by 10 percent that year.

However, China may not be that lucky this time, given unfavorable domestic and external economic conditions. So, with the novel coronavirus still on the rampage, the Chinese authorities must prepare for the worst.

Hope for the best, prepare for the worst

Chinese policymakers should respond to the current crisis in three ways. Their first priority must be to rein in the epidemic no matter what the cost. Because markets cannot function properly in emergencies, the country's leadership must play the decisive role. Fortunately, China's administrative machinery is functioning effectively.

At the moment, one of the most serious economic obstacles is the interruption to transport caused by local governments. While recognizing local officials' legitimate concerns about preventing the further spread of the virus, the central government must now intervene to facilitate smooth flows of people and materials, thus minimizing supply-chain disruptions.

Second, the government should devise ways to help businesses survive the crisis, focusing in particular on small and medium-sized service companies. While being careful not to create undue moral hazard, the government should cut taxes, reduce charges and compensate hard-hit enterprises. It should also consider establishing epidemic insurance funds so that society as a whole can bear businesses' virus-related losses.

Moreover, commercial banks should strive to ensure that there is no shortage of liquidity, including by rolling over loans to troubled enterprises and allowing them to postpone repayment. In addition, policymakers may need to resort to market-unfriendly measures such as targeted lending and moral suasion to steer the allocation of financial resources, as well as possibly loosening some financial regulations.

Third, the authorities should pursue more expansionary fiscal and monetary policies, even if such measures per se are not aimed at offsetting the negative impacts of supply-side shocks. The People's Bank of China, the country's central bank, should continue to lower interest rates as much as possible and inject enough liquidity into the money market. Although inflation has risen as a result of supply-chain disruptions and may yet climb further, tightening macroeconomic policy at this point would be counterproductive.

Likewise, although the government is unlikely to launch large-scale infrastructure investment projects before the virus is contained, the general budget deficit may nonetheless grow, owing to the epidemic-related increase in spending and decrease in tax revenues. And in its fight to control the virus' spread, the government should not worry too much about whether the budget deficit exceeds 3 percent of GDP.

GDP target could be reconsidered

The battle against the novel coronavirus epidemic will be very costly, and will reverse some of the Chinese authorities' recent achievements in reining in financial risks. For now, however, any potential problems related to debt, inflation or asset bubbles are secondary. Policymakers can worry about them once the situation has calmed down.

Late last year, I sparked a heated debate among Chinese

economists by arguing that the country's policymakers should not allow annual GDP growth to slip below 6 percent, because expectations of a slowdown are self-fulfilling.

In the light of the novel coronavirus outbreak, I concede that the 6 percent growth target must be reconsidered. But even if the epidemic lowers growth in 2020 by, say, one percentage point, this probably would not negatively affect people's expectations, because the slowdown would be the result of an external shock rather than some inherent weakness in the economy.

Chinese policymakers' most urgent challenge is no longer how to stimulate aggregate demand, but rather how to ensure that the economy functions as normally as possible without compromising the fight against the virus. Sooner or later, however, the epidemic will be conquered, and the Chinese economy will return to a normal growth path.

When that happens, the question of whether China needs more expansionary fiscal and monetary policies to achieve an adequate level of growth will return to the agenda. And the rationale for a looser stance will still apply. In fact, to compensate for the losses arising from the novel coronavirus outbreak, the authorities may have to adopt even more expansionary policies than I (and others) had previously suggested.

February 19, 2020

The author is a former president of the China Society of World Economics and director of the Institute of World Economics and Politics at the Chinese Academy of Social Sciences./Project Syndicate

Sacrifice, Toil and Tears — China and the World in the Fight against the Pandemic

Fundamental strengths

By Hu Angang/Liu Shenglong

Luo Jie/China Daily

Since its outbreak in China, the impacts of the novel coronavirus have been spreading. In addition to the negative effects on China's own economic development, there is now international concern as to how the outbreak will affect the global economy. China is currently the largest economy (based on purchasing power parity), ranking top in terms of industrial output, import volume of goods and energy and international tourism spending. Moreover, China is the largest trade partner of more than half of the world's countries and regions. Indeed, China is now the largest stakeholder in the world, and the country's ability to mitigate the economic impact of the outbreak will have huge implications for global economic expansion.

The dynamics between China and the world can be better understood through an illustration of the differences between China's international position today, compared with that during the 2003 severe acute respiratory syndrome (SARS) outbreak.

First of all, the percentage of China's GDP in world GDP grew from 8.7 percent in 2003 to 18.6 percent in 2018, an increase of 10 percentage points. In terms of global trade, China's trade volume (both imports and exports) is 5.43 times greater now than it was in 2003, while China's share of the world trade volume has increased by 7.1 percentage points, from 4.4 percent in 2002 to 11.5 percent in 2019. Consequently, China's impact on global trade is now 5.43 times greater in absolute terms, or relatively 7.1 percent.

However, as the novel coronavirus outbreak is a shock with a short-term and random nature, its actual global economic impact will be dependent on China's economic fundamentals, long-term factors and macroeconomic regulation capacity.

As the outbreak may possibly reach its peak by the end of February, the national economy in the first quarter will reduce sharply to 5 percent (year-on-year growth slowed by 1.4 percentage points). However, with effective macroeconomic control and the full recovery of production once people return to work, GDP growth will recover quickly in subsequent quarters. Therefore, the overall GDP growth in 2020 is expected to be 5.6 percent, 0.4 percentage points lower than would have been the case if the outbreak had not occurred.

The above data show that the outbreak cannot stop China's economic growth geared at medium high speed, nor can it change the upward trend of China's GDP as a percentage of the world total. China's status as the largest engine of world growth will remain unchanged.

In addition to the global impact of the outbreak, we have also calculated the outbreak's influence on seven major economies, namely the United States, India, Japan, Germany, Russia, the Republic of Korea, and Australia. Overall, the influence on these seven economies falls in a range between 0.1 percent to 0.3 percent, depending mainly on the gaps between their potential and actual economic growth, and on their macroeconomic regulation capacities.

For example, India's potential economic growth is around 6 percent, while its actual rate in 2019 was 4.9 percent; hence, even taking account of the effects of the outbreak, its growth will not slow down.

The US and China are each the largest trade partner of the other, and the economic integration between them is a basic trend. It should be noted that the bilateral trade volume in goods as a percentage of

US GDP grew from 2.8 percent in 2016 to 3.1 percent in 2018. If the phase one trade deal is implemented effectively, and the phase two trade deal is reached, trade and investment between the two countries will see a recovery growth rate, for example at about 10.4 percent as previously seen between 2016 and 2018. This will increase the trade dependence on each side, hence a higher degree of impact of the outbreak on the US economy.

The impact of the epidemic on Australia and the Republic of Korea is relatively large, because their dependence on China's trade is quite high. In addition, compared with other countries, they have a higher dependence on trade in services with China, especially education and tourism. Australia alone has 100,000 Chinese students.

Each country's growth is dependent on internal factors, such as development stage, potential growth rate, innovation factors, macroeconomic regulation capacity, and trade dependence.

February 27, 2020

Hu Angang is dean of the Institute of Contemporary China Studies at Tsinghua University. Liu Shenglong is a research associate of the Institute for Contemporary China Studies of Tsinghua University. The authors contributed this article to China Watch, a think tank powered by China Daily.

Outbreak to have limited impact on economy

By Mei Guanqun

Ma Xuejing/China Daily

The novel coronavirus outbreak not only poses a threat to public health but also has affected production activity and economic operations. Still, the epidemic's impact on the macroeconomy would be short term.

In China, the epidemic has had an impact on various industries and the overall economy. Globally, the novel coronavirus outbreak has mainly affected countries that have close market and industrial connections with China.

In terms of investment, as a consequence of the outbreak, many large-scale investment projects cannot start to work now, which will affect not only the manufacturing industry, infrastructure construction and real estate investment but also service sectors such as logistics and finance.

In terms of consumption, industries that rely heavily on customer flow, including catering, retail sales, tourism, films, airlines and hotels, may see a sharp decline in business.

And in terms of trade, China's exports of goods and services will decline in the short term because of the temporary closure of enterprises.

Among the three, consumption has been most affected by the epidemic, especially because Spring Festival is also the traditional peak period for retail sales. Since enterprises complete the export orders before Spring Festival and investment projects are suspended during the festival, they would suffer less because of the epidemic.

Also, in the short term, labor-intensive enterprises may find it challenging to increase production due to the epidemic. And small and micro businesses would find it more difficult to get financing until the economic and social order returns to normal. In particular, the lower-income group would suffer the most due to the increase in the prices of commodities and the uncertain job market.

As for the global economy, it will be directly affected, in the short term, if China's economy slows down, simply because the Chinese economy is the second largest in the world and closely connected with global economy.

In the trade and business field, since the United States and many European Union countries import consumer goods from China on a large scale, they too may see an increase in commodity prices.

China is closely connected with many economies including those of the EU, the US and Japan through the global industrial chain. As China is a major processing and manufacturing base for many of these countries' enterprises, the temporary closure of plants in China will disturb the industrial chain of upstream enterprises in those countries, especially in the electronics, information technology and auto industries.

In addition, foreign enterprises' businesses in China will be affected by the epidemic—in fact, Apple has already suspended its retail stores in China.

Also, some countries have imposed a travel ban on Chinese people and cancelled flights to and from China, which will undermine the flow of personnel and students. And the major overseas tourism destinations of Chinese people including Japan, Thailand and the Republic of Korea will suffer tourism revenue loss.

Since China is a major consumer of energy and other resources, global raw materials and financial markets will also be affected in the short term because of the closure of some Chinese factories due to the epidemic.

But the epidemic will not change the strong fundamentals of the Chinese economy which includes a huge domestic market, complete industrial and supply chains, good infrastructure and demographic dividend.

Moreover, unlike some US politicians' claim, manufacturing industries are unlikely to flow back from China to the US, because the cost of moving a complete industrial chain and cultivating industrial supporting capacity would be huge.

If the epidemic is contained by the end of March, China's economy is likely to stabilize by the second quarter of this year, and its impact on this year's economic growth will be minimized. And if more proactive fiscal and monetary policies are implemented to cope with the negative impacts of the epidemic, China can still achieve a GDP growth of 5.5 percent this year.

February 21, 2020

The author is a researcher at the China Center for International Economic Exchanges.

More govt funds needed to fight epidemic

By Yang Zhiyong

Swedish boiler manufacturer Alfa Laval Qingdao Ltd., located in Jiaozhou Economic and Technological Development Zone in Qingdao, East China's Shandong province, resumes production on Feb 10, 2020.

Provided by Alfa Laval Qingdao Ltd.

People across all walks of life in China are fighting against the novel coronavirus. And in a fight against any disease outbreak, public finance plays a key role.

Since the outbreak of the virus, Chinese provinces have implemented high-level public health measures, which require public funds. By Feb 14, governments at various levels had allocated 90 billion yuan ($12.86 billion) as epidemic prevention and control subsidies, meant to be used mainly for the treatment of those infected with the novel coronavirus and help medical institutions to fight the epidemic.

Since the epidemic is yet to be contained, the treatment of the growing number of patients, especially those critically ill, requires huge amounts of funds. The medical staff and epidemic prevention and control workers, too, need more financial help.

At this critical stage, more funds are needed to win the battle against the novel coronavirus. Since local financial situations vary, the fight against the coronavirus has put great pressure on the finances of some regions, especially undeveloped regions.

As such, the central government should provide special support for these areas, such as increasing special transfer payments. The central government could also help affected regions by announcing preferential tax policies. For instance, the authorities could exempt imported goods for fighting the epidemic from value-added tax and consumption tax, not impose import tariffs on medical imports, and forego taxes on medical products and equipment donated by enterprises or individuals to public welfare organizations and hospitals.

Public finance should also play its due role in supporting enterprises' operations to contain the epidemic, as prevention and control of a disease outbreak require the participation of all kinds of market forces.

The revenues of many industries, especially the catering, tourism, transportation and film industries, have declined because of the epidemic. And, in particular, small and medium-sized enterprises require fiscal support — even some large-scale enterprises face financial constraints.

Moreover, since the job market is closely related to social stability, a huge number of workers cannot return to work because of the epidemic, so public funds should be used to help enterprises restart their operations, which in turn will help stabilize the social environment and allow workers in many industries to return to work.

But enterprises have to ensure a safe and secure working environment to enable workers to return to their jobs, and since the enterprises' operational costs including human resources cost, epidemic prevention and control costs have greatly increased, they need the government's support. For instance, the authorities could consider exempting enterprises from income tax for a certain period, say a quarter, or reducing their taxes, administrative fees and rents.

The government should reduce other taxes, too, such as value-added tax and consumption tax. And the move to cut taxes, administrative fees and rents should be implemented according to the enterprises' actual situation to provide targeted help for them.

Since the financial expenditure of enterprises will greatly increase owing to the epidemic, the authorities should be prepared for lower fiscal revenue. Also, the government should not worry if spending crosses the bottom line of 3 percent of the budget deficit, because it is essential to provide sufficient fiscal support for epidemic prevention and control work.

Epidemic prevention and control work will test local governments' governance capability. But after the epidemic is contained, we should seriously reflect on the public finance issue. China has continuously increased financial allocation for public health service, but as the novel coronavirus shows, as a developing country, China has to further raise the financial allocation for public healthcare.

More importantly, the government needs to improve the efficiency of financial investment in the health sector to improve returns.

February 24, 2020

The author is a research fellow at the National Academy of Economic Strategy, Chinese Academy of Social Sciences.

Fiscal support to weather the storm

By Zhang Liqing

Ma Xuejing/China Daily

To respond to the unprecedented challenge of the novel coronavirus epidemic, the central government has unveiled a series of measures. The People's Bank of China, China's central bank, has injected an enormous amount of liquidity through multiple rounds of monetary policy measures as a timely response to buffer the shocks of the epidemic to economic and financial stability.

Provincial and local governments across China have been following suit in providing assistance in areas such as financing, rental and leases, taxes and utilities to companies affected by the epidemic.

These policy measures are essential to bring the situation under control and to alleviate the negative effects of the epidemic, and so far they have proven to be effective. Having said that, it is necessary to explore and release follow-on measures as the epidemic has not yet ended and the future remains uncertain.

First, fiscal policy should be prioritized among all policy options and be allowed to play a central role. In light of the scale and severity of the epidemic, fiscal policy can focus on further reducing taxes and fees on small and medium-sized enterprises and on providing direct subsidies to companies that play an outsized role in maintaining people's livelihoods, which have been hard hit by the outbreak. The State Council has announced measures to waive or reduce social security payments in phases and allow companies to delay contributions to the Housing Provident Fund. This policy is a timely measure, and will be fundamental for helping businesses in general and small and medium-sized enterprises in particular to survive the hardship.

In this vein, fiscal policies could also include raising the threshold on personal income tax so that people are left with more disposable income to spend. Such a policy would not only help with the current epidemic response but also contribute to the transition of the country's development model in the long run.

On the other hand, fiscal policies should also focus on boosting investment in infrastructure projects that are closely related to people's livelihoods. This can ultimately help expand aggregate demand. It is particularly important to drastically increase the fiscal commitment to public health to clear the bottleneck in the allocation of medical and health resources, as the outbreak brought in sharp relief investment gaps in prevention, medical staff and hospitals. Statistics show that China spent 6.6 percent of its GDP on health in 2018, while developed countries in Europe and the United States spent over 10 percent of the GDP on health. Per capita spending on health in China is even lower when one takes into consideration its vast population. Reversing this situation could help unlock high-quality economic growth and achieve our aspiration of a moderately prosperous society.

Currently, China's deficit stands at around 3 percent of GDP, a level lower than that of many developed and developing countries alike, which means that it still has some policy space. It may be wise to consider increasing the fiscal deficit to 4 percent of GDP in 2020 and issuing special treasury bonds to make up the difference.

Second, the People's Bank of China may consider additional reductions in the reserve requirement ratio (RRR) and benchmark lending rates, which would help SMEs to weather the storm through facilitating the release of liquidity on one hand and reducing the costs of borrowing on the other.

Third, since the start of the Sino-US trade conflict, foreign investors in some areas in China have been gearing up to move their supply chains to third-party countries. With stricter traffic controls in some cities and lockdowns of others since the outbreak of the epidemic, companies heavily dependent on global value chains (automakers, electronics manufacturers and pharmaceutical companies, for example) have been struggling to reopen after the Chinese New Year holiday or sell their goods. This may exacerbate the flight of foreign investors and heighten the risk of decoupling from the world economy. It may be time for the relevant government authorities to consider rolling out timely measures aimed at foreign investors that have been hard hit by the epidemic. These measures could include, for example, temporary relief on taxes, loans and foreign exchange. The key is to help these investors reopen their businesses and factories as early as it is safe to do so, so as to avoid prolonging the impact of the epidemic.

Fourth, expansionary fiscal and monetary policies can make effective short-term responses to downward pressures on growth. Having said that, fiscal and monetary policies can only be expansionary to a certain point, and the long-term consequences must be considered. In fact, another important tool (and one with longer-lasting benefits) to counteract downward pressures is market-driven supply-side reform, which can boost total factor productivity and help fully leverage the decisive role of the market in resource allocation, while at the same time mobilizing private enterprises by shoring up their business confidence.

The outbreak has been an emergency of extensive impact and duration. It has proven an enormous challenge for the current social governance model. Handled well, it could be a great opportunity for exploring and improving our way of responding to unexpected incidents in the future. Government authorities can draw lessons from other countries in this regard and heed the experts in their insights and recommendations. In this way, we can create more agile and evidence-based alert and response mechanisms that are based on enhanced exchange of information.

March 2, 2020

The author is Chief Economist of PwC China and professor of the School of Finance with Central University of Finance and Economics. The author contributed this article to China Watch, a think tank powered by China Daily.

Integrity as nexus must be maintained

By Fan Zhiyong

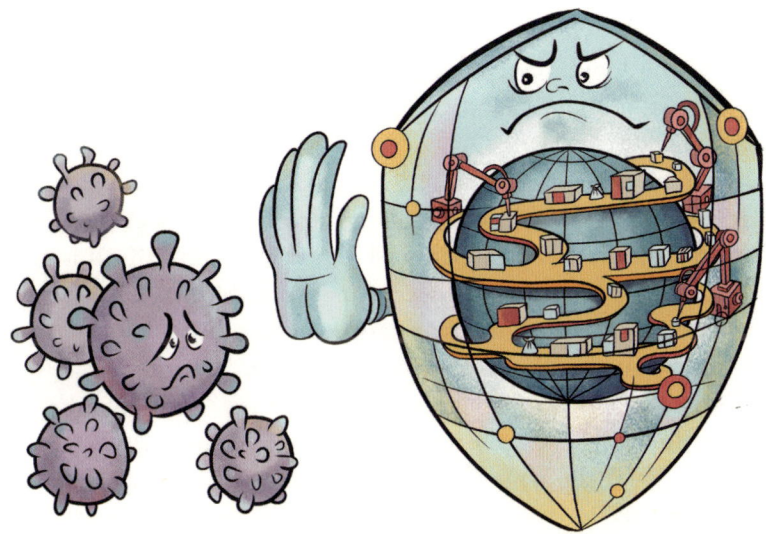

Ma Xuejing/China Daily

On Jan 31, the World Health Organization declared the novel coronavirus outbreak in China as a public health emergency of international concern (PHEIC), after which many countries began to impose restrictions on those traveling from China. But such restrictions are like a double-edged sword as they not only stop personnel exchanges, they also disrupt the normal economic order of the country which implement them. The economies of countries are now interwoven with each other through global production networks.

When US Commerce Secretary Wilbur Ross said the outbreak would speed up the flows of jobs back to North America, he was harshly criticized by Nobel laureate Paul Krugman, who said that in a world of global value chains, the majority of a country's imports are not consumer goods, but intermediate products for further domestic production. Anything that disrupts imports, be it tariffs or a virus, will drive production costs up and then harm manufacturing industries.

Entering the 21st century, China has gradually become a nexus linking different parts of the global production network together. It not only provides large numbers of final products to the world, but also supplies others with intermediate products. Therefore, the temporary stasis of the Chinese economy will have a profound impact on the global macroeconomic landscape, much more far-reaching than what the trade scale implies.

In recent years, some labor-intensive companies have moved their production bases from China to Southeast Asia. And this trend has been accelerated by the China-US trade frictions. But it is not the entire industrial chain or production network that has been moved. It is only some specific labor- and tariff-sensitive production parts that are shifting out of China. And such companies are still heavily reliant on China's supply of upstream intermediate products. Take Vietnam, for instance, Chinese companies are expanding investment in Vietnam, but at the same time, China's trade surplus with the country is on the rise.

Different from production network restructuring that comes from rising costs and trade frictions, the economic suspension caused by the outbreak of the novel coronavirus will have a direct impact on the crucial links or the nexus of the global production system. This impact will first be seen in China's dropping exports of intermediate products, and then some time afterward China's imports of such goods will also decrease. Take Hubei province for example. Although the province only accounts for about 4 percent of China's GDP, its capital city Wuhan is a hub for the country's electronic and auto manufacturing industries, as well as a strategic city for the semiconductor industry. Since it cannot get spare parts from Wuhan, Hyundai, headquartered in Soul, has shut down its domestic production lines. As the day for many workers to resume work after the Spring Festival holiday has been delayed, China's exports of intermediate products to Japan, the Republic of Korea, Europe and South America have also felt the blow. Some large multinationals are even considering expanding production outside China.

Restructuring of the global value chain may well begin after the epidemic ends. If such a reshuffle takes place, it will bring really serious challenges to the Chinese economy.

In which case, how to avoid a restructuring that is disadvantageous to China? First, the Chinese government should help companies to start production again as soon as possible to overcome the current difficulties. No country can guarantee that a contagious epidemic never happens on its land, but its response to an outbreak could reflect the resilience of its production network. Governments at various levels in China are now taking measures to help companies start work on the precondition that the epidemic is prevented and controlled in an effective manner. Initial progress has been made.

Second, the current outbreak has revealed the world's weaknesses in preventing and addressing a large-scale epidemic, and reminds the international community to pay attention to a possible systematic economic crisis. China should strengthen cooperation with international organizations to reduce the possibility of future epidemics and to improve the international public health and epidemic prevention systems.

Third, to deal with the outbreak, some multinationals are considering restructuring, which might decompose China's production network to some extent. In a certain sense, this outbreak can be regarded as a stress test of the global production network should it decouple from China. Accumulation of global manufacturing could of course increase production efficiency and lower costs, but by putting all the eggs in one basket, the stakes of systematic risks are also higher.

As for China, it should actively expand its outward investment so as to create copies of its core production networks and enhance the safety of them. The more copies of its production networks it has, the more secure it will be. Instead of weakening its strength, such practice will enhance the competitiveness of its production network.

The economic rise of China does not only come from the increasing size of its GDP, but also from the secure, open and efficient production network through which China supplies the world with intermediate products. To safeguard the openness and security of this network is an obligation that China must shoulder as a major responsible country. And this may also be a vital determinant and foundation for the internationalization of the renminbi and the success of development projects such as the Belt and Road Initiative.

February 27, 2020

The author is a researcher at the National Academy of Development and Strategy, and a professor at the School of Economics at Renmin University of China. The author contributed this article to China Watch, a think tank powered by China Daily.

Outbreak also offers opportunities

By Han Yonghui and Zhang Fan

China is gradually resuming economic activities, and judging from the stable pace of resumption and a healthy growth rate in 2019, we are confident that the Chinese economy will rebound in the second quarter in 2020.

But the novel coronavirus outbreak will still have a big impact on the Chinese economy this year. In fact, S&P has lowered China's growth forecast from 5.7 percent to 5 percent while Citi Bank has reduced it to 5.3 percent — with the export growth rate expected to be around 0 or even negative.

However, the coronavirus outbreak has also created some opportunities.

To begin with, the outbreak is expected to boost the development of the digital economy based on internet of things (IoT), as working online has already become common in many tertiary industries, especially big internet companies.

Manufacturing, though, still lags in digitalization and informatization, and this is the fundamental reason why the secondary industry has borne the brunt of the epidemic.

Yet embracing digitalization may be comparatively easy for tier-one companies but not viable for most small and medium-sized enterprises. As such, the epidemic has stimulated the demand for establishing a comprehensive IoT ecosystem, including cloud computing, data storage, data transmission and man-machine interaction.

Besides, the outbreak will accelerate the fusion of online and offline retail, as the innovation of "delivery without touch" has already redefined "the last kilometer" in online shopping. Delivery lockers, self pick-up warehouses, and unmanned stores are expected to become more prevalent. Also, online shopping may no longer just supplement offline shopping, as the fusion of the two is becoming a trend, and drones could soon enter the delivery market.

New technologies, such as artificial intelligence (AI) and big data, could become the next driving force for the economy. And the applications some companies have developed using big data to predict the spread of the virus in a particular area could help control the epidemic.

Since the essential use of big data is to feed AI, after the epidemic is contained, the government, companies and consumers are expected to focus more on data collection and data-driven decision-making, and thus propel the development of big data and AI.

Moreover, the health crisis has prompted internet giants to promote the concept of "sharing employees". Retail companies such as Freshhema, a subsidiary of Alibaba, and JD.com are sharing their employees with other service industries that have a low-entry threshold. The emergence of "sharing employees" has not only challenged the traditional organization of enterprises, but also created new possibilities for companies. A company may no longer mean a physical "location", as it could be a non-physical "platform". Further, a platform may not be one company, but a combination of companies or employees. And platforms can provide more and better job opportunities for the people.

To seize these economic opportunities, China should announce timely tax cuts, provide fiscal aid and, more importantly, push forward social governance reform. The most precious thing in the fight against a crisis is confidence, and the greatest source of confidence for China would be economic recovery and finding solutions to the problems that have emerged in the fight against the virus. In fact, by promoting social governance reform China can better utilize the economic opportunities that have emerged because of the epidemic.

The lesson from the outbreak is that solving domestic problems remains a priority for China, as the country's development is not determined by what the outside world thinks about it, but how China will choose its path. The focus should be on whether the Chinese governance system is capable of timely reforming, self-repairing and adjusting itself.

The disease control mechanism, for instance, should suit the reality of China and meet the demand of a mega-society that is rapidly modernizing. Since no country can serve as a model, China has to "cross the river by feeling the stones", but at a steady pace.

And by pushing forward social governance reform, China will be able to not only establish a more flexible and effective system, which would help it to solve its problems and use its economic and political strengths to advantage, but also maintain prosperity in the long run.

March 14, 2020

Han Yonghui is a senior researcher at the Guangdong Institute for International Strategies, Guangdong University of Foreign Studies, and Zhang Fan is an assistant researcher at the same institute.

Online emergency help

By Huang Yiping

Ma Xuejing/China Daily

As the novel coronavirus has proven to be highly infectious, quarantine has been the most widely practiced and most effective measure to curb its spread. But this has resulted in a big decline in consumption. Additionally, as the outbreak took place over the Chinese New Year, restaurants, hotels, amusement parks, museums and theaters have been heavily hit during what would have been their peak period, and countless meetings and forums scheduled for February have been postponed.

One silver lining in all this has been the digital economy, which has played a stabilizing role in consumption and the macro economy. With brick and mortar stores not accessible, online commerce has partially compensated.

Take restaurants, for example. During the epidemic, 40 percent of restaurants have worked hard to expand their online take-out business, with half of these restaurants not offering that option before. They were able to do this thanks to a robust infrastructure network that enables online purchase, delivery arrangement and mobile payment.

Both online and offline sales have suffered as a result of the epidemic, but the restaurant sector would have been devastated were it not for online business.

A comparison across different industries shows similar results. Amusement parks, museums and theaters have seen a 90 percent decrease in their business, if not more. At the same time, viewership of online movies, TV shows and short videos has experienced exponential growth, while online education has witnessed growth of upwards of 300 percent. As the spring semester has started but students are not yet allowed to go back to school, instructors are taking advantage of livestreaming or recorded online lessons to stay on track.

But with small and medium-sized enterprises being hit hard by the epidemic, it is important to prevent the effects of the outbreak escalating into systemic risks.

According to a survey conducted by Ant Financial, Alibaba's financial arm, over 70 percent of SMEs are struggling. While this number may not be exact, the risks could be systemic if over half of SMEs are struggling to survive.

While SMEs are no stranger to bankruptcy as around one-fifth fail each year under normal circumstances, when half or more SMEs fall on hard times and are at risk of failing at the same time, the economy as a whole will likely suffer. SMEs make up the majority of private enterprises in China and contribute 60 percent of our GDP and 80 percent of urban employment. At the same time, small and medium-sized banks, which have been providing most of the financing for SMEs suffer from poor asset quality. SMEs failing en masse would exert huge pressure on economic growth, employment and financial stability.

It is essential to prevent a vicious cycle of bankruptcy, rising unemployment and more non-performing assets. It is necessary for the government to take the initiative to prevent this cycle from happening. During the 2008 financial crisis, when the US federal government bailed out major financial institutions, the purpose was not to help these entities or their employees and shareholders but to prevent a systemic collapse of the US financial industry. Similarly, if the Chinese government were to take action now, the purpose would not be to save any SMEs in particular but to help the economy, jobs and the financial sector stay afloat.

The key to recovery is to help SMEs stabilize their cash flows. While businesses have reopened across many regions in China, it will take time for consumer confidence and the economy to bounce back. To avoid en masse bankruptcies, job losses and deterioration in financial asset quality, the key is preventing large-scale cash flow disruptions to SMEs. The Ant Financial survey points out that around 80 percent of SMEs are cash-strapped, and 70 percent of businesses say that they will not be able to continue operating if they cannot secure access to financing.

There are three ways to prevent cash flow disruptions: increase revenues, cut operating costs and obtain external financing.

Revenue growth will ultimately come from the recovery of the economy as a whole, and the most effective way to accomplish that is to get the epidemic under control as quickly as possible and restore business activities. The government and the central bank could also consider countercyclical measures, especially subsidizing low-income workers and the jobless, which would help safeguard social stability and also boost demand for the products and services of SMEs boosting revenue.

However, a more important measure is to help SMEs reduce their costs of operation. Over the near term, reducing fees may work better than tax relief, which only works when the businesses are making money in the first place. Recently there have been successful cases of cost reduction for SMEs in different areas, such as allowing a grace period on social security contribution payments, waving or reducing rentals for SMEs that lease State-owned property, waving or reducing utility bills, as well as private enterprise initiatives offering preferential treatment to SMEs.

When it comes to cash flow, past experiences show that companies will dig into their savings before taking out loans after an unexpected downturn. Compared to traditional banks, online banks are more competitive at offering financing options to SMEs, as no in-person contact is required, and risk management can be done even without collateral. Most of the traditional banks decided to close for business during the epidemic, while online banks did not see a decrease in applications for small and microloans. Data from Ant Financial also points to the fact that over half of SMEs have plans to apply for loans from online banks. Hence, the authorities could consider prioritizing these banks and city commercial banks in their support policies.

February 28, 2020

The author is deputy dean of the National School of Development and director of the Institute of Digital Finance at Peking University. The author contributed this article to China Watch, a think tank powered by China Daily.

Sacrifice, Toil and Tears — China and the World in the Fight against the Pandemic

China will emerge stronger after outbreak

By Michele Geraci

Neurosurgeon Ling Zhipei at the Chinese PLA General Hospital (301 Hospital) in Beijing uses 5G technology to prescribe treatment to a patient in North China's Hebei province on March 6, 2020.

Zou Hong/China Daily

Despite my training and my profession pushing me to make assessments based on data, analysis and econometric models, for once I would like to rely on a set of intuitions and experiences, which derives from the 10 years I lived in China, and venture to make a prediction: China will not only rise from this health emergency stronger than before, but also take advantage of these months of crisis to accelerate its social and economic transformation.

I expect China to learn vital lessons from the novel coronavirus epidemic and to become more prosperous and stable socially, economically and politically. After all, the history of China is dotted with crises that have been turned into opportunities: the banking crisis of the 1990s, which stabilized the banking system; the 2008 global financial crisis, which gave impetus to the development of a high-speed rail network. These are just two of the many examples.

China does more and speaks less

Contrary to how we act in Italy, China speaks less and does more, and does so to pursue its national interest objectives, exactly as any government should do.

I foresee that in the aftermath of the novel coronavirus epidemic, development will accelerate along two interconnected axes.

The first will comprise the proliferation of new software applications and services based on technologies that are already being widely used or being developed according to an already undertaken path.

The second axis will be that of upgrading management models, starting from the manufacturing and health sectors and leading up to the closure of live animal markets and an increase in the hygiene threshold in society.

Some examples will better clarify what I mean.

In the sector I am most familiar with, universities and higher education, the return of students and faculties to campus has been deferred several times; various forms of online teaching are being implemented and the most enterprising professors are already looking to adapt to a type of communication no longer ex cathedra, but via personal computers.

Concept of presence in class to change

University administrations will understand that the concept of compulsory presence will change, since each student will have the choice to watch the videos of lessons whenever he/she wishes and the teachers' performance will be under collective scrutiny, which will be an incentive to improve themselves.

But as in a Darwinian system, only the most flexible will adapt to the changes. Hopefully, the development and systemic improvement of online teaching will lead to an increase in the level of education in the poorest rural areas which even today have relatively little access to quality teaching. If done well, this will increase the standard of living and potential consumption, thus bringing economic benefits.

Remote working will extend to numerous other areas, starting right from remote medical diagnosis, a necessity during an epidemic and of great convenience at a lower cost in normal situations, which will also allow the less well-off to access medical treatment. Italian expertise in the medical field and remote diagnosis can help find interesting ways and satisfy the double-bottom approach: making profits while doing good.

Great advances in high-tech

Another example concerns the application of artificial intelligence. In a very short time, Chinese researchers seem to have developed much more refined facial recognition systems, which allow recognition even for those wearing a face mask. This does not require new technological developments, but simply a further optimization of the deep-learning process and backward propagation of technology and neural networks, that already exist.

An app has also been developed that allows anyone in real time to have a map of their neighborhood showing the homes of those who have contracted the novel coronavirus. Once a person enters a particular number on his or her mobile phone, an app service of Chinese telecom companies will give the names of all the cities he/she has visited in the last 15 days. Both are needed in Italy, especially at airports.

The philosophical debate between privacy and national security will no doubt be fierce in Italy and other European countries, but China is showing us that in time of crisis certain priorities can be readjusted, because national security comes first.

Booming online services proof of development

Within a few days, there has been an explosion of all online services — films and videos, financial services (playing on the stock exchange satisfies both economic and psychological needs), online games and much more — for those forced to stay at home. Most of the restaurants have been suspended, but food delivery services are skyrocketing.

These behaviors are facilitated by the fact that — unlike in the West where the internet was born in the laptop or desktop and, therefore, there is a clear separation between online and offline — in China the internet was born in mobile phones. Therefore, most Chinese users don't perceive the difference between online and offline because they are always online, except when they are asleep.

From crises arise opportunities, new ways of doing business and new markets because today's forced behaviors can easily become permanent in the post-crisis period. I believe that studying these phenomena and anticipating their trends will also be useful for our Italian companies that always struggle to penetrate the Chinese market.

March 7, 2020

The author is former under-secretary of state at the Italian Ministry of Economic Development.

Sacrifice, Toil and Tears | China and the World in the Fight against the Pandemic

No serious impact of virus on BRI projects

By Gao Yang

China-Europe freight train from Hefei, capital of East China's Anhui province, to Nuess, a city in the German state of North Rhine-Westphalia, resumes regular operations on Feb 13, 2020.

Zhong Xin/China News Service

II China's Economy Resilient

To contain the novel coronavirus outbreak, all provinces and municipalities in China have launched strict emergency health measures. And after declaring the novel coronavirus epidemic a public health emergency of international concern, the World Health Organization has released relevant suggestions regarding personnel, goods, containers and transportation vehicles.

Containing the spread of the novel coronavirus has now become a challenge for the entire international community. As the world's second-largest economy, China contributed 30 percent to global economic growth in 2019. Which means China remains the prime engine of global growth.

As such the outbreak will affect not only China but also other countries including those associated with the China-proposed Belt and Road Initiative. But despite threatening to reduce China's economic growth, the epidemic is likely to have only a temporary impact on the Belt and Road projects.

First, China's efforts to control the epidemic have begun to yield results, as the number of newly confirmed cases has continued to decrease. It would thus be fair to say that the spread of the virus has been effectively suppressed. In fact, on Feb 26, WHO Director-General Tedros Adhanom Ghebreyesus said that for the first time, the number of new cases outside China exceeded those within China.

Since the operation rate of more than 20,000 major production-oriented subsidiaries supervised by the State-owned Assets Supervision and Administration Commission exceeds 80 percent, and that of small and medium-sized enterprises is close to 30 percent, the negative impact of the epidemic on the overall economy could be controlled in the short term, which means the national economy has a strong chance of bouncing back to normal.

Second, the Chinese economy has great resilience, potential and vitality. In 2019, China's total GDP was close to 100 trillion yuan ($14.30 trillion) and grew by 6.1 percent. Although the growth rate was lower than 6.6 percent in 2018, it was significantly higher than the global growth rate. Besides, China's per capita GDP has now exceeded $10,000.

That China's exports have grown by 5 percent despite the Sino-US trade dispute shows not only the resilience of the Chinese economy but also the continuous optimization of its domestic business environment, which manifests the endogenous power of China's foreign trade. Stephen Roach, a senior researcher at Yale University, has said that the People's Bank of China has continued to inject liquidity into the market in recent days, indicating that the country has sufficient policy tools to meet the challenges. And the 40 economists Reuters interviewed recently said they were optimistic about China's economic outlook and believed that the Chinese economy would rebound rapidly in the second quarter of this year.

Third, the Belt and Road projects have a high localization rate. The Belt and Road projects have created hundreds of thousands of local jobs in the host countries. At present, 85 percent of the employees of State-owned enterprises' overseas branches are local employees, with the employment localization rate of many enterprises exceeding 90 percent. Petro-China's subsidiary in Indonesia and China Mobile's branch in Pakistan, for example, have hired almost 99 percent of their employees from among the local population.

And fourth, most of the Belt and Road partner governments are working with the Chinese government to reduce the impact of the epidemic. Since the Belt and Road Initiative was proposed in 2013, trade between China and other Belt and Road economies has been continuously expanding, with the accumulated trade value reaching about $6 trillion.

Since 2013, China has made direct investment of more than $100 billion in Belt and Road partner countries, and paid $2 billion in taxes. The Belt and Road projects have been playing a positive role in promoting the development of the local economy in the host countries, and these countries know that supporting China is good for their own economic growth. No wonder leaders of more than 160 countries and 30 international organizations have sent letters of support to China.

Although some countries have suspended air and rail services, and personnel exchanges with China, these restrictions are short term and will be lifted gradually as the epidemic is contained. Thanks to the preventive and control measures China has taken, the epidemic will not seriously affect economic and trade cooperation between China and other Belt and Road countries.

As International Monetary Fund Managing Director Kristalina Georgieva said recently, if the epidemic is controlled quickly, China's economy will rebound soon.

Hopefully, international cooperation will help contain the epidemic soon, and there is much to expect beyond the epidemic. China will continue to work with all Belt and Road partner countries to contain the epidemic and ensure high-quality cooperation in the future.

March 4, 2020

The author is a research fellow at the China Center for Contemporary World Studies.

Sacrifice, Toil and Tears — China and the World in the Fight against the Pandemic

It's still too early to gauge broad economic impact

By Jim O'Neill

Ma Xuejing/China Daily

Regarding the global economic impact of the novel coronavirus outbreak, it is still too early to state anything with certainty, though there are reasons for concern.

Throughout much of 2019, the world economy was slowing down, prompted by China's own slowdown and its trade dispute with the United States.

Countries tied to the China machine in terms of trade, such as Germany and Japan, saw significant slowing. Others, such as India, had their own domestic reasons for slowing, as did the United Kingdom, which was tackling the Brexit challenge.

In December and January, there was some evidence that the slowdown was abating, but the unexpected outbreak of COVID-19, and the need for China to restrict the movement of people, added to fresh concerns.

In the past week, the evidence of major outbreaks elsewhere in the world, notably in South Korea, Italy and Iran, has caused markets to fear the worst.

China, with a GDP of around $14.5 trillion, is around 18 percent of the world's GDP. If China's economy is hit, all those countries and companies that have benefited most from the rise of China are the ones that will suffer the most. For Germany, this is probably enough to push it into negative GDP growth, even if it did not have a major domestic virus outbreak.

The same is true for Japan. And it is especially true for Italy, which has had to shut down the north part of the country. This is now a real concern. Many countries that conduct trade, business and tourism with Italy, China, South Korea and Iran have to restrict all forms of human contact, which adds to the initial negative shock.

If the virus can appear in South Korea, quite rightly regarded as a successful country, the markets are fearing it could happen anywhere.

Then, of course, you add to the mix that in so many countries, conventional economic stimulus measures have been greatly exhausted by the consequences of the 2008 financial crisis and its aftermath. Markets are worried about this, too.

In this regard, the idea that interest rates being reduced might help offset some of the impact of the virus and its fears is sort of ridiculous.

It is quite clear from those countries that have had aggressive quantitative easing, and in some cases, negative interest rates, that it is not helping their economies. Quantitative easing is a policy in which a central bank buys predetermined amounts of government bonds to inject liquidity into the economy.

As for fiscal policy, it does seem to be, in circumstances where private business is so averse to major investment spending, the case for some governments to dramatically boost their own investment spending.

I would put Germany at the top of such a line, the UK not far behind, and include China. Much of this could be orientated toward so-called green investment spending and accelerated plans to stop climate warming, which the world needs anyhow. I am once more reminded of an old phrase, "Never let a crisis go to waste."

From the evidence that is reported in China in the past two weeks, it is clear that both the rate of reported infections and the reported recovery rate are improving relatively.

In some provinces, the rate of recovery is now more than 80 percent. South Korea, as of Feb 27, had a higher number of reported infections than any Chinese province other than Hubei. This suggests China is achieving some success at bringing COVID-19 under control, and may be allowing the economy to open up again.

The difficult question, which only time is going to give the answer to, is whether other countries can achieve the same success as China has apparently done. Let's hope so.

March 3, 2020

The author is chair of Chatham House, a London-based NGO.

Joint efforts needed to reduce global economic shocks

By Stephen S. Roach

Luo Jie/China Daily

The COVID-19 outbreak comes at a particularly vulnerable point in the global business cycle. World output expanded by just 2.9 percent in 2019 — the slowest pace since the 2008-09 global financial crisis and just 0.4 percentage points above the 2.5 percent threshold typically associated with global recession.

Moreover, vulnerability increased in most major economies over the course of last year, making prospects for early 2020 all the more uncertain. In Japan, the world's third-largest economy, growth contracted at a 6.3 percent annual rate in the fourth quarter — much sharper than expected following another consumption-tax hike.

In Germany and France industrial output fell sharply in

December, by -3.5 percent and -2.6 percent respectively. And although the United States, the world's largest economy in terms of GDP, appeared relatively resilient by comparison, 2.1 percent real (inflation-adjusted) GDP growth in the fourth quarter of 2019 hardly qualifies as a boom.

As for China, the world's largest economy in purchasing power parity terms, its growth slowed to a 27-year low of 6 percent in the last quarter of 2019.

Virus outbreak has had huge impact on economy

In other words, there was no margin for an accident at the beginning of this year. Yet there has been a big accident: China's COVID-19 shock.

Daily activity trackers compiled by Morgan Stanley's China team underscore the nationwide impact of this disruption. As of Feb 20, coal consumption (still 60 percent of China's total energy consumption) remained down 38 percent from the year-earlier pace, and nationwide transportation comparisons were even weaker.

The disruptions to supply are especially acute. Not only is China the world's largest exporter by a wide margin, it also plays a critical role at the center of global value chains. Recent research shows that the global value chains account for nearly 75 percent of growth in world trade, with China the most important source of this expansion. Apple's recent earnings alert says it all: the China shock is a major bottleneck to global supply.

Demand-side effects also affect global trade

But demand-side effects are also very important. After all, China is now the largest source of external demand for most Asian economies. Not surprisingly, trade data for both Japan and the Republic of Korea in early 2020 show unmistakable signs of weakness. As a result, it is virtually certain that Japan will record two consecutive quarters of negative GDP growth, which would make it three for three in experiencing recessions each time it has raised its consumption tax (1997, 2014 and 2019).

The shortfall in Chinese demand is also likely to hit an already weakening European Union economy very hard — especially Germany — and could even take a toll on a Teflon-like US economy, where China plays an important role as the country's third-largest and most rapidly growing export market. The sharp plunge in a preliminary tally of US purchasing managers' sentiment for February hints at just such a possibility, and underscores the time-honored adage that no country is an oasis in a faltering global economy.

Epidemiologists will have the final word on the endgame for COVID-19 and its economic impact. While that science is well beyond my expertise, I take the point that the current strain of coronavirus seems to be more contagious but less lethal than severe acute respiratory syndrome was in early 2003.

SARS was followed by strong rebound

I was in Beijing during that outbreak 17 years ago and remember well the fear and uncertainty that gripped China back then. But that the disruption was brief — a one-quarter shortfall of 2 percentage points in nominal GDP growth — followed by a vigorous rebound over the next four quarters.

In 2003, circumstances were very different. China was booming — with real GDP surging by 10 percent — and the world economy was growing by 4.3 percent. For China and the world, a SARS-related disruption barely made a dent. That is far from being the case today. COVID-19 has hit at a time of much greater economic vulnerability. Significantly, the shock is concentrated on the world's most important growth engine. The International Monetary Fund puts China's share of global output at 19.7 percent this year, more than double its 8.5 percent share in 2003, during the SARS outbreak.

Also, with China having accounted for 37 percent of the cumulative growth in world GDP since 2008 and no other economy stepping up to fill the void, the risk of outright global recession in the first half of 2020 seems a possibility.

Yes this, too, will pass. While vaccine production will take time — 6-12 months at the very least, the experts say — the combination of warmer weather in the northern hemisphere and unprecedented containment measures could mean that the infection rate peaks at some point in the next few weeks. But the economic response will undoubtedly lag the virus infection curve. Which means, at a minimum, a two-quarter growth shortfall for China, double the duration of the shortfall during SARS, suggesting that China could miss its 6 percent annual growth target for 2020 by as much as one percentage point.

Important to heed implications of trend

This matters little to the optimistic consensus of investors. After all, by definition shocks are merely temporary disruptions of an underlying trend. While it is tempting to dismiss this shock for that very reason, the key is to heed the implications of the underlying trend.

The world economy was weak, and getting weaker, when COVID-19 struck. The V-shaped recovery trajectory of a SARS-like episode will thus be much tougher to replicate — especially with monetary and fiscal authorities in the US, Japan and the EU having such little ammunition at their disposal. That, of course, was the big risk all along.

February 27, 2020

The author, a faculty member at Yale University and former Chairman of Morgan Stanley Asia, is the author of Unbalanced: The Codependency of America and China.

Panorama of Emerging Social Phenomena

Sacrifice, Toil and Tears — China and the World in the Fight against the Pandemic

TCM can help control spread of coronavirus

By Li Candong

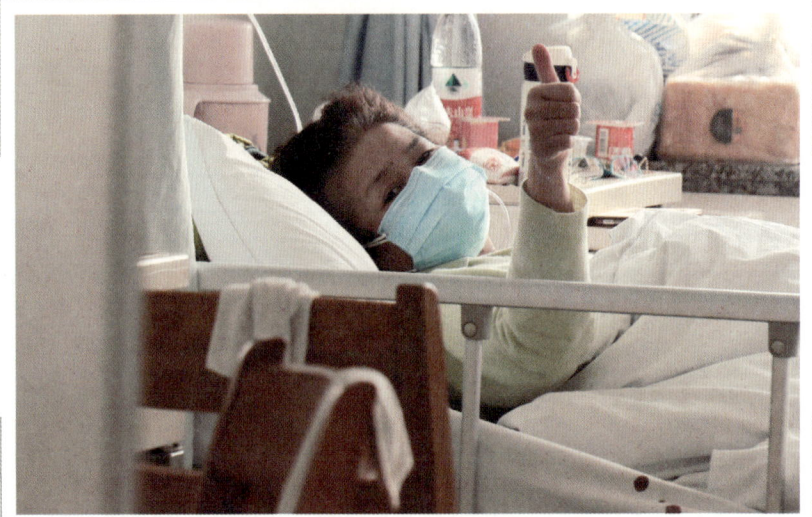

A patient infected with the novel coronavirus at the Tongji Hospital affiliated to Tongji Medical College of Huazhong University of Science and Technology in Wuhan gives the thumbs up to doctors from Beijing's China-Japan Friendship Hospital for their service, on Feb 3, 2020.

Zhu Xingxin/China Daily

In the fight against the novel coronavirus epidemic, traditional Chinese medicine has been proving relatively effective. But while highlighting TCM's efficacy and advantages, we also have to stress the risk of improper use of TCM to control and prevent the spread of coronavirus.

For example, some people mistakenly anchor their hope on some herbs or Chinese patent drugs to prevent infection. Since most people know little about the principles of TCM, they may relax their vigilance against the epidemic by randomly taking some traditional Chinese medicines and forego the mandatory safeguards such as quarantine and hospitalization in the fight against coronavirus.

According to TCM, exogenous diseases including epidemics are determined by the outcome of the fight of healthy *qi*, or internal energy, against pathogens. The healthy *qi* is the internal basis of the disease while pathogenic factors are external causes of the illness.

A person may contract a disease when pathogens defeat the healthy *qi*, which means pathogenic factors play a decisive role in causing a disease in a human being. Also, even if the healthy *qi* is very strong, it may not be able to win the fight against a strong pathogen.

So it is necessary for humans to take medically prescribed measures to avoid pathogenic transmission, especially when an epidemic breaks out.

But is it necessary to take TCM as a preventive measure during an epidemic?

First, those who have a yin-yang imbalance in the body, such as inner-body dampness ("damp evil") or dryness because of yin deficiency, can take some herbs as prescribed by TCM practitioners. For instance, if a person catches a cold after getting wet in the rain, it is advisable that he or she drink ginger soup. Such measures may prevent pathogenic transmission to some extent.

However, healthy people need not take traditional Chinese drugs to avoid contracting a disease.

Second, there is no need either for people to eat certain types of food to increase their immunity against coronavirus. According to TCM diet therapy, consumption of some types of food based on the body's requirement is good for physical health, but it is unnecessary to do so to prevent coronavirus infection.

Third, physical exercise including Tai Chi can help strengthen the healthy *qi* to fight against pathogens. But physical exercise is no substitute for medically prescribed safeguards against an epidemic.

Based on its theory and practice, TCM can prove effective in the treatment of influenza, including the novel coronavirus. Therefore, it is critical to highlight holistic treatment based on symptoms differentiation in TCM and necessary adjustments in line with different seasons, geographical conditions and individuals.

As such, the collection of clinical information for diagnosis should focus on not only some characteristic manifestations of the novel coronavirus but also factors including season, location and geographical condition, which are necessary for treatment based on symptom differentiation.

Prognosis, too, should depend on symptom differentiation. For example, since medical information on the novel coronavirus patients from different places points to the existence of "damp evil", the treatment should focus on drying the inner-body "dampness" while avoiding cold-natured medication as the overuse of heat-reducing and toxicity-draining herbs may hurt the spleen and stomach.

Taking into account the differences in geographical condition and climate is helpful for the treatment of infection. For example, Wuhan, capital of Hubei province and epicenter of the epidemic, experienced many rainy days following the epidemic outbreak, which caused the "damp evil".

So attention needs to be paid to all the early, middle as well as late recovery stages of people infected by the novel coronavirus, particularly because the healthy *qi* may not fully recover even after the disease is cured, owing to lingering fatigue, weakness and loss of appetite.

In short, to control and prevent the spread of the epidemic, it is important to sincerely follow all the principles of TCM while highlighting the integration of Chinese and Western medicines, and avoiding the abuse of herbs. Thanks to its holistic approach to medical treatment, TCM can help contain and prevent the spread of infectious diseases.

February 19, 2020

The author is president of Fujian University of Traditional Chinese Medicine.

III Panorama of Emerging Social Phenomena

Standardizing TCM will help it go global

By Harvey Dzodin

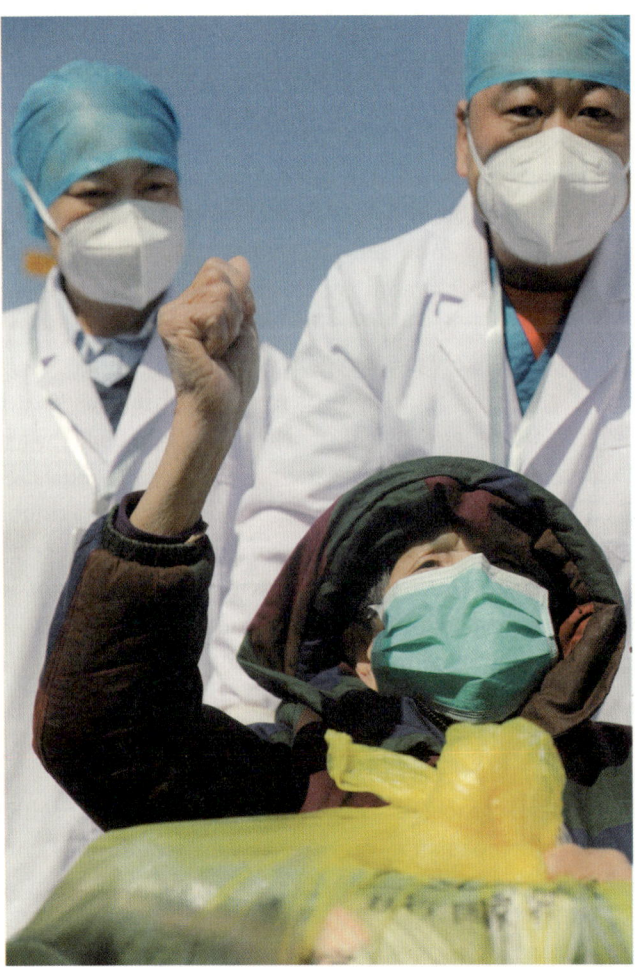

An 83-year-old resident of Wuhan raises her fist in solidarity after becoming first patient to recover from COVID-19 and be discharged from Leishenshan Hospital in Wuhan on Feb 18, 2020.

Wang Jing/China Daily

Sacrifice, Toil and Tears
China and the World in the Fight against the Pandemic

During these extraordinary days, it seems like the news everywhere is completely dominated by the latest developments concerning the novel coronavirus. But believe it or not, there are other medical stories that merit our attention. One of them is the great leap forward about to be made on the world stage by traditional Chinese medicine. That's important because long after the coronavirus is a distant memory, greater global adoption of TCM will boost the Chinese economy, contribute to global health and prove to be a shot in the arm for China's soft power.

TCM has many proponents in China and abroad and it is practiced, especially acupuncture, massage and cupping, in over 180 countries. However, TCM does have many skeptics, especially in the foreign medical and pharmaceutical communities. Some of their negativity is obviously from self-interest in avoiding competition, but many are also well-motivated by wanting to see rigorous scientific evidence that TCM is both effective and safe. When the skeptics are satisfied, TCM will likely grow exponentially.

One of the first giant steps toward this was the official establishment a year ago of the world's first evidence-based TCM Medical Center in the Chinese Academy of Chinese Medical Sciences. Proof of efficacy requires having statistically significant double-blind clinical trials in which a large number of patients get either a placebo or the medical treatment or medicine with the doctors not knowing which one any given patient gets, so as to not bias the results.

The second step is being taken now but knowledge of it has been eclipsed by the necessary laser-like focus on containing and defeating the novel coronavirus. This involves setting government-sanctioned industry standards for TCM ingredients.

Experts have criticized some TCM ingredients, of which there are thousands, for consistency, purity and for sometimes containing poisons, heavy metals and other toxins. Part of the reason was that a traditional TCM pharmacy was, well, traditional, certainly a sight to behold — full of dried seahorses, bird feathers and other exotic ingredients hand measured by the pharmacist and taken away to be prepared as a (usually foul tasting) soup or decoction — with no consistency from one batch to the next. So now the government is requiring the manufacturers to meet minimum standards, starting with the first 160 most commonly used ingredients, largely abandoning the soup and requiring that each ingredient be made into what's called concentrated TCM granules. This will not only ensure a healthy level of safety but help avoid problems for TCM neophytes like me. When I first tried TCM in New York decades ago, I wasn't told to make a soup and instead ate the ingredients, amazingly I survived none the worse for wear.

In addition, in 2022 the World Health Organization will include TCM in its compendium International Classification of Diseases. While this doesn't imply an official endorsement of efficacy it certainly will put TCM on the map in a number of ways. According to WHO spokesperson Tarik Jasarevic, its inclusion will promote TCM internationally by improving international comparability of practices, diagnoses and outcomes, and even enable TCM's integration into insurance coverage. One additional major advantage will be to save lives by for the first time globally tracking data on TCM-western medicine drug interactions which have sometimes caused unforeseen severe problems for some patients when used in combination.

These three steps will inevitably be the catalyst for TCM to go global in a massive way. It's already a big business domestically, as well as in countries with substantially Chinese populations. For example, according to a Chinese government white paper published in December 2016, the TCM pharmaceutical industry's output value increased by 20 percent year-on-year from 2010 to 2015, reaching 786.6 billion yuan ($113.3 billion) in 2015.

But it's not merely about growing the Chinese economy. It's also about improving people's health around the world with treatments that have not merely stood the test of time but that have also been subjected to the most rigorous scientific efficacy and safety testing. It also will improve China's image and soft power as Dr. Tu Youyou, China's Nobel Prize winner, did when she created the antimalarial drug Artemisinin based on a TCM herb described in a 1,600 year old Chinese medical text, saving countless lives globally.

And coming full circle back to the latest novel coronavirus outbreak, with these enhancements perhaps next time there is a public health emergency here or elsewhere, traditional Chinese medicines and their ever growing number of practitioners at home and abroad will be able to make critical contributions to averting a catastrophe. Keep in mind that two millennia before the West did, China developed an inoculation against smallpox and has never stopped innovating.

February 11, 2020

The author is a senior fellow at the Beijing-based think tank Center for China and Globalization.

Wildlife trade ban will protect health

Li Min/China Daily

Amid the nationwide fight to contain the spread of the novel coronavirus, the Standing Committee of the 13th National People's Congress, China's top legislature, made the decision to ban the illegal trade in wildlife and eliminate the consumption of wild animals — so as to guarantee people's lives, health and safety — at a bi-monthly session on Monday.

Which has raised hopes that the existing law on wildlife protection will be amended by lawmakers in the near future to give it teeth so that the trade in wild animals will be made illegal and banned permanently.

It is worth noticing that for the first time lawmakers have elevated wildlife protection to the prominent level of ensuring public health and safety, underlining a firm resolve to defuse the threat of wild animals transmitting viruses to humans.

Scientists believe that more than 70 percent of newly emerged infectious diseases can be traced back to animals. For example, civet cats were thought to be a source for the severe acute respiratory syndrome outbreak in 2002-03, and pangolins are suspected of being the host that transmitted the novel coronavirus to humans.

Pangolins, one of the world's oldest mammal species, have seen their numbers decline by 90 percent over the past two decades in China, according to statistics from the Convention on International Trade in Endangered Species of Wild Fauna and Flora. Police seized 23 metric tons of smuggled pangolin scales, estimated to be extracted from 50,000 pangolins, in a single case they cracked in Zhejiang province in December.

The rampant wildlife trade can be attributed to loopholes in existing laws and regulations, which have yet to categorically prohibit the eating of wild animals.

This has fueled increasing demand for wild species on the dining table because of the huge profits involved. The now-shuttered Hua'nan Seafood Wholesale Market in Wuhan, reportedly advertised more than 70 kinds of wild species.

Many of the country's licensed wild animal breeding farms, established as centers for wildlife protection and research, have actually degenerated into accomplices in wildlife trading due to lax supervision and law enforcement.

The authorities temporarily banned the wildlife trade in the event of SARS outbreak 17 years ago, but the trade rebounded once the ban was relaxed. Lawmakers must see to it that the same mistake will not be committed once again, given the sufferings being inflicted on the nation by the novel coronavirus.

After all, how animals are treated has a direct bearing on the well-being of human society as well.

February 24, 2020

China Daily Editorial

Panorama of Emerging Social Phenomena III

Better protecting wildlife good for all

Li Min/China Daily

Editor's note: The Standing Committee of the National People's Congress, China's top legislature, passed a decision on Feb 24 on thoroughly banning illegal wildlife trade. What needs to be done to protect wildlife as well as public health? Three experts share their views on the issue with China Daily's Liu Jianna. Excerpts follow:

Legislation revision to strengthen protection of wild animals

That the top legislature passed the decision on the total ban is encouraging news, especially because some people have been making huge profits from the trade in wildlife at the expense of China's reputation and Chinese people's health while the wildlife protection department is forced to take the blame.

Many animals including bats are not included in the country's wildlife protection list, which has not been updated for 30 years except for some small adjustments. The existing wildlife protection law focuses on protecting the species of rare and endangered wild animals, keeping out a big number of terrestrial vertebrates from the protected list.

Therefore, it is necessary to update the wildlife protection list and forbid the taming and breeding of all wild animals, except those that can be legally bred and sold in the market. This will help stop the sale of more wild animals and prevent humans from coming in contact with them and thus greatly reduce the chances animal-to-human disease transmission.

As China's ban on ivory trade in 2018 shows, keeping legislation abreast of the times can significantly promote wildlife protection and prompt people to change their habits of wildlife product consumption.

In fact, after the severe acute respiratory syndrome outbreak in 2002-03, wildlife trade has largely diminished in Guangdong province.

In short, the wildlife protection law should be further strengthened and publicized to prevent consumption of wild animals. And the public should be endowed with supervision rights so they can play a bigger role in wildlife protection.

Zhang Li, a professor of ecology at Beijing Normal University and general secretary of the Society of Entrepreneurs and Ecology Foundation

Enforcement of law more crucial in protection

The wildlife protection law should be expanded to cover all wildlife, not just the ones on the protection list. Wild animals like hares and pheasants should also be protected, albeit differently from the way rare and endangered animals are protected.

As a matter of fact, the biggest problem with wildlife protection lies not in legislation, but the lax enforcement of the law, mostly because of a lack of grassroots law enforcement personnel. Many local governments don't have forestry bureaus, which are in charge of wild animal protection.

Besides, the many departments involved in wildlife protection including the forestry and grassland administration, industrial and commercial administrative departments, public security departments and agricultural departments should have more clearly defined responsibilities.

The institutional restructuring goal of "one thing should be managed and resolved by one department" has not proved as effective as expected. In practice, wildlife is divided into terrestrial and aquatic animals, which are managed by the forestry and agricultural departments, respectively. But who is responsible for amphibians such as frogs?

There is also confusion over the management of wildlife in between the natural habitat and the market, as the commercial administrative departments deal with wildlife only when they enter the market. The loopholes in law enforcement need to be plugged.

While the new law on wildlife protection should clearly define wildlife, artificially bred wild animals, such as sika deer and giant salamander, should be viewed as domesticated animals and managed like pigs and chickens. They should be raised, quarantined and tested according to strict standards to ensure their safe use. And all trading and eating of wildlife, irrespective of whether they are on the protection list, should be banned.

The coronavirus outbreak is warning that the detection of wildlife epidemic and disease is related to the disease control system, and it needs significant improvement. Until now, attention has been paid only to controlling the spread of disease among domesticated animals such as the spread of avian influenza and swine fever, while the control of viruses and bacteria at source remains weak. Wild animals, especially bats, marmots and muroids should be tested for the viruses they carry to prevent them from endangering public health.

Tang Xiaoping, deputy director of the National Park Management Office affiliated to the National Forestry and Grassland Administration

Both wild and domesticated animals must be protected

Prioritizing protection of wild animals, China's wildlife protection law also emphasizes the limited and proper use of wild animals. For instance, some practitioners of folk art make a living by taming monkeys and using them in performances. If all commercial use of wildlife is banned, these people would lose their livelihoods and folk art forms would die an untimely death. Therefore, the principle of proper use, not zero use, of wildlife should be upheld.

And the Criminal Law, which prescribes heavy punishment for those killing and indiscriminately capturing wild animals, should be strictly enforced. Besides, the compensation mechanism should be improved to better manage the cases of wild animals injuring or killing people or disrupting their livelihoods.

Prohibiting the indiscriminate trading in and consumption of wild animals is necessary, especially given the coronavirus outbreak, which is speculated to be connected with the consumption of wild animals. But instead of indiscriminately punishing everyone suspected of trading in or consuming wild animals, the authorities should find the root cause of the issue.

To end the chaos surrounding wildlife protection, a comprehensive animal protection law not limited to wildlife, but also including pets, domesticated and performing animals, should be introduced and classified management and protection implemented.

Qiao Xinsheng, a professor of law at Zhongnan University of Economics and Law.

February 24, 2020

The vulnerable need more support

By Peng Siqing

A sales clerk prepares supplies for residents at a supermarket in Hongshan district of Wuhan during the outbreak.

Wang Jing/China Daily

The novel coronavirus epidemic has had a severe impact on society, with many people facing great difficulties in their lives or business operations. Although the difficulties they face may only be temporary, the social consequences caused by the epidemic could last for a long time. People who are struggling need the support of the whole of society in this difficult time.

The impacts of the epidemic have been felt in multiple aspects of social life. The virus has spread around the world and it is hard to predict when it will end. The negative sentiments caused by the epidemic and some crude practices in epidemic prevention and control enforcement could damage social relationships and even divide society, giving rise to disadvantaged groups, albeit temporarily.

The first vulnerable group is comprised of those infected with the virus and their families. Those infected with the virus are not only victims but also the sources of new infections. They not only suffer from the virus, but also face discrimination and exclusion. The public's anxiety over the epidemic could transform into alienation and hostility against those who have had the virus. Even after their rehabilitation, these people could be excluded from normal life for a period.

The second vulnerable group includes those from Hubei province, especially the capital city Wuhan, the epicenter of the epidemic. People living in smaller epidemic areas, such as the residential communities or working units where infections are found, are considered part of the dangerous population. Most of the people inhabiting the epidemic areas are healthy people. But they are labeled as "dangerous" merely because of their home addresses. Moreover, some of them who stay at home in self-isolation as a preventative measure see their homes marked out as a warning. In such a special period, such measures are understandable, but their side-effects should be monitored.

Since the outbreak of the virus, restrictive measures have been carried out in some places, creating barriers for certain groups of people, who constitute the vulnerable groups whose rights are restricted. With cities locked down, roads blocked and residential communities sealed off, many people find they cannot enter a city because they are not locally registered residents, or cannot enter a residential community because they are not property owners. They might have decent jobs and stable incomes in the cities where they work and are local taxpayers and builders, but now they are discriminated and marginalized because of the lack of local *hukou* (household registration) or property ownership.

Moreover, face masks have been in short supply since the outbreak began, leading to those who have no mask being shunned. These people were not well prepared at the beginning of the outbreak, and found face masks had been sold out everywhere. At the peak of the epidemic, those who do not wear a mask draw uncomfortable glances wherever they go. And in some places, people are banned from taking public transport without wearing a mask.

In terms of business, many enterprises in catering, tourism or entertainment have been forced to suspend their operations during the epidemic.

The owners of these enterprises may see their businesses on the brink of going bankrupt. Enterprises in some places are required to pay salaries to their employees despite the delay of business operations, further exacerbating their plight. Many small and medium-sized enterprises are close to bankruptcy because of a lack of funds.

The closedown of SMEs will lead to unemployment. Those who are laid off in the epidemic are likely to be reduced to impoverished status. These temporary disadvantaged groups arising during the epidemic are fragile. They are not able to weather the impacts in social life like ordinary people do, and find it difficult to defend their legitimate rights and interests. In some cases, these vulnerable ones may have been ones with status in society, who have lost their original positions in society because of the epidemic.

The epidemic will have extensive and long-lasting influence on a large proportion of the population. The above-mentioned six temporary vulnerable groups cover a great number of people. If their difficulties cannot be solved in a timely manner, it will not only affect their quality of life and sense of happiness, but also undermine social harmony and stability, causing a social divide and crisis.

Therefore, we call for greater attention to be given to these epidemic-induced vulnerable groups and measures to be taken to help solve their difficulties and mitigate social division.

There are some effective practices implemented by the governments in some places that we can learn from. For example, Suzhou in Jiangsu province has rolled out policies to support SMEs to help them overcome their difficulties; Hebi in Henan province proposed to "isolate but not estrange, and treat people returning from Wuhan like families". We also call for helping hands be lent to those without a face mask by sharing or distribution them from work units or neighborhood communities.

We believe that so long as the governments at all levels and the society reach a consensus on helping those vulnerable groups, we can overcome the difficulties, win the combat against the epidemic, and transform the crisis into opportunities, further promote social harmony and bolster people's sense of gain and happiness. If so, the above-mentioned vulnerable groups will not be permanent and they will show more adoration for the country and more trust in the government.

March 3, 2020

The author is a professor with the marketing department of Guanghua School of Management at Peking University. The author contributed this article to China Watch, a think tank powered by China Daily.

Discarded masks must be properly disposed of

By Yao Yuxin

Li Min/China Daily

Editor's Note: With people wearing face masks to help protect themselves from being infected with the novel coronavirus, a concern now is how they are disposing of their used masks. Two experts share their views on how to correctly dispose of used masks with China Daily's Yao Yuxin. Excerpts follow:

Prevent used masks being recycled

As used face masks may carry germs involving the coronavirus, they shouldn't be randomly discarded as waste.

Since the virus can survive for one or two days in humid conditions, the used masks may become a new source of infection.

If the waste masks are tossed in a confined space such as an elevator, they may contaminate the environment, posing a potential threat to people within it.

Also, it is inappropriate to mix contaminated masks with household waste.

Given the garbage sorting is currently implemented in only a few cities, mixed waste commonly exists. The mixture of polluted masks and recyclable waste may cause a potential danger to rubbish collectors when they put hands in the waste bins to collect recyclable items.

Worse, if someone just throws a used mask on the street, someone might pick it up, or worse try to collect them to sell second-hand.

Thus, it is necessary for the government to encourage people to make sure the used masks are safely recycled and disposed of. Special trash cans should be set up in communities as centralized disposal points for the used masks of residents.

If no special garbage bins are available, residents could spray disinfectant on both sides of their used masks and fold them up before putting them into a sealed plastic bag in the dustbin.

For the safety of others and themselves, residents have to take care of their used masks. Disinfecting them will help ensure the used masks do not become a second source of the coronavirus.

Jiang Rongmeng, chief physician at the Infection Center of Ditan Hospital

Masks should be treated as medical waste

The protective gear already used by medical staff and patients is already designated as medical waste. The medical waste management regulation was enacted the same year as the outbreak of severe acute respiratory syndrome (SARS) in 2002-03, which sets out clear rules on the classification, collection, transportation and disposal of infectious medical waste.

Given the regulation, hospitals in China already have a mature procedure to follow in dealing with medical waste. However, with the outbreak of the novel coronavirus, there has obviously been a high demand for protective equipment such as face masks among ordinary people, with the subsequent generation of a huge quantity of what may be considered medical waste.

Thus, the problem is how to cope with this mass of medical waste, particularly the used face masks discarded outside of hospitals.

Communities should place some special trash cans around to collect used masks. If not available, people had better wrap the waste into plastic bags before throwing them away, so they are not exposed to the air.

However, stricter rules must be implemented once cases of novel coronavirus are confirmed in a community. Once those affected are found, people need to handle polluted masks in such communities according to regulations on disposing medical waste.

According to the regulation, only licensed companies should collect, transport and do the final disposal of medical waste. For example, the medical waste must be collected in special containers, and be transported by special vehicles by qualified people.

As the main hazard of medical waste is infectivity, disinfection, no matter whether by steam, chemicals or microwave, is very important.

Since the SARS outbreak in 2003, many cities have built special disposal sites for medical garbage. After disinfection, the hazardous waste can be sent for incineration in the special facilities, or sent to the incineration plants or landfills set for household rubbish.

Jiang Jianguo, a professor specialized in hazardous wastes at the School of Environment, Tsinghua University

February 5, 2020

Sacrifice, Toil and Tears — China and the World in the Fight against the Pandemic

AI can make big difference in fighting virus

By Zhang Junsheng/Sun Yunchuan

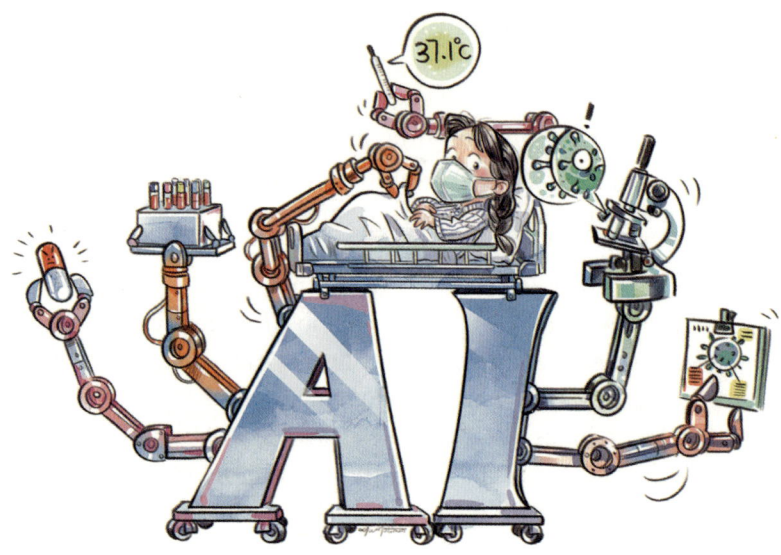

Li Min/China Daily

High technologies, represented by artificial intelligence and robots, will widely and deeply change people's lives and work. At the moment, China, in the middle of a grim fight against the novel coronavirus, could well make use of these technologies to help contain and treat the epidemic.

First, AI, along with big data, could support the prevention and control of the virus. The misreporting of the daily infection data, which is probably inevitable with manual statistics, could be reduced by AI. For instance, we could quickly ascertain the movements made by those infected by plotting their cellphone positioning. While knowledge about the infected people's close contacts and the possible transmission scope and route could be gained by using the big data from tourism and transportation. Furthermore, facial recognition could be used to reduce or prevent unnecessary flows of people. Although people's privacy must be protected in the process.

Second, AI could help make projections of the epidemic situation. By monitoring and analyzing virus transmission and the effectiveness of treatments, it could thus guide the ongoing prevention, control and treatment work based on transmission, treatment and quarantine. In this way limited medical resources could be used most effectively.

Third, AI could be employed to help monitor, control and guide public opinion. Internet technologies could be used to reassure the public and recognize and stop rumors, as well as advocate effective prevention and protection measures. Using AI and big data, false information and rumors can be identified effectively before they spread online. Besides, medical chat robots could provide information about the outbreak and give suggestions, saving medical resources.

The use of robots could largely reduce infections through contact. It is essential to reduce the contacts between people. Limiting outside activities and implementing home quarantine and observation are required. In rural areas, unmanned aerial vehicles could be used to monitor quarantines.

But people still need to replenish daily necessities, and there are a lot of application scenarios for robots not only in treatment and services for the people infected with the virus but also logistics services for the healthy.

For example, hospitals could use robots to deliver meals and medicines to medical staff and patients, which not only saves manual labor but also reduces the chance of infection. In terms of education, online classes should be promoted in the fight against the coronavirus outbreak. For jobs that don't need close contacts, telecommuting is a preferred solution.

AI could also help coordinate the distribution of medical supplies and reduce the man-made unreasonable distribution, which has provoked the loudest public outcries in the outbreak. If the scarce materials are allocated unfairly and the medical staff are not protected effectively, the battle against the outbreak will be significantly hindered. AI technology could be employed to analyze the material demand of each department and implement smart distribution according to the medical supply stock, thus facilitating the smooth containing of the virus.

Finally, AI can help expedite the research and development of antiviral medicines. It could be used in simulations of various treatment methods and techniques and figure out the characteristics of the virus. A number of reports in recent years on smart medicine R&D indicate that AI will be more widely applied in areas including genetics and pharmaceutical manufacturing.

Therefore, AI should play a strong supportive role in the fight against public health threats, guide public opinion in the event of an emergency, even though the difficulty in data accumulation and acquisition may somewhat restrict the role that AI can play.

AI and robotics will certainly exert more influence in the future and Chinese people's experience in fighting the novel coronavirus will have enduring effects in a number of areas such as health care, transportation and education.

February 11, 2020

Zhang Junsheng is a research fellow at the Institute of Scientific and Technical Information of China. Sun Yunchuan is a professor at and director of International Institute of Big Data in Finance of Business School of Beijing Normal University.

Panorama of Emerging Social Phenomena

III

Working from home, distant dream for Chinese

By Liu Jianna

Song Chen/China Daily

Editor's note: With people asked to stay at home during the novel coronavirus epidemic, many of those who can are working from home. Will the outbreak be the turning point of telecommuting in China? Two experts share their views on the issue with China Daily's Liu Jianna. Excerpts follow:

Change of management philosophy imperative

Paperless offices and home offices were proposed in the early days of the internet more than 20 years ago. Yet home offices have never been well implemented in China despite their advantages, such as reducing commuting and congestion and cutting operating costs for businesses.

Given the relevant technology is mature enough, the lackluster promotion of working from home can only be attributed to an outdated management philosophy. Unfortunately the unwillingness to change has led to a huge waste of resources. For instance, college admission letters could be replaced by emails if the department in question changed its management ideas and adopted a more resource-saving attitude. The same goes with college admission interviews which require the applicants to be onsite, no matter what.

Some oppose telecommuting arguing that working from home may prove to be a drag on efficiency. Yet Zhu Qingshi, former head of the University of Science and Technology of China, said that he was the most efficient during the severe acute respiratory syndrome (SARS) outbreak, thanks to a significant reduction in the number of meetings he had to attend.

Therefore only when people's management philosophy is fundamentally changed can telecommuting be popularized. However, no sign of change has been spotted yet.

But blind promotion of telecommuting should also be avoided as only certain types of work are suitable to be done at home. Those providing process-oriented services, such as civil servants, and those in delivery, catering and tourism could never work from home. In a word, telecommuting should be welcomed and promoted targetedly and progressively.

Xiong Bingqi, deputy director of the 21st Century Education Research Institute

Telecommuting unlikely to go mainstream

At the moment, the biggest advantage of working from home—less aggregation of people—can greatly help the fight against the spread of the novel coronavirus. For the moment at least, telecommuting should be encouraged since the priority now is to contain and control the spread of the outbreak.

But telecommuting is not expected to be a mainstream work model despite its obvious merits. Mainly because most Chinese prefer face-to-face interactions which are more effective and make it easier for participants to build trust. That online education could not rival, not to say surpass, on-the-spot teaching, partly speaks of the dilemma that telecommuting is confronted with.

Albeit the people qualified to telecommute could be encouraged to work from home. For example, researchers and writers could largely choose this kind of work style without compromising their work results and efficiency. But for people in the service industry and assembly line workers, telecommuting is not an option.

Looking ahead, some people working in specific sectors may be able to work at home if their employers approve. But generally most people will return to their offices and resume their normal work just as they did after the SARS outbreak ended.

Nevertheless, this epidemic has given people a chance to reflect on their way of working. Hopefully it will be a turning point for employers and employees to try to look for a better work model to improve efficiency.

Mao Shoulong, a professor at the School of Public Administration and Policy, Renmin University of China

February 15, 2020

Online classes can't replace classrooms

By Xiong Bingqi

Cai Meng/China Daily

This week should have seen the beginning of a new semester. Instead, China has been witnessing a different kind of new semester because of the novel coronavirus outbreak: many Chinese schools have suspended the new semester and moved the classrooms online.

On the first day of school, DingTalk, a virtual workplace developed by Alibaba Group, held online classes for an estimated 50 million students nationwide, from primary to high school level.

The huge demand prompted many to assume that online

classrooms are the source of future prosperity. But according to a guideline issued by the Ministry of Education on Feb 12, "postponement of school without suspension of learning" is not equal to learning through online courses. As the education authorities have said, it is unnecessary for every teacher to record online courses to be evaluated for quality. Also, kindergarten classes cannot be held online.

Therefore, it is still too early to say this is the onset of "spring" for online education.

To prevent the spread of the novel coronavirus, schools have postponed the new semester, and after-school training institutes have been closed. This has made online education an indispensable medium for students to take lessons, leading to an explosion of viewings on online educational platforms.

Yet online classes can never replace real classes. Whether online education would continue its explosive growth even after the epidemic is contained would depend on the quality of courses it offers. If user experience is poor, the rapidly growing traffic on online education platforms will contract in the near future, bringing little profit for the online education companies.

In fact, despite the huge flow of capital into online education platforms, merely 5 percent of the platforms are making a profit. Although online education platforms have taken up the grand mission to replace the traditional teaching mode, they exhibit little superiority over the traditional education institutions except that they can overcome the time and space limitation.

More suitable to impart knowledge and skill because of their unfettered access to resources and students, online courses have been found wanting when it comes to educating students in aspects such as morality, social responsibilities and physical exercise, which play a big role in the development of a person.

Besides, because of poor interaction, knowledge teaching may be compromised online. Also, complaints by students, teachers, parents have exposed the weaknesses of online education. For example, paying little attention to the online teachers, many students have been reported to be busy chatting or posting messages online. And a class of 60 students is said to have clicked hundreds of thousands of likes for their teacher during a single live-streaming lesson.

Moreover, parents are under pressure to fully cooperate with the online teachers as they have to monitor and tutor their children at home to ensure they are not distracted while attending online classes.

It is also harmful to urge teachers who are not qualified to do so to start live-streaming. The poor quality of education they impart may have the opposite effect on the students, which may affect the students' development in the long run. Such problems also exist in some traditional educational institutions which have hastily switched to online platforms to cut costs, without paying attention to quality.

The epidemic, however, may accelerate the demise of some offline institutions whose performance has been poor. But that does not mean online platforms are having an easy time, because most of them are offering free lessons to compete with rivals and attract more students. And although the epidemic may have prompted more subscribers to join online education platforms, it would be far-fetched to assume that online education institutions are making big money.

Basically, it is content rather than the form of education that plays a decisive role in the education sector's competition. So, poor quality online education platforms are likely to have a short life despite the increase in traffic due to the epidemic.

February 22, 2020

The author is the deputy director of the 21st Century Education Research Institute.

Therapy key to ease outbreak-induced stress

By Wang Bin/Fu Haojie

Medical staff and patients exercise at the "Wuhan Livingroom", a makeshift hospital in Wuhan on Feb 15, 2020.

Zhu Xingxin/China Daily

People across the country have responded positively to measures such as quarantine to prevent the spread of the novel coronavirus epidemic. As a result, the epidemic is effectively under control in China, with the World Health Organization praising China's contributions to the global fight against the virus. China is still fighting to win the battle against the epidemic, though, but in doing so it has contributed a lot to global fight against the virus.

Yet to strike a balance between prevention and resumption of manufacturing, the fight against the epidemic should be extended from hospitals, medical treatment and preventive measures to psychotherapy including counseling in order to ease people's stress and trauma, as the epidemic has triggered fear, anxiety and depression, and loss, guilt, exhaustion and different levels of insecurity among the people.

According to American psychologist Abraham Maslow's theory of "hierarchy of needs", there are different levels of human needs, which from bottom to top are physiological (breathing, food, water, sleep, sex), safety (security, order, stability), love/belonging (friendship, family, sexual intimacy), esteem (self-esteem, confidence, respect of and by others) and self-actualization (morality, creativity, problem solving, lack of prejudice, acceptance of facts). The high-level needs emerge after the low-level needs are satisfied to a certain extent, and the satisfaction of multiple levels of needs forms a relatively stable pyramid in our daily life.

But the epidemic has disrupted the stable pyramid of the hierarchy of needs. As the novel coronavirus is highly contagious, more and more people are seeking security, safety and order. Quarantine and masks have disrupted social networking, undermining many people's sense of belonging. As the epidemic poses a threat to people, most residents staying at or working from home find it hard to maintain their self-esteem.

The failure to meet multi-level needs gives rise to panic and anxiety among people. Surveys show that despite the different rates of infection, residents in Wuhan, the epicenter of the outbreak in Hubei province, and Chengdu, capital of Sichuan province, show a similar rate (as high as 20 percent) of moderate and severe "acute stress response" because of the outbreak.

To prevent acute stress response from turning into chronic post-traumatic stress disorder, intervention should be taken as soon as possible, because it is extremely important to instantly reduce the number of people with negative emotions and the degree of their acute stress response.

Since the epidemic outbreak, hundreds of hotlines across the country have been opened for residents to seek psychological support services, which offer many kinds of psychotherapy such as lecture series, online counseling and self-help manuals.

Yet the services being offered have some last-mile problems such as simple repetition, differences in the quality of counseling and a lack of sustainable mechanism. For instance, "Psychology Teacher", a nonprofit organization in Sichuan, has been providing psychological support services for people since the Wenchuan earthquake in 2008. But despite therapists being on hotline duty every day, the number of phones being answered is less than 10 on average, which could undermine voluntary work.

According to a conservative estimate, 80 percent of the hotlines nationwide have a relatively small number of people to answer phone calls, yet they consume a huge amount of manpower and materials.

The epidemic has created a huge demand for psychotherapy, as according to a survey, more than 40 percent of the residents said they needed counseling to change their mood. Notwithstanding the high demand for psychotherapy, however, more than two-thirds of the residents may not voluntarily seek such help. Yet, if approached by counselors, more than half of them will accept counseling or other forms of psychotherapy.

Normally, Chinese psychologists wait for patients to approach them or visit them in their office. By contrast, there are door-to-door services for diagnosis and treatment of ailments in the traditional Chinese medical system, which "barefoot doctors" used as their working model in the 1970s and 1980s.

Thus to overcome the last-mile problem without compromising the principles and ethics of psychotherapy, it is necessary to use innovative methods and directly offer psychological support services to those who need them. And bridging the gap between supply and demand will help make the psychological support services more effective.

In addition to psychotherapists, it is also necessary that different parties including the health and education departments, media outlets and NGOs properly coordinate the services in order to fulfill the multi-level psychological needs of the people.

March 11, 2020

Wang Bin is executive director of the Psychosocial Services and Mental Crisis Intervention Research Center jointly established by the Institute of Psychology at Chinese Academy of Sciences and the Southwest University of Science and Technology. And Fu Haojie is a lecturer at the psychological counseling center at the same university.

Sacrifice, Toil and Tears — China and the World in the Fight against the Pandemic

We-media shouldn't be a plague of false news

By Jia Wenshan

Shi Yu/China Daily

The popularity of social media apps such as Facebook, Twitter and WeChat as alternative news-sharing platforms has also seen them become tools for the circulation of fake news and misinformation. Whenever there is an emergency or crisis, some users of these apps tend to generate and circulate more news and information, and also, inevitably, more fake news and misinformation.

With the outbreak of the novel coronavirus in Wuhan, capital of China's Hubei province, WeChat users have been active in not only editing, modifying and truncating reports from other sources, but also in fabricating and circulating news and information, including fake news and disinformation, that is shared among thousands and potentially millions of people in a variety of forms such as one-on-one, in WeChat groups, each of which is capped at 500 members, in WeChat Moments, in WeChat public accounts and so on.

In this way, one can communicate one-on-one, one to a group, and one to the public using written, audio, visual, audiovisual means in one, two, or even many languages.

People do this for fun, to gain popularity or to make a profit. WeChat users have been actively communicating with their relatives, friends, colleagues, and even strangers to show their concern, love, and support to those infected with the new coronavirus in Wuhan and elsewhere. Social media apps such as WeChat have become an organizing device to collect donations from different communities.

But the positives aside, some WeChat users have also been promoting fake, incomplete, distorted partial and biased news, and misinformation and unreliable information about the virus have spread and so damaged the public information and public opinion environment.

For example, a rumor which won the trust of almost 100 million Chinese netizens claimed that the virus was lab-made, stoking up a conspiracy theory that there had been a biological attack against China. Even with the biologists and health scientists deconstructing the reasoning behind the theory, it has still persisted.

Another notable rumor was that the novel coronavirus is not only communicable via breath droplets and physical contact, but also through eye-contact between two individuals. According to the Dingxiang Medical Team, this is Rumor#23 for which the rumormonger has been arrested. Rumor #24 on the List of Rumors of the Dingxiang Medical Team which currently lists 99 popular rumors, is that China has been designated as a so-called "Plague area" by the World Health Organization.

In fact, the WHO has not announced China as "a plague area". As a mere warning, not as a mandatory request for personnel evacuation or personnel move stoppage, the WHO has declared the coronavirus outbreak in China as a Public Health Emergency of International Concern (PHEIC), a designation created by the WHO in its International Health Guidelines (2005). Its goal is to warn the international community to guard against the potential risk of infection.

While China itself has not been designated as "a plague area", self-media such as WeChat have descended into a plague of fake news and misinformation with regard to reporting about the virus. WeChat has become a double-edged sword in the public information and public opinion arena. It has been both an asset and a liability.

WeChat users and WeChat account managers and content creators have different education levels, income levels and ideological orientations. Most of them have received little formal training in journalism and communication. While some of the rumors are concocted out of the political or economic calculations of the WeChat users, most of the rumors probably occur due to the users' lack of sufficient knowledge, absence of logical reasoning and paucity of critical thinking skills.

Thus a majority of the WeChat users who spread rumors are innocent or innocently "ignorant" people. Only a very small number of them harbor malicious or ulterior motives. Compared with traditional media, WeChat communication is more spontaneous, speedier, more personal and compassionate, but less organized, and less professional.

In order to quickly recover from the coronavirus outbreak, and in order to create a trustworthy public arena of information and opinion exchanges in China and the world, the plague of fake news and misinformation should be cleaned up by offering guidelines for users to follow.

February 7, 2020

The author is professor of communication at Chapman University and distinguished guest professor, Shandong University.

People's health knowledge requires a boost

By Lu Weimin/Wang Kan

During the novel coronavirus outbreak, misinformation has fueled the spread of fear. Some people might be unsure of how to tell facts from rumors, so enhancing the public's health knowledge is a critical step to help people take the right protective measures and avoid unnecessary panic.

As the battle against the novel coronavirus continues to be waged, it appears that people's awareness of how to protect themselves from the virus and infection differs according to age, and whether they are urban or rural residents.

Based on the present epidemic situation, people's awareness needs to be upgraded.

For example, in the face of the epidemic, some people may feel panic to some extent because they are not aware that there are effective prevention and protection measures they can take.

Therefore, it is urgent that people's public health awareness is raised. To do this, a number of things can be done.

The education authorities should strengthen science popularization among the public especially among teenagers. For example, primary and middle schools should emphasize scientific education, and they could invite medical professionals to teach students about the scientific protection measures they should adopt.

As regards governmental departments, they can carry out projects to popularize health knowledge, and encourage people to participate in the move for improvement of the public scientific literacy, including in different townships, districts and communities.

In addition, relevant science and technology institutions also have the responsibility to innovate measures and set up coordinated systems to implement a health awareness campaign, so more people are aware of the benefits of scientific prevention and protection measures.

Sacrifice, Toil and Tears — China and the World in the Fight against the Pandemic

Since the improvement of public scientific literacy is of great significance and concern, medical and healthcare departments should learn the lessons of this epidemic, continue to build well-established and professional teams comprised of paramedic staff, particularly grassroots units that are dedicated to promote the public health literacy should be formed.

Science and healthcare institutions should pool their resources to meet the public's knowledge demand. They should establish and refine ways to boost the public's scientific prevention and protection knowledge.

Moreover, it is also important for healthcare institutions to diversify the channels for spreading scientific public health knowledge, and mull over effective policies to upgrade the mechanism to deal with emergencies, so as to ensure that it can swiftly respond to a public health emergency and provide authoritative information on the situation and the appropriate response.

Keeping the public apprised of specialized and scientific public health knowledge in a timely manner will help prevent public panic and contribute to the prevention of public health crises.

February 20, 2020

The author is vice-president of Tianjin Science and Technology Association. This is an excerpt of his interview with China Daily's Wang Kan.

Anti-Prejudice Best Prescription for Joint Fight

Sacrifice, Toil and Tears | China and the World in the Fight against the Pandemic

World must give China support against virus

By Moaaz Awan

Shi Yu/China Daily

As China fights to contain the viral outbreak centered in Wuhan, where medical supplies are increasingly under stress, the Pakistani government has sent its first consignment of aid to China to facilitate the Chinese government's fight against the novel coronavirus.

The Pakistani government has allocated 300,000 medical masks, 800 hazmat suits and 6,800 pairs of gloves from stocks of public hospitals around the nation and transported the aid to China. Medical supplies from Pakistan arrived in China on Feb 1. The official Twitter account of China's Ministry of Foreign Affairs said, "To help China fight against novel coronavirus, Russia, Pakistan, ROK, Belarus, France, Germany, Malaysia and UNICEF and many others are providing assistance and support to China. Thanks to you all! A friend in need is a friend indeed."

IV Anti-Prejudice Best Prescription for Joint Fight

This move by Pakistan is a gesture by the Pakistani state and people to show solidarity with their brethren in China. The people of Pakistan are also standing with the Chinese nation. Usman, a Pakistani teacher at Changsha Medical College, has volunteered to go to Wuhan to help out with the medical emergency. Usman graduated from Hunan University of Traditional Chinese Medicine with a bachelor's degree in 2012, and a master's degree in medicine at Central South University in Changsha. After graduation, he became a foreign teacher at Changsha Medical College. During the four years since his return to his hometown, he has been unable to forget China and Changsha, and said China has provided him with good opportunities for education and employment and helped him realized his dream.

In ancient times, the Chinese used to say "The mountains are high and the emperor is far" to represent the lack of coordination between central and local governments. This time, however, as soon as the intensity of the outbreak was reported by the local government, the central government sprang into action. First, Wuhan and its 11 million inhabitants were quarantined. Then eight adjoining cities were shut down, too, making the total number of people under quarantine 56 million.

The China Development Bank, one of the country's major policy banks, offered emergency loans worth 2 billion yuan ($288.3 million) last Friday to Wuhan for prevention and control of the novel coronavirus. The country's finance ministry allocated 1 billion yuan to support Hubei's battle against the virus. Authorities in Wuhan decided to build two makeshift hospitals — Huoshenshan with 700 to 1,000 beds, and Leishenshan with a capacity of 1,300 to 1,500 beds, to treat infected patients.

The Chinese authorities have declared all the facts, even making an updated website for the continuous sharing of information regarding the viral outbreak. The WHO has shown complete trust in China's efforts to contain the virus, which shows the global body's trust in the Chinese authorities.

Even in this dire situation, there is good news, too. First, the fatality rate of the virus is approximately 2.1 percent, compared to 10 percent with SARS. Second, the Chinese learned some painful but valuable experiences during the SARS epidemic, which was useful for prevention. Third, due to the involvement of technology in the Chinese system, it has been easier to identify the movement and spread of the virus. Various apps have been launched to the public so they may identify potential carriers and keep themselves and their families safe.

China, acting as a mature and responsible global player, is voluntarily bearing the brunt of the viral outbreak in physical, emotional and economic terms. Some of the responses have been rather severe, but are necessary to stop the virus from further spreading. The world has to acknowledge these steps and support and strengthen the Chinese fight against the virus. Support can come through medical equipment, expertise and information sharing. The world must get its act together to save humanity.

February 6, 2020

The author is an observer and a researcher at Tianjin University.

Racist reports symptom of West's Sinophobia

By Maitreya Bhakal

Westerners have offered three different responses to the recent virus outbreak in China. Some have empathized with the victims and expressed the hope that the outbreak ends soon. Some have taken advantage of it to indulge in stereotypes and memes. And some have delighted in the opportunity to disparage the Chinese government.

There were similar responses during the SARS outbreak in 2002-03. Yet those were the early days of 24-hour news coverage, and social media was almost non-existent. Today's technology has made sensationalizing these responses imperative to grab an audience.

Upon hearing the story that the virus may spread through bats, the Daily Mail, a British tabloid, published a video of a Chinese woman eating bat soup. It didn't matter that the video was from Palau, not China, and was filmed in 2016.

Following such reports, children started being harassed in school just for looking like Chinese.

In France, a Twitter hashtag-JeNeSuisPasUnVirus (I'm not a virus) — was started by the Chinese community to counter such racist reports.

It's not entirely fair to say that the "Yellow Peril" was back. It never left. Racism has always been central to Western culture. Why change now?

The more people the virus has killed, the more the Western media has killed journalistic values. The New York Times has led the horde, braying that the Chinese government's response exposed "core flaws", assuming perhaps that "democracies" handle health crisis better. Another article bellowed that the crisis could "humble China's strongman" (their favorite word to describe Chinese top leader). The Wall Street Journal was more direct, simply saying that China's censorship helped spread the virus.

And it is worth noting that in the initial days of an epidemic, obtaining accurate data is difficult. Everything cannot be irresponsibly released without verification. Moreover, in this case, symptoms matched normal flu symptoms, making the virus difficult to detect. Yet the reluctance of local officials to jump to conclusions has been interpreted by some in the West as some sort of nefarious conspiracy to silence critics at the cost of public health.

Do the Western democracies handle health crises better? One way to find out is by focusing at what the Western media won't: facts.

When they preach about "free speech", are they holding up the United States as the model for transparency on public health crises? This is where officials in the Michigan town Flint initially hid the true extent of lead poisoning, and where children and adults continue drinking poisoned water even today, and where seasonal flu kills tens of thousands of Americans each year.

Or do they mean India, where last year more than 67,000 people were diagnosed with a preventable disease like dengue? Where 1,108 children on average have died every year since 2014 in a single hospital in the city of Kota?

By contrast, in China, the response was sanctioned and mobilized at the highest level of government (a level which, in the "US democracy", is generally reserved for killing civilians using drones).

China has put people over profits, taking the most un-American, un-capitalist steps to battle the outbreak: More than 50 million people and 15 cities have been quarantined. In one of them, Wuhan, Hubei province, where the outbreak was first reported, a 1,000-bed hospital has been built within a couple of weeks. To help curb new infections, the Lunar New Year holiday was extended by three days and people encouraged to stay at home, with movie releases postponed and train and flight cancellation charges refunded for that purpose. The Shanghai and Shenzhen stock exchanges have been suspended. Delays in loan repayments are being accommodated and virus-related insurance claims prioritized. And online sellers of protective masks have been banned from raising prices.

In the US, such moves would be unthinkable. Imagine the corporate losses if whole cities and the stock markets were shut down.

US banks would probably have increased interest rates in such a crisis.

And these moves are paying off. While deaths have been rising (425 at last count), patients are also being cured. Experts estimate that the peak of the outbreak could be reached in 8-10 days. The WHO has praised China's efforts relentlessly—denting celebrations in prejudiced Western newsrooms.

The crisis will pass, but the Sinophobia won't. Those who have the disease of Sinophobia will always find something else. The Western media will continue questioning the legitimacy of the Chinese government. As China succeeds and rises, it will experience more jealousy. More Sinophobia. More Schadenfreude. That is a disease that will prove more difficult to eradicate.

February 5, 2020

The author is an Indian commentator.

Sacrifice, Toil and Tears — China and the World in the Fight against the Pandemic

Discrimination against Chinese a virus

International students at Wuhan University, Elvira Zhaidarova from Kazakhstan (left) and Svetlana Zhigalova from Russia, shout "Wuhan, Jiayou" (roughly meaning "Stay strong, Wuhan"), in the city on Feb 1, 2020.

Zhu Xingxin/China Daily

Discrimination of any kind is undoubtedly heartrending and hurtful for people. Especially when it is directed at those from a region or a country that are doing all they can to fight against the spread of an infectious disease, such as the current novel coronavirus.

If they are not willing to extend a helping hand, the least other people can do is not show any resentment toward them.

IV Anti-Prejudice Best Prescription for Joint Fight

Yet, signs of discrimination have surfaced both within the country against people from Hubei province and in other parts of the world against Chinese people or even those of Asian origin.

The fear of the disease which has spread rapidly throughout China has provoked racial abuse against anyone perceived to be Chinese.

And it is not just individuals who are guilty of such prejudice, some media organizations have really gone too far by using inflammatory language and discriminatory visuals when reporting on the outbreak.

Australia's Herald Sun blazoned "China Kids Stay Home" on its front page. A French local paper ran articles headlined "New Yellow Peril" and "Yellow Alert". In some parts of Europe, some people of non-Chinese Asian heritage have even felt the need to make clear that they are not Chinese.

Throughout history, the seemingly inexorable nature of such health threats has led to those perceived as unleashing it being scapegoated.

And as João Rangel de Almeida, a member of the epidemic response group at the London-based medical charity Welcome Trust told The Financial Times: "Diseases are a great tool to magnify social trends and tensions."

We know that such discrimination will never vanish. Even some well-educated people have deep-rooted phobias against people of particular groups or ethnicity.

But while it would be naive to think that such prejudice will completely disappear, that does not mean it should be tolerated or everyone is willing to turn a blind eye to it.

That many people in Berlin came to the rescue of a Chinese girl who was attacked for wearing a face mask shows that not everyone has succumbed to a phobia of anyone Chinese or who looks Chinese.

When China is making all-out efforts fighting against the novel coronavirus, it needs help from the rest of the world. That is why Chinese people appreciate the increasing number of countries extending a helping hand to it in its efforts to contain the spread of the virus.

While this speaks volumes about the concern and sympathy of their counterparts in other countries, more empathy needs to be shown to those for whom sympathy has been lacking. No matter the origin of the outbreak, even if a few people were at fault, not everyone from that place should be tarred with the same brush.

February 4, 2020

China Daily Editorial

Opportunistic racists find a golden opportunity within the outbreak

By Joseph Lam

When a 60-year-old man collapsed outside a popular Thai restaurant near Sydney Chinatown on Tuesday last week, no resuscitation attempts were made.

He had died of apparent cardiac arrest, but there were fears he was infected with novel coronavirus, which kept bystanders from responding, a local tabloid reported.

The story likened the lack of help to videos and pictures that emerged showing Chinese citizens allegedly collapsing in the street due to the virus.

On the same day, AFP Indonesia fact checked a picture depicting a similar incident. The report found the image was from a 2014 art project in Frankfurt, portraying victims of the Nazi's Katzbac concentration camp.

As of Friday, there were 15 confirmed cases of novel coronavirus in Australia, five recoveries and one unassociated death.

The man who died was not a victim of the virus but rather one of Sinophobic behavior and fears that have spread in recent weeks, it seems.

Since the outbreak of the novel coronavirus was first reported, fake news has traveled much further than the virus, and its aftermath is proving harmful.

In Australia, it has spread in the form of fake press releases issued by nonexistent government departments. These have targeted areas with large Chinese populations and restaurants, prompting responses from government health departments and politicians.

Chinese-owned businesses are feeling the effects, and some, mostly restaurants, have decided to shut to cover financial loss, while others operate with minimum staff as some employees are scared of returning amid the outbreak.

Unfortunately, it doesn't stop at fake news or reduced business.

Sacrifice, Toil and Tears — China and the World in the Fight against the Pandemic

For 25-year-old Chinese-Australian journalist and writer Yen-Rong Wong, as she wrote on Twitter, "This is the first time I've ever felt physically unsafe in Australia because of my race. I thought we were over this ... but obviously not."

Wong isn't alone. Chinese citizens and people of Chinese descent around the world have reported increased hostility, accounts of discrimination, racism and xenophobic behavior in the last few weeks amid the outbreak.

Meanwhile at home in Hong Kong, Tammy Ho Lai-Ming, editor of Asian Cha Journal, tweeted, "I can understand people's frustration about the current #coronavirus situation (I'm frustrated & worried) but this portrayal of mainlanders as zombie-like is offensive & unnecessary. Can we resist the urge to generalize & stigmatize a whole nation of people?"

The director of the Australia-China Relations Institute James Laurenceson, who has seen increased hostility towards Chinese Australians as China's influence in Australia continues to grow, said, "these reports are not a one-off anecdote".

In times of crisis, amid fear and panic, a lack of leadership and questionable quarantining of Australians who were in Wuhan hasn't helped, he said.

On Monday, a plane carrying 243 Australians fleeing Wuhan arrived on Christmas island, the home of Australia's off-shore detention centers. On Thursday, 35 more Australians joined them.

On this decision, Laurenceson noted, "I don't think they're racist in their policy response, but I haven't seen another country do the same thing to their own."

In a time where people of Chinese ancestry around the world are feeling discriminated against, treated like outsiders and blamed for a virus, leadership is important, as is calling out baseless xenophobic behavior.

Instead, the job is being left to journalists, academics and institute directors like Laurenceson in the form of opinion editorials, as well as international students like Katie, a former Wisconsin and Hong Kong student, who asked only to be referred to her first name.

A Facebook post she wrote on Jan 30 detailing live updates on the virus and information from her experience from Henan province in China has been shared 289 times, liked by almost 500 people and received 86 comments.

Katie said she felt compelled to share information after seeing several memes make light of the virus and comments blaming Chinese people and some saying it "is deserved".

"Some people are using their personal feelings about the Chinese government to respond to the virus outbreak, which is irrational, rude and disrespectful," she said.

She noted there are thousands of people across China, like her father, who instead of spending Chinese New Year with his family are on call working long hours in factories to produce medical supplies and contain the virus or treat victims.

"I have friends who are doctors and who are fighting on the front line right now," she said.

Chinese-Australian architect Shuwei Zhang, a former Queensland resident, was stuck in Guangzhou until Saturday and said people aren't simply paranoid about the virus, but are being taken away and confined with potentially infected victims.

"I think being inside is affecting people because they read everything on the internet, which essentially drives them to hysteria," he said.

Laurenceson concedes there's a lot of "insensitivity towards people who are in an extraordinarily difficult situation through no fault of their own".

"At the moment it seems clear that the greatest danger in Australia isn't from the spread of the virus — it's from behaviour driven by fear, not facts," he said.

February 11, 2020

The author is an Australia-based freelance writer.

Racism behind coronavirus paranoia

By Mitchell Blatt

Luo Jie/China Daily

While China was quickly building hospitals in Wuhan and people from around the world were donating masks, some politicians and pundits in the United States were lashing out at the nation that is already on the front lines of combating a global epidemic.

In addition to questioning the death toll, Arkansas Senator Tom Cotton went so far as to suggest the virus was manufactured in a "level four super laboratory." What expertise does he have in medicine or epidemiology to make this claim?

It doesn't matter; that's the same Tom Cotton who claimed the earth's temperature is not warming, a science-denying statement, despite having no expertise in climate studies. So he apparently is unwilling to accept the fact viruses can spread between living organisms.

But this is a man who is influential in American policy making. He is a rising figure within the Republican Party, and President

Donald Trump appears to take his advice. Cotton, appearing on Fox News' Tucker Carlson Tonight on Jan 29, said he "urged the Trump administration" to "stop commercial air travel" from China. Donald Trump, who one week ago claimed "We have it totally under control," banned Chinese and other foreign nationals from entering the country if they had spent any time in China, a policy that impacted Chinese students and even more business travelers, researchers and tourists.

Cotton is not the only one in the US to make dodgy claims and spread fear. But Cotton is one of the highest ranking, and he should know better.

His words impact others. When supposed authority figures make loose comments, they risk inducing panic and spreading misinformation that could counter the effort to fight coronavirus. What the world needs is a rational response based on evidence, not fearmongering and partisan politicking. Unfortunately quite a few bloggers jumped on Cotton's conspiratorial comments in order to claim the virus was "man-made."

It's possible to argue he was taken out of context. But he was perfectly clear about his recommendation to ban flights from China, and perfectly clear about his idea the number is much higher than reported.

Carlson, star of the right-wing Fox News lineup, also asked, with his unique brand of snark and feigned surprise, "So far, travel between the US and China is completely unaffected. Why? Who knows?"

Well, maybe because the World Health Organization advises against it, and the vast majority of policy experts agree travel bans don't work. But the US announced the travel ban just a few days later. (Trump spends a lot of time watching Fox News, too, so it's possible he took his advice from Carlson.)

What's behind the overbearing response and paranoia? There is the well-known fact people fear the unknown more than the routine. "Exotic" viruses that seem to come about suddenly are scarier than influenza, for example. A shooting on a long-distance bus in California in the early morning of Feb 3, which killed one and wounded five, does not alarm people in the US when there are hundreds of random public shootings every year.

But there may be some other motives influencing some people's attitudes toward coronavirus, on account of its having originated in China.

Sacrifice, Toil and Tears
China and the World in the Fight against the Pandemic

As a member of the Foreign Affairs Committee, Cotton frequently criticizes China. He is right to be on the lookout for what he feels is in the national interest of his country, but when it comes to matters of public health one ought to drop his animus and solve a problem that affects all of humanity. Indeed, stopping it now will also decrease the likelihood of it spreading in the US.

The diagnosis for Carlson, I'm afraid, is a good deal more grave. Here is a man who blames "immigrants" for dirtying America's environment: "litter is left almost exclusively by immigrants," he said in a December 2019 interview. In 2018, he blamed immigrants for the fact that, in his view, America is becoming more divided. In one segment, he warned that "immigrants" are "replacing" "Americans."

Does any of that sound racist to you? Don't worry, it's not. Carlson, after all, also said in 2019 that white supremacy "is not a real problem in America," it's a "hoax." Glad that's been cleared up.

The problem of racism with regard to coronavirus response is not limited to the United States, but has been expressed in other countries, in Asia and Europe and elsewhere. In South Korea, some restaurants posted signs saying "no Chinese."

When a student who appeared to be of Chinese descent was seen walking to class at the University of Sheffield wearing a mask, she was verbally attacked by multiple students, according to a report published at Guancha.

Now, you might ask, as Tucker Carlson did, what, at all, does "racism" have to do with the response to coronavirus? There's your answer.

February 11, 2020

The author is a columnist and a recent graduate of the Johns Hopkins School of Advanced International Studies.

Anti-Prejudice Best Prescription for Joint Fight   IV

Something's not right when they criticize China

By Mario Cavolo

Song Chen/China Daily

When the United States 2009 H1N1 swine flu emerged, it eventually infected 60 million people in the US and killed a minimum of 18,449 cases worldwide that year. But the final story of the H1N1 global pandemic was far worse than that, with close to 300,000 deaths in the world, according to the final tallies in 2012 reported by the United States Centers for Disease Control and Prevention.

But during that outbreak, I don't recall xenophobic anti-American attacks across the globe, do you? In fact, do you recall it took six months for the US to declare a national emergency? Did any government from the onset in April 2009 through the end in April 2010, including the month of June, when H1N1 was declared an international emergency global pandemic, then send out a notice to its citizens that they should leave the United States? Close their borders to American travelers? Nope, there was not a peep.

- 179

Sacrifice, Toil and Tears

China and the World in the Fight against the Pandemic

Yet I am reading hateful vicious attacks on the Chinese government for their supposed intentional underreporting of the number of infections, even though that is exactly and always the case with such flu outbreaks no matter where, and the CDC reports illustrate that crystal clear. The US H1N1 swine flu numbers were vastly underestimated and updated three years later, because that is the nature of such viral outbreaks, which don't care which country they emerge in. There is never enough manpower, there are never enough test kits, there is never enough medicine or medical supplies. China is not trying to hide these hardships, they are well known, they are being reported on the news daily in China. There are always people who die in an epidemic, many of whom we'll never know if they died of a particular virus. Those are the facts, not any problem unique to China's healthcare system or government.

Not a conspiracy, but a tragedy

It's not a conspiracy, it's a tragedy.

According to the June 27, 2012 research report followup three years later, it gets much more disturbing when you learn about the CDC's final estimate of the H1N1 virus global death toll. This article can be found on the Center for Infectious Disease Research and Policy website, the CDC's 18,449 total deaths number was "...regarded as WELL BELOW THE TRUE TOTAL, mainly because many people who die of flu-related causes are not tested for the disease."

So during the 2009 outbreak, was anyone accusing the US medical and government authorities of hiding the numbers? Were Americans with hidden cameras strolling into the Mayo Clinic to prove how many people were really dying? The absurdity of these vicious attacks are that whether or not a person specifically does have the novel coronavirus or some other viral bug presenting as pneumonia, the treatment is the same supportive treatment anyway.

Something's not right here folks. The world should be applauding China's unprecedented, broad, aggressive response.

Instead of looking at the will of an entire system of government acting faster than any other government on the planet could, there are some still busy bashing a few local government officials in Wuhan where the outbreak was first reported. True, perhaps they should have said something sooner, but that's not an indictment of an entire country's government. On this point, every provincial government has sent out a notice to its government officials pretty much saying that if they try to hide anything, they will face harsh punishment.

And here's the mic drop for you: "The CDC researchers estimate that the H1N1 2009 pandemic virus caused 201,200 respiratory deaths and another 83,300 deaths from cardiovascular disease associated with H1N1 infections." Total: 284,000 deaths. Shocking, isn't it?

Was there a travel ban for any length of time to and from the United States?

Did China, Germany, Japan or any other country close their border to American travelers?

Following the United States Department of State policy suggesting US citizens leave China, the United Kingdom embassy released the same recommendation to UK citizens. In 2009, did UK subjects in America get a notice to leave America? No.

Did the world suggest we isolate from America? Close the US borders? No.

Did Americans get xenophobically attacked and targeted by anti-American sentiments like the Chinese are experiencing now? Um, no.

Chinese people will defeat the virus at last

Fascinating and disturbing to say the least. And the truth is you couldn't be safer than in this country, where almost everyone is staying home and dutifully isolating themselves with awareness. Not to mention that the Chinese government's decision to safeguard people is coming at a devastating economic cost in the hundreds of billions.

I have a friend in Mesa, Arizona. He told me earlier that the big popular China City buffet, a huge busy place, has no customers. Does that make any sense at all?

If you were in Miami and you heard that there was a virus outbreak that started in Milan, in central Italy, would you cancel your dinner reservation at the Italian restaurant that night in South Beach? No. Would you buy a pizza next week at Joey's Pizzeria in Delray Beach?

Sacrifice, Toil and Tears
China and the World in the Fight against the Pandemic

If you were in Singapore and you heard there was a virus outbreak in Dallas, Texas, in the central US, would you stop going to your favorite local Texas southern BBQ restaurant in Singapore?

Finally, here are some straight up, sensible accurate descriptions of this new coronavirus which were detected in Wuhan, China. It's not called the China virus and neither was H1N1 called the America virus.

Just like every flu season. However, don't misunderstand me. The extra caution and the remarkable response by the Chinese government and people together to quell the spread of this virus was warranted because, yes it is correct that this coronavirus is nastier than the usual annual flu bug, as was H1N1 in 2009.

This coronavirus is highly contagious, it spreads easily. It binds to lung tissue and so in particular, likes to cause pneumonia, that's what infection of lung tissue is. That's more severe than a respiratory infection which is only in your throat or bronchial tubes.

The virus currently has a 2 percent death rate. That's a lot higher, around 20 times higher, than a typical annual flu virus with a death rate of 0.1 percent. However, a 2-percent death rate is still much lower by comparison to the severe acute respiratory syndrome (SARS) virus which had a 9 percent death rate or the Middle East respiratory syndrome (MERS) virus with a really nasty 37 percent death rate.

The novel coronavirus is causing severe symptoms in 10-15 percent of cases, with 80-90 percent of deaths elderly patients, most with other existing health problems. That characteristic by the way, is in contrast to the America 2009 H1N1 swine flu virus which in fact had a higher death rate amongst younger people including children, rather than those over 60 years old.

China identified and shared the novel coronavirus genome in record times, in only days, and of course, immediately shared it with all international health and disease organizations. Medical researchers are already discovering that certain existing anti-viral medications may be effective against this coronavirus.

It's impossible not to marvel at China's broad and aggressive domestic response directed by the provincial level governments to restrict movement, transportation, and business operations for a period of time combined with the voluntary dutiful cooperation of its 1.4 billion citizens who are in the majority quietly staying at home these weeks to let the virus pass; this model response is already being hailed by the international community as a remarkable unprecedented response setting a new standard in understanding what is possible for future outbreaks in whatever country they may occur. Is it inconvenient and costly. You bet.

Whether in a couple of weeks or months later, this nasty flu type coronavirus will begin declining and the joy of spring will arrive. Between now and then if you don't have anything good, anything supportive to say about China or Chinese people, how about you just keep your mouth shut.

February 11, 2020

The author is a freelance author and commentator.

Racist reports infect the truth with prejudice

By Hannay Richards

Despite repeated warnings from experts that a global pandemic was likely, most people probably didn't spend much time worrying about the threat of a new infectious disease until recently.

After all, it appeared to be a hypothetical risk and there were plenty more immediate threats to worry about, why worry about what to do in such a seemingly remote eventuality.

Now that the new coronavirus has emerged, it is a different story, of course.

Deep-seated fears in the collective memory implanted by previous pandemics have come rushing to fore, and the possibility of a disease sweeping through populations like some indefatigable horseman of the apocalypse remorselessly scything down whoever he encounters has triggered worldwide panic.

Not unreasonably perhaps, since the natural human response to any life-threatening situation is to either flee or fight, and for many people neither of those seem feasible against such an inexorable and invisible threat.

In China, where the latest outbreak has appeared, the quarantining of much of the population, forced in some areas but generally self-imposed, means people's fears have been largely contained indoors or else allowed to run wild in cyberspace. This has to some extent helped stop panic feeding panic, since panic itself is highly contagious.

In the West however, people's fear is being whipped up into near hysteria by sensationalized media reports.

Not surprising, given these media outlets' form and purpose, these reports are usually also racist; fostering and pandering to anti-Chinese prejudice.

Although an infectious disease can emerge in any corner of the world, as shown by the H1N1 pandemic that originated in the United States, the Ebola outbreak in West Africa and the Zika emergency in

Brazil in recent years, the reporting on the novel coronavirus outbreak in China by much of the mainstream media in the West has been distinguished by its bigoted refueling of the "Yellow Peril" stereotyping of the civilized West being overrun by uncivilized Chinese hordes.

While the search for a scapegoat has accompanied other infectious disease outbreaks, seemingly throughout history, the Sinophobia exposed by the "Yellow Peril" reporting on the new coronavirus is symptomatic of the broader fears in the West about China's rise, where it is viewed by some as a sort of infectious disease that will debilitate Western civilization, like a tumor corrupting Western values.

People's fears are easily directed in this direction because the pathogens that cause contagious diseases are viewed as foreign invaders overwhelming even a healthy body's defenses.

The bigotry in such reports seek to link the emergence of the disease with notion that there is weakness or inferiority in the Chinese character that enabled the outbreak to happen, much like the media portrayals of the Chinese in the early decades of the last century when characters such as Fu Manchu were malevolent villains intent on ruling the world. Once again showing that the more things change the more they stay the same.

There are always those who hurry to hunt down others who can be blamed for the woes they have inflicted on themselves.

But to borrow an observation attributed to Marie Curie, nothing in life is to be feared, it has only to be understood — that applies to infectious diseases and China's rise.

February 11, 2020

The author is a senior editor with China Daily.

Sacrifice, Toil and Tears
China and the World in the Fight against the Pandemic

A sincere letter to friends of China

By Zlatko Lagumdzija

My dear friends, colleagues, People of China,
People who are suffering and struggling with novel coronavirus.

First, as a friend of China and Chinese people, I would like to offer my deepest condolences for the lives lost in this epidemic. I want to share with you my profound respect for all that you are doing under such a terrible and almost impossible circumstances.

Your courage and patience, hard work and empathy, knowledge and wisdom are not only hope for saving your great nation, but also the rest of the world as well. Today you are the first line of global defense for humanity facing the grim threat of an epidemic.

This is not fight for your future alone. It is a fight for all our futures.

The novel coronavirus threatens all of us today. Are we ready, willing and capable for having a shared future or shall we have no future at all?

The new coronavirus does not care about our borders, our norms and rules, our economic or political disputes. All of us wherever we are, are confronted with this deadly threat. This is not the first but it could be one of the last viruses threatening.

Viruses like this one are not only a common threat, but also an opportunity to come together in the fight with shared leadership, shared values, shared security, shared responsibility, shared benefits and a shared vision for a shared future.

Even when the world is wide awake and aware, I see hope in this serious situation. The unity of China and willingness to tackle this horrible virus at the same time, but also a huge desire to find a solution, the cure, and save lives, gives me a hope and also a great respect for the people of China.

You are fighting not only against this deadly unknown virus but against ignorance, selfishness, prejudices and even fake news that at times are spreading faster than the virus itself.

In this battle you are set, once again, to be an example to the world with your excellent organizational and mobilization capabilities.

Your 5,000 years of accumulated culture, selfless dedication and unity based on accumulated wisdom, and last four decades of historically unrecorded enormous growth directed at eradicating poverty while building the knowledge centers of global excellence, give me full confidence in your capacity to win this battle.

I believe that one day, soon, your struggle with the epidemic will be another building block for a community with a shared future for humanity. It will be logical consequence of Chinese accumulated thousands of years of culture and recent achievements in global poverty eradication, economic and technological heights.

I'm sure that China has a strength under the leadership of President Xi Jinping to prevail over this epidemic and overcome the threat confronting all of us. Determination driven by the force of shared future in dignity and prosperity for all, is the reason why I believe that better days are ahead.

I believe that you, and we, can make right choices for our shared future to ensure the brighter days to come.

In closing, I salute you, with the wise words of a poet:

> *There is a tide in the affairs of men.*
> *Which taken at the flood, leads on to fortune.*
> *Omitted, all the voyage of their life is bound in shallows and in miseries.*
> *On such a full sea are we now afloat.*
> *And we must take the current when it serves, or lose our ventures.*
>
> *—William Shakespeare*

February 10, 2020

The author is former prime minister of Bosnia and Herzegovina.

"Yellow peril" virus more contagious and condemnable

By Yury Tavrovsky

Cai Meng/China Daily

"The Chinese! The Chinese are coming!" Two men were running and shouting at the entrance of the Exhibition subway station in Moscow. I looked around and saw a group of Chinese tourists taking pictures of the elegant and gigantic Monument to the Explorers of Space.

The two men were wearing the uniform jackets of street cleaners and looked like migrant workers from Central Asia. Other people near the very busy subway station were not at all surprised or terrified at the view of a dozen of tourists wearing masks. People in Moscow know about the novel coronavirus epidemic in China, discuss it, watch TV programs and sympathize with people of Wuhan and other parts of the stricken country.

IV
Anti-Prejudice Best Prescription for Joint Fight

Of course the Russians at first were full of fear that the lethal virus will reach their cities and they will look like the "deserted streets" of Wuhan. But pretty soon the mainstream mass media explained that the situation in China is under control and the sacrificial efforts of Chinese medics and the efficient measures of the government to control further spread of disease are showing the desired effects.

As an expert on China, I have been asked to write many articles and speak on several national TV shows recently. I have explained that the novel coronavirus is just another natural calamity for the mankind like the floods in Siberia and Europe, forest fires in Australia and California or previous epidemics before. Specialists on viruses and epidemics have stressed the relatively low mortality rate of the new coronavirus and the dedication and professionalism of Chinese medical workers. Still some experts on the shows started to blame Chinese people saying that their way of life is the main reason for current and previous epidemics. "There are too many of them. They are concentrated in huge cities. Their air, soil, and waters are polluted. They lack food and have to eat bats and snakes …"

Comments of this sort can be found nowadays in many countries, especially among netizens. They concentrate on national or even racial aspects of the coronavirus epidemic in China. It looks like even after this epidemic is over we will have to fight another disease spreading around the world. It is called "yellow peril". It is very old. It is very contagious. We can trace "yellow peril" back to the Opium Wars in the mid-19th century. We see it in the infamous "Chinese Exclusion Act" of 1882 in America. We hear racist explanations of the inevitable "Cold War" with China from high-ranking officials of the US State Department. There are already reports of xenophobic attacks on the streets of cities in the United States, Germany, England and Italy.

The novel coronavirus has triggeed the new "civilized" edition of the "yellow peril". It is based on envy and fear of the Chinese Miracle. The results of the reform and opening-up over the past 40 years have been formidable. The efficiency of socialism with Chinese characteristics in the past seven decades cannot be denied. The future great rejuvenation of the Chinese nation is inevitable.

The entire history of mankind is full of the rise and fall of different civilizations. Some people analyze the Chinese experience and try to use elements of the Chinese Dream for the benefit of their own nations. Yet there are people who do not want to share room at the top. They are not happy with the Chinese winning the game according to the rules set by themselves. They are changing the rules in the middle of the current party and say the winners are not playing fair. Being adepts of the monotheistic Judeo-Christian religion they cannot permit another nation to rule the world, especially if that nation is "godless". That way the competition inevitably spills over the boundaries of the trade war into civilization and race.

China is not Alice drinking her potion in Wonderland. It cannot become bigger or smaller at anybody's whim. Its industrial, scientific and technological development cannot be stopped or even slowed. Still there is one thing China can and should do. It can still be modest. Of course, it is impossible now to "stay in the shadows" according to Deng Xiaoping's advice. But Chinese people who work in international communication sector should not mix internal and external stories. "Triumphalism" is often counterproductive overseas. Chinese experts should not overestimate Chinese wisdom against European wisdom at international conferences.

International and interracial matters are very delicate. It is utterly irresponsible to speculate on them. Especially at a time of epidemics or other natural calamities.

February 12, 2020

The author is head of the Russian Dream and Chinese Dream Research Center of the Izborsk Club, Moscow.

Novel coronavirus outbreak puts fresh spotlight on media's racism

By Chen Weihua

Shi Yu/China Daily

While covering the World Health Organization news briefings in the past days, I was struck by how many times WHO officials have reminded people to refrain from using the novel coronavirus to stigmatize people.

Tedros Adhanom Ghebreyesus, WHO director-general, Michael Ryan, executive director of WHO's Health Emergencies Program and Sylvie Briand, director of WHO Global Infectious Hazard Preparedness have all expressed that message.

The main content of their briefings, of course, is how to rally the world to fight the virus given the short window of opportunity that

Sacrifice, Toil and Tears

China and the World in the Fight against the Pandemic

is available, an opportunity created by the serious measures China is taking in Wuhan and other cities, according to the WHO.

When the WHO on Tuesday named the disease caused by the novel coronavirus as COVID-19, it stated that it wanted to find a name that did not refer to a geographical location, an individual or group of people.

The WHO chief stressed that having a name matters to prevent the use of other names that can be inaccurate or stigmatizing. He was clearly referring to racially charged terms used by some news outlets and politicians.

For example, a Feb 3 Wall Street Journal column titled "China Is the Real Sick Man of Asia" by Walter Russell Mead, a senior fellow at the conservative Hudson Institute, displayed a total lack of sensitivity and journalistic ethics, especially at a time when people across China were combating the novel coronavirus.

When reporting the controversy, some Western media, such as the Euronews, still don't get why such a headline would constitute an insult to all Chinese since they never knew how that term has been used by Western imperialists, including Japanese invaders during World War II, to humiliate the Chinese. Using that kind of racial slur is as offensive to Chinese as using N-word for African-Americans, which the newspaper would not use. It is truly despicable for a respected newspaper like the Wall Street Journal.

The same is true when French newspaper Le Courrier Picard and its online edition ran respective headlines titled "Yellow Alert" and "New Yellow Peril?", triggering an immediate outcry from the Asian community in France.

A racist color-metaphor to describe East Asians by Western colonial powers, such a headline should be condemned by every reader with a conscience and every journalist with professional ethical standards.

However, the two papers are quite different. Le Courrier Picard has since apologized while the Wall Street Journal has not.

As journalists, we all know what words to avoid when it comes to people of disability, and people who are lesbian, gay and transgender and various ethnic groups. It is not about restricting freedom of press but rather upholding ethical journalism and a basic human conscience.

Germany, for example, places strict limits on speech and expression when it comes to neo-Nazis. It is illegal to produce, distribute or display symbols of the Nazi era — swastikas, the Hitler salute. Holocaust denial is also illegal in Germany.

However, when Jyllands-Posten, a Danish daily paper, printed a cartoon of the Chinese national flag with virus-like symbols in place of the five stars, it infuriated the Chinese who regard blasphemy of their national flag as an insult to all Chinese.

While the newspaper editor refused to apologize, what makes things worse was Danish Prime Minister Mette Frederiksen who jumped out to eagerly defend the paper's freedom of speech instead of denouncing its insult.

The outbreak of the novel coronavirus is unfortunate and a "common enemy" for the world to fight as the WHO has urged. But it also exposes how racism is still a serious disease that plagues human society in the 21st century.

February 14, 2020

The author is chief of China Daily EU Bureau based in Brussels.

Bias undermines solidarity in virus fight

Olivier Guyonvarch, French consul general in Wuhan, leaves an office building in the city on Feb 13, 2020. The French consulate in Wuhan insisted on remaining open during the outbreak.

Zhu Xingxin/China Daily

That outside of Hubei province, the most hard-hit area, the number of new novel coronavirus infections has dropped each day for 12 days in a row, to 166 as of Sunday, indicates the epidemic situation is largely being brought under control.

Even in Hubei, the number of new infections each day has dropped over the past four days, to below the level before the complicated genetic lab diagnosis was replaced by faster CT scans, which led to a jump in the number of confirmed cases. This is heartening news as the province has borne the brunt of the epidemic which broke out in the provincial capital Wuhan in late December.

But while the epidemic situation in the province as a whole may be easing, the fact that the city's share in the province's number of

Anti-Prejudice Best Prescription for Joint Fight   IV

deaths remains at about 79 percent and it accounts for 83 percent of the people infected in the province shows that it is still suffering the most and remains the stronghold of the virus.

Undoubtedly, it was the lockdown of Wuhan since Jan 23, that has helped the country to keep the virus contained largely within the city; and it is the country's efforts — the whole nation has come to a virtual state of standstill for nearly a month — that has helped win the world a window of opportunity to curb the virus' spread.

This opportunity has been won at a huge cost — 1,666 people had been killed by the virus in China as of Sunday, according to the National Health Commission, which does not include those who passed away before being confirmed of infection with the novel coronavirus due to the lack of sufficient testing kits in Wuhan and elsewhere in the province. And by Friday, a total of 1,716 medical professionals had been infected with the virus, among whom six have died.

People throughout the country extend their condolences to the families and friends of those who have died, and their appreciation for the self-sacrifice of Wuhan residents.

But some outside the country, prefer prejudice to empathy and they vilify the Chinese people, the country and its governance system. These China-bashers turn a blind eye to the country's efforts to prevent the virus spreading — efforts whose scale and efficiency are enabled by its system — and point to the infections outside the country, about 1 percent of the total, to hype up the epidemic as symptomatic of the China threat they are peddling.

And it is because of them that the World Health Organization has repeatedly had to urge some developed countries to share their data and join in the war against the virus.

Such biased and immoral views are against the interests of the world, as they directly shake the foundation for the international solidarity that is needed to defeat the virus.

February 16, 2020

China Daily Editorial

Sacrifice, Toil and Tears
China and the World in the Fight against the Pandemic

China should be praised not insulted

By Yukteshwar Kumar

Ma Xuejing/China Daily

The Chinese economy seems to be marking time because of the novel coronavirous epidemic and it will take time to get the engine of Chinese growth on the right track again.

This is not the time for other countries to rejoice in China's misfortune, yet there are some indulging in schadenfreude as the country reels under the calamity.

US Secretary of Commerce Wilbur Ross immediately jumped on the outbreak, saying, "I think it will help to accelerate the return of jobs to North America." He went even further, disparagingly claiming that China "has a long history of covering up real risks to its own people and the rest of the world".

China is trying its best to determine the number of infected people and the death toll from the virus, and it constantly makes it known, both at home and abroad. Chinese people can even pinpoint how far they are away from the site of a known infection via a map on their smartphones. Where is the cover-up?

The highly admired American newspaper The Wall Street Journal recently published an article with an underlying racist tone with the headline, "China is the Real Sick Man of Asia". And it is not only the media in the US that are exposing their bigotry, some European media outlets have also been expressing disdain for the Chinese government and the state. A Danish newspaper, the Morgenavisen Jyllands-Posten, replaced the five stars on the Chinese flag with five symbols depicting the new virus.

The French newspaper Le Courrier Picard also used the headline "Alerte Jaune", which means "Yellow Alert" and the German magazine Der Spigel declared on its cover "Coronavirus — Made in China".

While all this prejudice has been on display, the Chinese people have been suffering.

When the West wants to take pride in being the champion of liberty and an "all accommodating society", why not show it can be that? Should the editors and publishers of these newspapers and magazines have shown more wisdom, maturity and not resorted to racist-laden phrases and words?

It was highly disappointing to read some online attention-seeking news articles that claimed Chinese officials were seeking approval from the Supreme People's Court to start the mass slaughter of 20,000 people infected with the new coronavirus to contain the disease. My own mother called me from the impoverished state of Bihar in India to know the truth and so did some of my students. How can one even publish such vicious "fake news"? Just to get online presence and attract some attention? Ridiculous indeed. This double standard on epidemics is not helpful in fighting diseases.

The response by the US government during 2009 H1N1 epidemic outbreak was extremely slow and it took the US almost half a year to

Sacrifice, Toil and Tears
China and the World in the Fight against the Pandemic

declare it as a national emergency. China informed the World Health Organization of the outbreak soon after it emerged and it has kept it up to date on developments. While the Chinese people are doing all they can to stop the spread of this nasty virus, too many in the West seem intent on making nasty attacks on China.

The West and the whole world need to understand clearly that no matter in which country a public health threat emerges, no country is powerful enough to have all the resources, all the medical facilities, all the manpower, all the expertise and all the kits available to combat against these sorts of epidemics within a few days. China needs to be congratulated for erecting two hospitals in Wuhan within the span of some 10 days for each, and it should be appreciated for the all-out efforts it is making to contain the virus, at great cost to itself.

Under these kinds of abnormal circumstances, strong actions need to be taken which may not be welcomed by everyone. Whatever the government does, there will be always some people who will criticize the government without knowing the exact situation.

The whole world should show solidarity, and jointly fight against this invisible enemy with China. The West does not need to criticize or ridicule the Chinese government or denigrate the Chinese people.

February 17, 2020

The author is a senior academic at the University of Bath.

Epidemic exposes West's colonial mentality

By David Monyae

Xenophobia, ideological bias and the West's fear of China's rise are the triple burdens that hinder the fight against the novel coronavirus outbreak in China. Recently, Kevin Rudd, the former Australian prime minister and president of the Asia Society Policy Institute in New York, wrote, and I quote: "The wider world should show sympathy and express solidarity with the long suffering Chinese people. These are ugly times, and the racism implicit (and sometimes explicit) in many responses to Chinese people around the world makes me question just how far we have really come as a human family".

Indeed, Rudd's take on the need for a people-centered global approach in the fight against the epidemic resonate with a well-known African idiom commonly used among the Nguni dialects which says, Inxeba lendoda alihlekwa. It simply means that, "The wound of a man is not laughed at".

In reporting on the new coronavirus, The Wall Street Journal carried an article by Bard College Professor Walter Russell Mead titled, "China Is the Real Sick Man of Asia". The learned professor and the newspaper in question are quite aware that the term "sick man of Asia" is a derogatory phrase that emanates from China's century of humiliation at the hands of Western and Japanese powers. It was commonly used by foreign forces that conquered China to justify their inhuman treatment of Chinese people.

This colonial language was also common in Africa when colonial masters considered their religion, culture and general lifestyles to be superior to those of the ingenious people whom they perceived to be disease-ridden and unclean.

There have also been attacks against the attempts by the Chinese authorities to speedily control the outbreak that are cloaked in ideological clothes. There have been numerous opinion pieces across

Sacrifice, Toil and Tears — China and the World in the Fight against the Pandemic

the Western media that are using the breakout of this disease to directly attack the Chinese system.

The main aim of such attacks is to advance the long-held view that liberal democracies handle and manage epidemics and general crises much better than what is considered an authoritarian regime in China. The weakness of such an argument lies in the fact it is ahistorical. The United States itself is littered with endless mismanagement of epidemics and general crises confronted by its people. A recent example is Hurricane Katrina in New Orleans in 2005. The George W. Bush administration failed dismally to respond to the crisis that affected almost 80 percent of the city's mainly black population.

The British Guardian newspaper carried an article by Emma Graham-Harrison on Jan 31, in which she said that, "China soon won international plaudits for a huge mobilization, including the near impossible feat of building two new hospitals in as many weeks, even as Wuhan became an international byword for a new epidemic". She further settled for ideological point-scoring: "Yet as information about the early days of the outbreak has slowly filtered out of China, it has become increasingly clear that the same political system that allowed Beijing to order such a dramatic response, also initially allowed the virus to foster."

Also, some elements in the Western media and US officials are using the epidemic as a tool in their bid to limit the rise of China. On Jan 24, Foreign Policy magazine unashamedly carried an article titled, "Welcome to the Belt and Road Pandemic".

And US Secretary of Commerce Wilbur Ross responding to the epidemic in China was quoted as saying: "I think it will help to accelerate the return of jobs to America."

At this critical juncture of the fight against the novel coronavirus, there is a need to build a united front in combating the spread of the disease as well as finding a cure. The African continent in particular has worked tirelessly with China within the Forum on China-Africa Cooperation on managing communicative diseases. Africa can assist China in its efforts to manage the virus. Africa has responded soberly to the outbreak of the novel coronavirus in China without causing unnecessary panic. But more efforts ought to be taken to strengthen

Africa health workers' ability to respond to the novel coronavirus should it spread to the continent. Africa should also reject the triple Western diseases of xenophobia, ideological bias and the fear of China's rise.

February 18, 2020

The author is the director for the Centre for Africa-China Studies at the University of Johannesburg.

Epidemical discrimination violates spirit of human rights

By Wang Xigen

The sudden outbreak of the novel coronavirus in China is threatening the lives and health of people in China, and its impacts go beyond the country.

In the spirit of humanitarianism, people from all over the world have offered assistance and cares to China in various ways. With the spread of the epidemic, some countries, however, have made insulting, discriminatory remarks against China and the Chinese people, such as "Coronavirus, made in China", "Chinese virus", or "yellow peril", and "China is really the sick man of Asia". Some countries have overreacted by excluding tourists from China or discriminating against local Chinese, which has had a bad influence in the international community, so much so that even some Westerners themselves find it hard to tolerate such acts and condemn them.

Some countries have realized their mistake and made an open apology to China, but some have shown no sense of regret, and even tried to use so-called freedom of speech to whitewash their words and acts. Under the guise of freedom of speech they are violating human rights. Is it fear of the virus, or malicious discrimination against Chinese? In essence, these words and acts have gone far beyond normal preventive measures to curb the spread of the virus or a fearful response to a potential pandemic. They are, in essence, the spread of racial discrimination on the back of such fears, which constitutes exploitation of the epidemic for discrimination that aims to subvert the human rights values of equality and non-discrimination, and challenge the international human rights system.

As UN Secretary-General Antonio Guterres pointed out while some people look at a virus from a discriminatory perspective and have an inclination to violate human rights, Article 3 of the International Health Regulations stipulates that human dignity, human rights and fundamental freedoms should be fully respected. After a visit to China, WHO Director-General Tedros Adhanom Ghebreyesus stressed that the way to fight the epidemic is "solidarity and cooperation", "not stigmatization".

To combat discrimination is the basic principle of the international system of human rights with the UN Charter at its core. Discrimination on the basis of nationality, race or specific groups of people is strictly prohibited by international framework for human rights. The UN Charter emphasizes the promotion of respect for human rights and fundamental freedoms of all human beings, irrespective of race, sex, language or religion. The 1948 Universal Declaration of Human Rights proclaims that mankind shall be treated in a spirit of brotherhood and shall be free from any act of discrimination in violation of this declaration and from any act that incites such discrimination. Article 2 of the 1966 International Covenant on Economic, Social and Cultural Rights also states that the rights proclaimed in this covenant shall be universally applied without any distinction as to race, skin color, sex, language, religion, political or other opinions, nationality, or social origin, property, birth, or other status. In order to highlight the special significance of anti-discrimination for all human beings, the international community has adopted a series of international human rights conventions specially designed to combat discrimination, in which the principles of equality and non-discrimination are red lines that must not be crossed.

Indeed, at a time when a natural disaster seriously threatens human life and health, in order to deal with the crisis, it is necessary that countries take specific preventive and restrictive measures, shoulder their obligations to protect their citizens and strengthen the protection of their right to health and safety. However, such obligations are not without boundaries and the red line of nondiscrimination should not be crossed, as stipulated by the International Covenant on Civil and Political Rights. According to Article 4 of the Covenant, under no circumstances shall discrimination because of race or skin color be allowed, and even if there is a life-threatening state of emergency, there can be no discrimination based on race or skin color. Any insulting remarks and acts against China and the Chinese people under the guise of self-protection against the novel coronavirus completely deviate from a country's obligations set by international human rights conventions and are a violation of the spirit of international law that demands respect for the dignity of people.

After the outbreak of the new coronavirus, some foreign media outlets have made use of it to publicize and arouse dissatisfaction and discrimination against the Chinese people, which constitutes the incitement of discriminatory behavior, as defined by Article 7 of the Universal Declaration of Human Rights.

Since the coronavirus outbreak, China has made the highest-level response and taken the fastest and most stringent prevention and control measures that go beyond the standards set by the International Health Regulations. Just as WHO chief Tedros said, China deserves gratitude and respect for fighting the virus so resolutely. Under such circumstances, any attempt to add fuel to the fire or to throw stones into the well with discrimination toward China and the Chinese people is clearly incompatible with the spirit of the international human rights law.

February 20, 2020

The author is the dean of the School of Law, Huazhong University of Science and Technology.

Coronavirus and world responsibility

By Shabir Mohsin Hashmi

Zheng Xinyao /For China Daily

The novel coronavirus, also known as COVID-19, has become a global concern. Chinese efforts in curbing the virus have widely been recognized. Even the World Health Organization has lauded the efforts of the Chinese government and advised the world to learn from China in fighting the disease.

To stop the outbreak, China has made extraordinary efforts. Wuhan, the epicenter of the disease in China, has been completely quarantined along with other cities where the number of infected people was growing rapidly. Apart from this, the central government has mobilized all its resources, with teams of doctors and medical supplies being directly sent to the affected place in the shortest period of time. House-to-house temperature checks have been initiated. People were asked to report to the authorities immediately if they have

Sacrifice, Toil and Tears — China and the World in the Fight against the Pandemic

any sign of fever, cough or pneumonia. To ensure a smooth supply of food and daily necessities, special arrangements were made. Were it not possible for the people to acquire daily necessities, the government had ensured that the masses would be provided food, clothing and shelter at the expense of the government. To meet with the sudden demand for hospitals in Wuhan city, two were built in less than two weeks, equipped with state-of-the-art technology, while makeshift hospitals were also established.

Due to such government efforts, the number of infected people and fatalities has been reduced significantly. Moreover, the Chinese government has decided to reopen schools but students will be given lessons online. For the factories and workers, the government has decided to bring workers in shifts and that will also depend on the conditions. Official meetings and other day-to-day work are being minimized and where necessary; officials are asked to avoid direct contact and instead hold online meetings. For trade and commerce, human contact is minimized and machines and robots are given tasks to perform duties. Thanks to such policies, we have seen a sharp decline in the spread of the virus and number of fatalities. The Chinese experience with fighting against virus has largely been successful and many countries have praised the efforts.

Despite this, a few countries still showed some hostile behavior toward China. The worse example of such hostility is that some nations refused to provide medical equipment, machines, technical staff and face masks. Above all were the comments of the US commerce secretary. He reportedly advised American companies to shift their manufacturing units out of China because China is dirty. Such remarks never suit a responsible statesman. Besides, there have been numerous reports in the media that Chinese people have been humiliated or harassed in different countries only because they are from China. Such behavior is inhuman and highly condemnable.

In contrast, some countries have provided all possible support to China. Chinese Foreign Minister Wang Yi has appreciated Pakistan's help to China in this difficult time. But regretfully, the US, India and their allies are spreading baseless rumors to distort the truth and propagating conspiracy theories which have no scientific basis.

China is a responsible country and has played its due role during world crises. We should not forget the role of China during fight against the Ebola. It was Chinese scientists who were on the front lines. No matter if it was a global warming conference, an earthquake in Haiti, UN peacekeeping forces or hurricanes in Philippines and Indonesia, China was in the forefront. We know difficult times never remain the same. But this makes nations more resilient and united. All Chinese are together, telling the world that we are united and we will win the war against the coronavirus.

February 25, 2020

The writer is a professor and director of the BRI Research Center at Yancheng Institute of Technology, Jiangsu, China.

Coronavirus not China's Chernobyl

By Lan Shunzheng

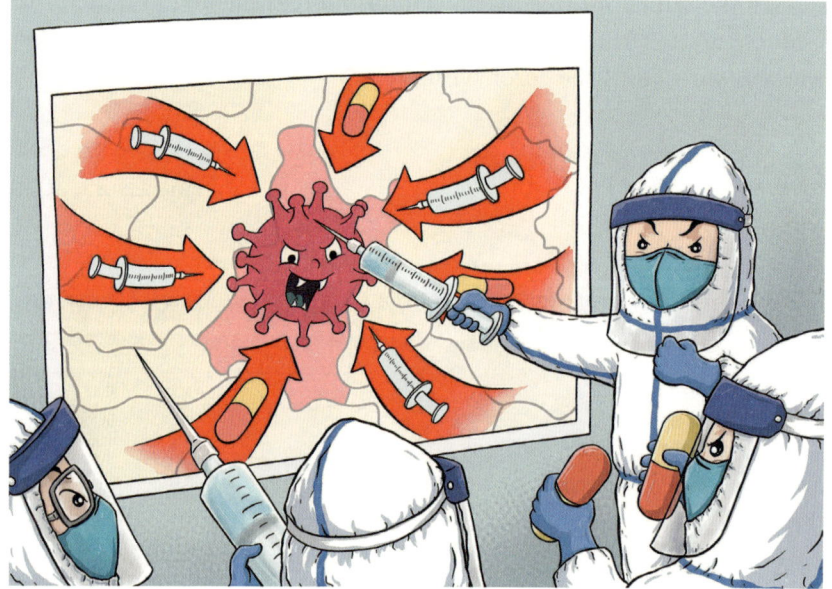

Hao Yanpeng /For China Daily

At a time when China is trying to contain the novel coronavirus epidemic, some Western media outlets have exposed their anti-China bias by claiming the situation is "China's Chernobyl".

The nuclear disaster in Chernobyl, Ukraine, in the then Soviet Union in 1986 remains the worst nuclear accident till date. It was caused by the meltdown of the No 4 light water graphite moderated reactor in the Chernobyl nuclear power plant.

Apart from the initial casualty of more than 30 people and hundreds being hospitalized for radiation exposure, tens of thousands of people were exposed to leaked radiation and the disaster resulted in tens of billions of dollars in direct and indirect economic losses. Radioactive dust and cloud from Chernobyl traveled from Ukraine to the then western Soviet Union, mainly Belarus, all the way to Europe. Ultimately an area around the nuclear plant — with a radius of 30 kilometers — was declared an exclusion zone.

Also, the Soviet authorities didn't immediately inform the residents around the Chernobyl plant or the international community about the serious consequences of the nuclear accident. The disaster raised global censure, especially because many in the international community believed the Soviet authorities didn't appropriately respond to the emergency.

But order was established after the central government realized what was happening, it immediately implemented strict measures to contain the epidemic by setting quarantine norms, mobilizing the national medical corps, ordering the local government and health department to swing into action, and building two makeshift hospitals in about two weeks. And all the while, China maintained transparency as far as releasing information and updating data on the epidemic were concerned.

So, by comparing the coronavirus outbreak to the Chernobyl disaster, some Western media outlets are trying to create panic across the world and giving a bad name to China's political institutional measures when they should be focusing on working together to contain the epidemic.

It's a pity that their Cold War mentality is prompting some Western media outlets, especially those in the United States, to hype up the epidemic as part of their "China threat" fallacy even in these trying times. A report, titled "Rising to the China Challenge: Renewing American Competitiveness in the Indo-Pacific", released on Jan 28 by the Center for a New American Security, US think tank, said Western governments and companies should consider competing with China by, for instance, attacking what it perceives as the problems with Chinese institutes.

Besides, US State Secretary Mike Pompeo tried to derail the cooperation between China and countries such as Ukraine and Kazakhstan during his visit to the two countries on Jan 31 and Feb 2.

Some US officials continue to claim China poses a threat to the world, in order to fulfill their narrow political goals, even as China has intensified its fight against the epidemic. US Secretary of Commerce

Wilbur Ross, for example, said on Jan 30 that the epidemic might help jobs return to the US.

Governments should accord top priority to cooperation at all times, particularly when a country is fighting a deadly disease outbreak. But some Western media outlets and politicians have been violating this long established global rule.

Since China is the world's second-largest economy, the novel coronavirus outbreak in the country has already impacted the global economy. For example, global stock markets have been volatile, oil prices have dropped because China's demand for oil has declined and exports of auto components from China have been restricted, and Nissan decided to shut down several production lines.

Yet China has taken effective measures to contain the spread of the novel coronavirus. And new cases have shown a declining trend, even as the World Health Organization has warned the risks of novel coronavirus transmission beyond China might cause serious global problems.

In short, the epidemic is by no means China's Chernobyl and the international community should work together to contain the epidemic as soon as possible so as to strengthen global security and stability.

February 21, 2020

The author is a research fellow at the Charhar Institute and a member of the Chinese Institute of Command and Control.

Anti-Prejudice Best Prescription
for Joint Fight

IV

Headlines in New York Times are misleading

By Philip J. Cunningham

Li Min/China Daily

With tens of thousands sick and more than two thousand lives lost, among them a growing number of front-line medical workers, the struggle to contain the coronavirus has put China on edge.

It's understandable that people's nerves are on edge at a time like this. That's why the Wall Street Journal's "China is the Real Sick Man of Asia" provoked a strong reaction among ordinary citizens and officials alike. Many members of the WSJ reporting staff were also unhappy with this unfriendly and infelicitous "sick man" word choice, and said so, but the editors did not budge.

Chinese officials asked for an apology which was not forthcoming. Unfortunately, the reaction was to kick out three decent rank-and-file reporters when the hand responsible for the offending headline was in the WSJ home office in New York.

Americans take press freedom, including the freedom to insult, quite seriously and most of the time it's a value worth defending. However, gratuitous insult designed to kick someone when they are down is not easy to defend or forget.

It's instructional to look at The New York Times headlines about China in the past two months, bearing in mind that the home office, not the reporters in the field, pen the headlines in question which includes several opinion and editorial pieces as well.

The headlines are generally much less offensive than the WSJ "sick man" zinger that rattled media relations, but the New York-based editorial touches are distant, insensitive and sometimes arrogant.

While the consistent use of the neutral term "coronavirus" is an editorial improvement over "China flu" and "Wuhan virus" which can be seen elsewhere, the epidemic was cast by the NYT as an essentially Chinese thing from the start:

"To Understand the Wuhan Coronavirus, Look to the Epidemic Triangle"

"Why Did the Coronavirus Outbreak Start in China?"

Let's talk about the cultural causes of this epidemic. A Wuhan wet market where wildlife was on sale was initially, and still not confirmed as the outbreak ground zero, but the facts didn't stop the persistence of the "Chinese eat weird things" trope which exploded on social networks and managed to find its way into mainstream press reports:

"In Coronavirus, China Weighs Benefits of Buffalo Horn and Other Remedies"

"As New Coronavirus Spreads, China's Old Habits Delayed Fight"

Scientists and serious journalists have long since debunked the "it's a bioweapon from the labs in Wuhan" meme, but that doesn't stop the malicious insinuation from getting repeated.

What's the Greek rhetorical term for indirectly mocking someone by bringing attention to someone else's "fringe" theory?

"Senator Tom Cotton Repeats Fringe Theory of Coronavirus Origins"

As coronavirus spreads, so does anti-Chinese sentiment. And there's more. China's singular misfortune to be the nation hardest hit by a virus that knows no nationality, yet it was the nation state that provided a field day for headlines mocking China:

"Coronavirus Crisis Exposes Cracks in China's Facade of Unity"

"Coronavirus Exposes Core Flaws, and Few Strengths, in China's Governance"

Naturally the NYT headline writers are not exactly adept at seeing through their own smug prejudices. They are quite confident, however, in poking big holes in China's media.

"The Coronavirus Story is Too Big for China to Spin"

It's interesting to note that the pattern of China-bashing themes implicit in the NYT headlines began to soften when the disease jumped borders to spread to Japan, the Republic of Korea, Iran and Italy. It was no longer a uniquely Chinese problem, and there was more blame to go around. Tokyo's feet of clay were exposed during the debacle of the cruise ship quarantine. Ditto the United States, where few test kits are available.

When face to face with an epidemic, human frailty, irrational fear and bureaucratic bungling are universal qualities, as Camus memorialized in his powerful novel *The Plague*.

Fear has hit the stock market and the world economy is starting to look wobbly. The US Centers for Disease Control and Prevention's recent clarion call to ready the nation for the epidemic spread of the virus has found the US woefully underfunded and unprepared to deal with a crisis even with the fraction of intensity of that in Wuhan, Hubei province. There are not enough facemasks or testing kits, let alone beds and special equipment.

The bad news was almost immediately counteracted by a tweet from the US president who retorted:

"Low Ratings Fake News MSDNC (Comcast) & @CNN are

doing everything possible to make the Caronavirus look as bad as possible, including panicking markets…USA in great shape!"

(The misspelling of "coronavirus" is in the original tweet.)

Let's hope The New York Times does a better job of covering the US chapter of the coronavirus tragedy than it's done so far in China.

February 28, 2020

The author is a media researcher covering Asian issues.

This is not the time to play the blame game

By Zhang Jinling

Physician Ni Xiaohui surveys from a vantage point the makeshift hospital at the Wuhan Sports Center on March 1, 2020. Ni and 29 of his colleagues from Nantong, East China's Jiangsu province, were stationed at the makeshift hospital to treat the COVID-19 patients.

Wang Jing/China Daily

China has been making its utmost efforts to fight the COVID-19 outbreak, and the strict measures it has taken to rein in the epidemic are gradually yielding results, except perhaps in Hubei province.

But since an epidemic is a common threat to humankind as a whole, the international community should help China tide over the difficulties by sharing their experiences and advanced methods to prevent and control the epidemic, because by so doing they would be helping the entire humankind.

But many Western politicians and media outlets have spared no efforts to vilify China's political system, especially the leadership of

Sacrifice, Toil and Tears — China and the World in the Fight against the Pandemic

the Communist Party of China at a time when China has been using all the resources at its disposal to fight the epidemic. For instance, US Senator Marco Rubio, over the weekend, once again claimed China has failed to "share necessary information" that could have contained the spread of the novel coronavirus and blamed it for putting the world at risk as more countries reported their first deaths from the virus.

Indeed, the local authorities in Wuhan, Hubei province, didn't handle the epidemic properly in the initial days of the outbreak. But later, the central authorities mobilized resources nationwide to fight the disease and closely coordinated with the World Health Organization to take measures to control the disease.

China did share its experience with the rest of the world as it imposed strict quarantine measures on the epicenter of the outbreak in Hubei province. Strict and effective quarantine and lock-down measures in certain places are a scientific way of preventing cross-infection and containing the spread of the epidemic. However, some Western media outlets see the Chinese government's community quarantine measures as a manifestation of "high-handed" rule.

Such distorted, malicious reports are an apt example of irresponsible behavior. Such reports and comments from Western politicians and media outlets have not only hurt the feelings of Chinese people, but also misled the international community, which undermine international cooperation and solidarity in the face of a global medical emergency.

It is true that China's political, economic, social and cultural systems are different from those of many other countries, but they are the choice of the Chinese people, and the inevitable outcome of China's historical development that suits its national conditions. The prevention and control of the epidemic is not only medical and health problem but also a comprehensive crisis management problem. In this unprecedented war against the novel coronavirus, the Chinese system has fully displayed its advantages in terms of decision-making, mobilization and execution abilities, and its ability to correct mistakes.

The Chinese government mobilized the social mechanism within a very short time despite the COVID-19 outbreak affecting Wuhan, a densely populated city, during the Spring Festival travel rush season. From locking down the epicenter, sending medical aid teams and completing emergency construction of medical facilities to organizing the supply of emergency medical products and coordinating efforts to prevent and control the epidemic are all a reflection of China's institutional advantages.

The authorities have taken prompt measures to correct the mistakes of some officials who didn't perform their duties properly in the initial stages in some regions, punished relevant personnel according to Party disciplines and the law, and have thus ensured that the measures to control the spread of the novel coronavirus are implemented strictly and effectively.

The novel coronavirus, as the name indicates, is a new type of virus, which is still to be properly understood by the scientific community. Yet, despite being hit by the epidemic, China has been resilient enough to try to bring production back to normal. More important, people in Hubei province have been making great sacrifices to enable the nation to win the battle against the epidemic.

As such, this is not the time for people to play the blame game. Instead, members of the international community should coordinate their efforts to contain the rising cases outside China. As for China, it too has the responsibility and obligation to promote international cooperation in preventing and controlling epidemics and conducting scientific research to find cures for viruses.

March 5, 2020

The author is a researcher at the Institute of European Studies, Chinese Academy of Social Sciences.

Neither "Wuhan virus" nor "Los Angeles virus"

By Yan Lun

Cai Meng / China Daily

Is China trying to deny its "disgraceful role" in a "global pandemic" by strongly opposing the use of "Wuhan virus" or "China virus" to describe the novel coronavirus? And has China put the whole world on edge because of its inability to contain the virus in Wuhan, Hubei province, in the initial stages?

Yes, claim many Western media outlets and politicians.

But has the world heard of "Los Angeles virus" or "US virus"?

In June 1981, a rare type of pneumonia was detected in five previously healthy young men in Los Angeles. Epidemiologists had to conduct studies for 18 months to identify the acquired immunodeficiency syndrome (AIDS) and its major risk factors.

The lethal disease has spread from the United States to the rest of world in the past 39 years. According to UNAIDS, in 2018 an estimated

Anti-Prejudice Best Prescription for Joint Fight **IV**

37.9 million people, including 1.7 million children, were living with HIV and 770,000 died of AIDS-related illnesses. And since the first cases were reported, a total of about 74.9 million people have contracted HIV and 32 million people have died of AIDS-related illnesses.

Has anyone used "Los Angeles virus" to describe HIV? Have people attacked the US for failing to keep the deadly disease within its borders? Do people panic over the disease that claimed 770,000 lives in 2018 alone?

The answers are no. It was in 2007, 26 years after the first AIDS cases were reported in Los Angeles, that biologists at the University of Arizona put forward a hypothesis that HIV was carried from Africa first to Haiti and then to the US way back in 1969.

Have people rejected the hypothesis, saying the US is trying to cover its "role" in "creating and spreading" HIV/AIDS?

No. On the contrary, the hypothesis has been widely accepted.

To determine where a new kind of disease or virus originated, scientists need a long time to track down the pathogen, "patient zero", or "ground zero". And even a century after the influenza pandemic of 1918-20, more widely known as "Spanish flu", killed about 40 million people, there are different hypotheses about its place of origin—from France to the US, to even China.

The opposition to linking the novel coronavirus with Wuhan, the epicenter of the outbreak in China, is not China's attempt to shirk its responsibility as COVID-19 cases outside China continue to rise sharply, but because epidemiologists and other experts need time and arduous research to find out where it originated. In early February, in the initial stages of the outbreak, at least 12 people in Japan had contracted the disease despite not having a travel history to China or coming in contact with a Chinese national. And at the hearing in the US House of Representatives on Wednesday, the Centers for Disease Control and Prevention Director Robert Redfield admitted that it was possible some Americans who appear to be dying of influenza may actually be dying for the novel coronavirus as the CDC's surveillance system for pneumonia does not cover every city, every state, every hospital.

The novel coronavirus is the common enemy of humankind. And people who have suffered and even lost their lives in the epidemic should not be blamed for that. Before the puzzle of determining the

Sacrifice, Toil and Tears
China and the World in the Fight against the Pandemic

place of origin of the virus is solved, people shouldn't display their ignorance by casting aspersions on others, especially the victims. If some media outlets and politicians such as US Secretary of State Mike Pompeo continue to link the virus with "Wuhan" or "China", they would be spreading racial hatred.

Take a look at the chain of discrimination that is emerging because of prejudice. In a recent column in The New York Times, a Chinese author described how a woman of Vietnamese origin in an Asian community in the US yelled at her for "eating weird food and bringing it here". Asians have become an eyesore for many Westerners now. A college student from Singapore was beaten up in London by a group of men who told him that they didn't "want your coronavirus in my country". Such biased attacks will undermine the joint efforts to fight the pandemic, and they should stop.

True, all 15 makeshift hospitals in Wuhan were closed on Tuesday, suggesting China is closer to reining in the outbreak. But let us not forget what China has sacrificed in the battle against the disease: the whole Hubei province is under lockdown, China's economic growth may slip to as low as 3.5 percent in the first quarter. Nor should we forget the contribution of more than 40,000 medical staff from across the country who went to Wuhan to take care of the patients. And the measures China has taken to control the epidemic will not only better protect its people, but has also created a window of opportunity for other countries to fight against the disease, as WHO said.

Indeed, China should learn many lessons from the anti-virus fight, including how to strengthen public health governance in the early stage of an outbreak. Such painful lessons, as well as experiences, are valuable reference for other countries tackling an epidemic.

Wuhan's sacrifices, Hubei's sufferings, China's battles. The stories of the city, the province, and the country should not be demonized. And calling the novel coronavirus "Wuhan virus" or "China virus" is the worst form of demonizing. It should stop.

March 13, 2020

The author is a writer with China Daily.

International Coordination Essential to Deal with Global Risks

Sacrifice, Toil and Tears: China and the World in the Fight against the Pandemic

Global solidarity essential to defeat outbreak

By Tedros Adhanom Ghebreyesus

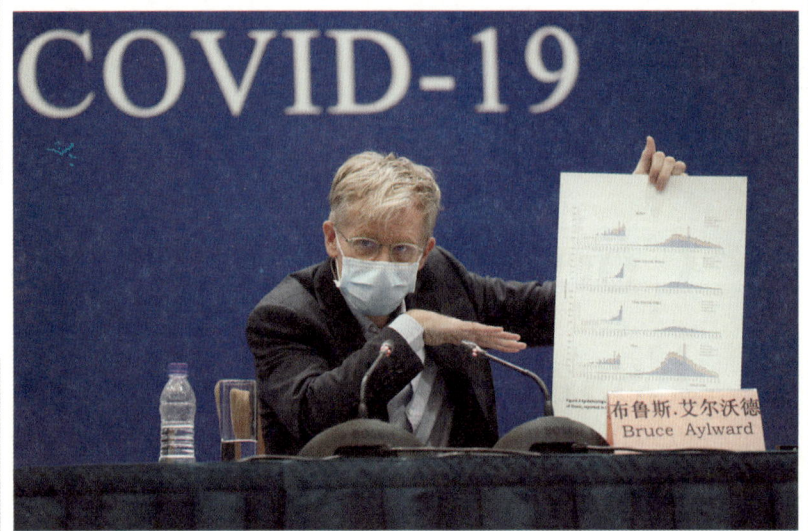

Epidemiologist Bruce Aylward, who heads the WHO mission team to China, speaks at a news conference of the WHO-China Joint Mission on COVID-19 in Beijing on Feb 24, 2020.

Wang Zhuangfei/China Daily

I have already said a lot about the outbreak of the novel coronavirus, at the Executive Board yesterday and at the PBAC meeting last week.

But allow me to underline a few key points.

The latest data we have is that there are 20,471 confirmed cases in China, including 425 deaths.

Outside China there are 176 cases in 24 countries, and one death, in the Philippines.

It's important to underline that 99 percent of the cases are in China, and 97 percent of the deaths are in Hubei province. This is still

International Coordination Essential to Deal with Global Risks

first and foremost an emergency for China.

We continue to work closely with the Chinese government to support its efforts to address this outbreak at the epicenter. That is our best chance of preventing a broader global crisis.

Of course, the risk of it becoming more widespread globally remains high. Now is the moment for all countries to be preparing themselves.

WHO is sending masks, gloves, respirators and almost 18,000 isolation gowns from our warehouses in Dubai and Accra to 24 countries who need support, and we will add more countries.

We're sending 250,000 tests to more than 70 reference laboratories globally to facilitate faster testing.

We're sending a team of international experts to work with their Chinese counterparts to increase understanding of the outbreak to guide the global response.

We're convening a global research meeting next week to identify research priorities in all areas of the outbreak, from identifying the source of the virus to developing vaccines and therapeutics.

Tomorrow, I will brief the Secretary General and the UN senior management team.

Today we held a call with all 150 WHO country offices, to discuss the measures they need to take to be ready. On Thursday we'll have a similar briefing with all resident coordinators in the UN system.

We are also increasing our communications capacity to counter the spread of rumours and misinformation, and ensure all people receive the accurate, reliable information they need to protect themselves and their families.

And we plan to hold daily media briefings.

Today I have three key requests for Member States:

First, I call on all Member States to share detailed information with WHO-including epidemiological, clinical severity and the results of community studies and investigations. This is the responsibility of all countries under the International Health Regulations.

Of the 176 cases reported outside China so far, WHO has received complete case report forms for only 38 percent of cases. Some high-income countries are well behind in sharing this vital data with WHO. I don't think it's because they lack capacity.

Sacrifice, Toil and Tears — China and the World in the Fight against the Pandemic

Without better data, it's very hard for us to assess how the outbreak is evolving, or what impact it could have, and to ensure we are providing the most appropriate recommendations.

Today I am writing to all ministers of health to request an immediate improvement in data sharing.

As I said yesterday, we can only defeat this outbreak with global solidarity, and that starts with collective participation in global surveillance. The commitment to solidarity starts with sharing information. Solidarity, solidarity, solidarity.

Second, we reiterate our call to all countries not to impose restrictions inconsistent with the International Health Regulations.

Such restrictions can have the effect of increasing fear and stigma, with little public health benefit.

So far, 22 countries have reported such restrictions to WHO.

Where such measures have been implemented, we urge that they are short in duration, proportionate to the public health risks, and are reconsidered regularly as the situation evolves.

And third, facilitate rapid collaboration between the public and private sectors to develop the diagnostics, medicines and vaccines we need to bring this outbreak under control.

We have a window of opportunity. While 99 percent of cases are in China, in the rest of the world we only have 176 cases. That doesn't mean that it won't get worse. But for sure we have a window of opportunity to act. Because 176 in the rest of the world is very small, there is no reason to panic or fear. Of course, people are worried — they should be.

There is a window of opportunity because of the measures China has used at the epicenter, at the source. Let's not miss this window of opportunity.

February 6, 2020

The author is director-general of WHO. This is his opening remarks at the technical briefing on 2019 novel coronavirus at the 146th session of the Executive Board on Feb 4.

International Coordination Essential
to Deal with Global Risks

V

Region shows solidarity in anti-virus fight

Shi Yu/China Daily

The outbreak of the novel coronavirus again reminds us that this is an era in which a regional or national issue can easily evolve into a global one. In a highly interdependent world, countries must join hands to fight a public health incident of such magnitude.

Hence, it is heartening to see that the foreign ministers of China

Sacrifice, Toil and Tears — China and the World in the Fight against the Pandemic

and the members of the Association of Southeast Asian Nations are meeting in Vientiane, Laos, from Wednesday to Friday to strengthen regional cooperation to address the public health threat. It is expected that they will build upon their existing national measures with an orchestrated response and collective actions.

China and ASEAN accumulated useful experience in this respect with their cooperation during the severe acute respiratory syndrome outbreak in 2002-03.

With China fighting an all-out war to contain the outbreak, people from various countries have expressed confidence and offered assistance. In a statement released on Saturday by Vietnam, which is chairman of the regional bloc this year, ASEAN expressed its "solidarity and heartfelt support" for China, as well as other countries fighting the virus.

The statement also affirmed ASEAN countries would maintain an open-door policy with quarantine work conducted and coordinated at the border gates of the member countries.

Epidemics know no boundaries, and the novel coronavirus, like any highly contagious disease, is a common enemy of humanity. That well explains why the cruise ships Diamond Princess, docked in Japan's Yokohama Port, and Westerdam, docked in Cambodia's sea port of Sihanoukville, have drawn global concerns.

While the Diamond Princess has contributed a large proportion of Japan's confirmed cases, one passenger onboard the Westerdam also tested positive last week. Now that passengers onboard both ships have begun to disembark, it has raised concerns about the further spread of the virus.

In Southeast Asia, the alarm was already sounding, as six out of the 10 ASEAN members have reported a combined total of 154 confirmed infections, according to Tuesday's World Health Organization report.

Although China is bringing the outbreak under control, vigilance is still needed. The special foreign ministers' meeting in Laos will help shore up regional solidarity and confidence that the virus can be contained, as it will enhance coordination at the regional level for a synchronized approach.

In contrast to the rising trend of unilateralism and isolationism in some parts of the world, more and more countries, China and ASEAN members included, are harnessing support for multilateralism as they know it is the best way to protect the well-being of their peoples.

February 19, 2020

China Daily Editorial

Sino-Mongolian true friendship endures amid outbreak

By Meng Gencang

Mongolian President Khaltmaagiin Battulga paid a special one-day visit to China on Feb 27, 2020, as the first foreign head of state to visit China since the outbreak of COVID-19, representing the profound friendship between the two countries at the current stage of the fight against epidemic. During his meeting with Chinese President Xi Jinping, he quoted some old Mongolian words of wisdom — "a needle in need is of greater use than a camel in prosperity" as an implication of "adversity reveals true friendship".

President Xi Jinping expressed his warm welcome as President Battulga paid this special visit only one day after Mongolia's traditional White Month holiday and appreciated the Mongolian government and people for their valuable support and assistance to China in fighting the epidemic. Moreover, he noted that President Battulga's one-day visit to express consolation and support to the Chinese people over the outbreak of the virus vividly showed that the two countries stand closely together in difficult times.

After both sides exchanged views on joint efforts to curb the spread of the novel coronavirus, President Battulga announced to President Xi Jinping a donation of 30,000 sheep to China, implying that the assistance will be measured by the significance of its size. This sincere and down-to-earth assistance has received wide attention and warm appreciation from the netizens of both countries.

Firm support reveals true friendship

President Battulga's one-day visit during this special period of time fully illustrated the Mongolian government's firm support for China's efforts to fight against the epidemic. The Mongolian government provided China at the earliest possible time $200,000, which was Mongolia's largest amount of cash assistance for a foreign country in recent years. Meanwhile, the Mongolian government's senior officials and some other party leaders sent letters to China, expressing their condolences and highly praising the effective measures taken by the Chinese government to battle against the epidemic.

During his meeting with President Xi Jinping, President Battulga addressed his appreciation of China's nationwide joint efforts to fight against the epidemic.

No wonder this meeting at this special time between the heads of state of the two countries will be an important step toward maintaining the regular bilateral high-level visits, strengthening mutual trust, and consolidating the comprehensive strategic partnership between the two countries.

"A friend in need, a friend indeed"

Since the unprecedented outbreak of the virus, the Mongolian people have launched humanitarian fundraising activities to support China's fight against the epidemic, and received active responses from all walks of life, indicating the profound friendship between the two peoples. The Mongolian people have paid great attention to China's anti-epidemic situation and expressed their kindness to stand with the Chinese people and try their best to provide support and help in many ways.

According to the Chinese embassy in Mongolia, the charitable funds raised by all sectors of Mongolian society have reached nearly 5 million yuan, and donations also include medical supplies such as masks and medical protective clothing that are in short supply in China, reflecting the profound friendship between the two peoples.

There is no isolated island in front of an epidemic. During the meeting, President Xi Jinping emphasized that China will continue to work with countries including Mongolia to fight the epidemic and safeguard regional and global public health security. Since the Mongolian people have been equally concerned about the outbreak, as Mongolia shares the longest land border with China, it is very necessary that the two countries stand closely together to curb the spread of the novel coronavirus.

President Battulga's special visit during the ongoing nationwide fight against the epidemic presented cooperation between neighboring countries to the world, and the vision of a community with a shared future for humanity will be deeply rooted in the hearts of the two peoples.

February 29, 2020

The author is an assistant researcher at the Inner Mongolia Academy of Social Sciences.

International Coordination Essential
to Deal with Global Risks V

Show of solidarity

By Li Yonghui

Jin Ding/China Daily

Since the outbreak of the novel coronavirus in China, its largest neighbor, Russia, has expressed its support for and solidarity with China in surmounting the difficulties. The support from the Russian government and civil society has warmed the hearts of Chinese people and injected vigor into China's efforts to fight the epidemic, while reflecting the strong people-to-people exchanges between the two sides, and the deepening of the Sino-Russian Comprehensive Strategic Partnership of Coordination for a New Era.

After the outbreak of the epidemic, Russian President Vladimir Putin sent a letter to Chinese President Xi Jinping to express his condolence and praise China's efforts in preventing and controlling the epidemic. Russia sent epidemic control experts to China, and donated 23 tons of medical and relief supplies, including 2 million pieces of face masks and other protective equipment. It also carried urgently-needed medical supplies to Wuhan, the epicenter of the outbreak, on a military transport aircraft deployed to evacuate Russian nationals living in the city on Feb 5.

The Russian authorities have voiced support for China on multiple occasions. On Jan 31, Putin expressed the willingness to assist China in combating the coronavirus in a telegram message sent to Xi. In the message he said the Russian authorities would cooperate closely with China to ward off the shared threat as soon as possible. Putin said the Chinese authorities had taken decisive measures to control the spread of the coronavirus and minimize the impact of the epidemic. On the same day, Putin ordered relevant government departments to provide necessary assistance to China. On Feb 4, Putin expressed his concern over the epidemic as well as his confidence that China would win the battle against the epidemic when meeting with activists in Cherepovets in Vologda region. On Feb 5, he again voiced support for China at a ceremony in which the ambassadors of 18 countries presented their credentials. Putin told Zhang Hanhui, Chinese ambassador to Russia the Chinese authorities are taking decisive and vigorous measures in order to stop the epidemic and Russia stands ready to provide the friendly Chinese people with all kinds of assistance. On Feb 12, Russian Foreign Ministry Spokesperson Maria Zakharova voiced support for China's efforts in fighting the coronavirus in the Chinese language.

The two sides have ramped up cooperation in prevention and control of epidemic since the outbreak. The Sino-Russian Comprehensive Strategic Partnership of Coordination for a New Era, which was established in a deal signed by the top leaders of the two countries in June 2019, enriched the bilateral relationship. The document broadened the scope of cooperation between the two countries on health issues, including strengthening collaboration in responding to public health emergencies caused by natural or human reasons and minimizing the medical consequences; and further expanding cooperation in diagnosis and treatment of contagious diseases and epidemic prevention and control. Under the framework of the partnership, the two sides will step up coordination in research on and the monitoring of dangerous viral and infectious diseases with natural foci, as well as in academic research on risk assessment of environmental elements affecting human health.

On Feb 5, five Russian epidemic prevention experts went to Wuhan to work together with Chinese peers on researching vaccines and test kits for the novel coronavirus. Five days later, virus test kits developed by the Russian experts passed assessment. The test kits can be preserved at a temperature of 4 C, while similar test kits developed by other countries need to be preserved at minus 20 C. The testing is easy to do, with only smear samples from nose and pharynx required to be collected, and the test outcome can be seen in four hours. Russian experts said the test kits, which are based on molecular genetics, are able to identify new strains and pathogens responsible for the SARS. The scientists of the two countries are now working on co-developing vaccines for the virus.

Russian media have voiced their support for China in combating the epidemic. On Feb 10, Rossiyskaya Gazeta, a leading Russian newspaper, published an editorial and touching posters to show its solidarity with China, demonstrating the close friendship of the two countries. Russian people, including businessmen, tourists, students and foreign officers, voiced their support for China and Wuhan on Chinese social media platforms, with many video clips from Russia having warmed the hearts of Chinese people. More than 10,000 Russians live in China, and they stay here because they believe China can overcome the epidemic.

The Russian authorities will cooperate closely with China to ward off the shared threat. The relationship between the two countries has proved to be one featuring mutual assistance and mutual support in this difficult time. The epidemic will not disrupt the further development of two countries' relationship. Instead, it will showcase to the world the true meaning of the Sino-Russian Comprehensive

Strategic Partnership of Coordination or a New Era, which is supporting each other in difficult times.

February 19, 2020

The author is a senior researcher of the Institute of Russian, East European and Central Asian Studies at the Chinese Academy of Social Sciences. The author contributed this article to China Watch, a think tank powered by China Daily.

Russia supports China's fight against outbreak

By Sergey Glaziev

Russian students Shashikian Manae (left) and Manae Oorzhak Manae display Chinese knots they made in Wuhan University's international student apartment, on Feb 1, 2020.

Zhu Xingxin/China Daily

Measures taken by the Chinese government to fight the coronavirus epidemic are impressive. The whole world is delighted with the speed and scale of the measures taken to prevent the spread of infection, as well as the cohesion and discipline of the Chinese people facing a new health threat.

I think the whole world can learn from China how to organize work to overcome an emergency, especially because the epidemic threatens humankind as a whole.

Sacrifice, Toil and Tears — China and the World in the Fight against the Pandemic

We see that governments of all countries around the world have taken urgent measures to control the spread of the virus. These measures can be divided into two types: isolation from China and preparing specific measures to combat the epidemic.

I consider the first direction to be useless, and, as far as I know, the World Health Organization, too, does not support it.

In the second direction, work is underway in Russia, primarily to develop a vaccine against the novel coronavirus.

Here we need to combine scientific and technical resources, and organize international research to combat all biological threats to the existence of human civilization.

Today, the entire medical industry is working according to the needs of China, supplying various kinds of medical items. As for measures to limit contacts with China, they have not gone beyond the standard recommendations for tourists and are aimed at informing people and reducing the channels for spreading the epidemic.

As far as I know, all the leading Russian airlines maintain their regular flights to and from China, with the possible exception of ports closed by the Chinese government itself. By the way, I just made a transfer in Wuhan recently, and spent two hours at Wuhan airport, where none of the passengers seemed to be worried about their own safety.

For us (Russia), China is a strategic partner with a long friendship and cooperation. The two heads of state have repeatedly talked about mutual friendship, cooperation and support, highlighting the importance of joint opposition to external threats by using such Chinese expression as "back to back" and the Russian expression as "shoulder to shoulder".

That's why we do not hesitate for a second before accepting as a common problem the misfortune that has befallen the people of China. In the fight against the epidemic, the Chinese people can rely on the help of Russia.

I am sure that the epidemic will not have any serious negative impact on Sino-Russian trade and economic relations. Of course, temporary quarantine measures may be introduced in accordance with World Trade Organization standards and our agreements. This may concern, first of all, products of animal origin. But in other areas, on the contrary, cooperation has sharply intensified, as in the already mentioned medical industry.

And in the long run, the epidemic has highlighted the importance of the need to deepen cooperation in areas such as high-tech industries including bioengineering technologies, pharmaceuticals and procurement.

February 22, 2020

The author is the minister for integration and macroeconomics of the Eurasian Economic Commission, and a member of the Russian Academy of Sciences. Chongyang Institute for Financial Studies at Renmin University of China also contributed to this article.

Hardships more bearable with help of friends

By Xing Haiming

Support of neighbor warms hearts of Chinese people as they battle the novel coronavirus outbreak in the cold of winter.

On Jan 30, the sixth day of the first lunar month, I embarked on a new mission to the Republic of Korea. I have worked in the ROK several times as a diplomat. But this time, helping to defeat the novel coronavirus is my top priority.

The outbreak of the pneumonia came suddenly and coincided with the traditional Chinese New Year holiday. The virus spread faster than expected, and the ROK government is very concerned about the outbreak and has paid great attention to the measures the Chinese authorities have taken to prevent and control it.

On the day of my arrival, reporters from several mainstream ROK media gathered around me as I walked out of the airport, asking for information on the epidemic. I told them: "The Chinese people are fighting against the virus under the in-person command of President Xi Jinping. We have made fruitful progress in all aspects of the work. We are confident and capable of overcoming the epidemic as soon as possible. We thank the government and people of South Korea for their support, and will continue to strengthen cooperation with the international community in an open, transparent and responsible manner. Also we will ensure the health and safety of all foreign nationals in China."

Over the next few days, I gave interviews to the ROK media and held a live news conference at the Chinese embassy to provide information on China's comprehensive measures to combat the virus. Major ROK media outlets broadcast the news conference live during prime time, and messages such as "the Chinese government has taken the most comprehensive and rigorous prevention and control

V. International Coordination Essential to Deal with Global Risks

measures" and "the epidemic is completely preventable, controllable and treatable" were widely shared by the ROK public opinion.

In the face of the outbreak of the virus, the ROK government and people have extended to China active support. In a telephone conversation with President Xi Jinping on Feb 20, ROK President Moon Jae-in expressed the ROK's sincere condolences to the Chinese people over the outbreak, saying that the ROK would stand firmly with China, continue to provide assistance for the fight against the virus and carry out epidemic prevention cooperation with China. In fact, in the early days of the outbreak, President Moon publicly declared on Feb 3 that China's difficulties are our difficulties. On Feb 7, he told me at a ceremony to receive my credentials: "To help one's neighbor is to help himself. We believe that under the leadership of President Xi Jinping, the Chinese people will overcome difficulties soon and achieve greater development."

The ROK government has provided emergent assistance to China and arranged flights to transport relevant materials to the frontline. On Feb 20, The ROK's new consul general in Wuhan, Kang Seung-seok, arrived to take up his post. In addition to government donations, the ROK enterprises and people have also extended helping hands: some helped purchase epidemic relief supplies, others donated meals for the frontline anti-epidemic personnel. The Chinese embassy has opened a special donation account and has received messages of support and donations from ordinary people from all walks of life in the ROK.

In the ROK, you can see "Come on China, Come on Wuhan" everywhere. Government officials, celebrities, ordinary people have all offered sincere blessings to China and Wuhan. Famous actress Lee Young-ae recorded a video extending her support to Chinese medical workers, and Park Wonsoon, the Seoul mayor, made a special video in which he said "it is time for Seoul to show its gratitude to China". The Lotte World Tower, the ROK's tallest skyscraper and a famous landmark, was illuminated with China's national flag and "Come on Wuhan". Former UN secretary-general Ban Ki-moon, former ROK prime minister Han Seung-soo, director of the Oscar winning movie *Parasite* Bong Joon-ho and actress Song Hye-kyo have also made videos offering their support to the Chinese people. What moved me most was an ordinary Korean kid who sent a letter to the embassy, hoping it could be passed on to the Chinese kids. He said: "I believe that difficulties will eventually pass and beautiful flowers will bloom wherever the wind blows."

During the severe acute respiratory syndrome (SARS) outbreak in 2002-03, many foreign leaders' schedules and international events held in China were suspended or postponed. But in July that year Roh Moo-hyun, the then ROK president, paid a state visit to China. I was involved in the reception as the division chief of China's Foreign Ministry. Roh said: "A long road seems shorter if you walk with good friends." In May 2015, Middle East respiratory syndrome (MERS) broke out in the ROK, and many countries restricted their tourists to the ROK. However, based on an objective and scientific judgment, China did not take restrictive measures. The chairman of China's National People's Congress Standing Committee visited the ROK in June on schedule. I was in the retinue for that visit. A Korean friend spoke highly of this visit, saying that China showed it was a great and trustworthy neighbor.

The outbreak of the novel coronavirus is an international public health emergency. Recently, the number of confirmed cases in the ROK has also increased. China will actively share its experience and provide corresponding support. We believe that standing together, China and the ROK will be able to overcome the epidemic.

Since the establishment of diplomatic ties in 1992, with the care of the top leaders of the two countries and the joint efforts of both sides, China-ROK relations have developed by leaps and bounds. As China and the ROK have kept watching and helping each other, our relations have made remarkable achievements. With cooperation, both countries can overcome the virus and start a new chapter for our relationship.

February 27, 2020

The author is Chinese ambassador to the Republic of Korea. The author contributed this article to China Watch, a think tank powered by China Daily.

International Coordination Essential
to Deal with Global Risks

V

Future of China-Japan ties lies in peaceful coexistence

By Yang Bojiang

Li Min/China Daily

Since the outbreak of the novel coronavirus pneumonia, now named COVID-19, China's stringent measures to combat the epidemic have not only attracted the attention of millions of Chinese, but also foreign governments.

Among the many countries that have come to China's aid,

neighboring Japan has responded with remarkable speed.

The Japanese government as well as the country's private sector responded quickly. As early as Jan 23, Prime Minister Shinzo Abe said at the plenary session of the House of Representatives, the lower house of the Diet, Japan's parliament, that the country should fully support China's fight against the epidemic.

Ito-Yokado, the Japanese supermarket chain, transported 1 million masks to Chengdu Shuangliu International Airport in Sichuan province on Jan 25.

Japanese Foreign Minister Toshimitsu Motegi said Japan is willing to make every effort to provide China with all-around support to help tide over the situation.

Local governments have started to provide "targeted support" to their Chinese sister cities. For example, Oita, the capital of Oita Prefecture, has been providing support to Wuhan. Other cities providing help to sister cities are Tomakomai, to Qinhuangdao, Hebei province; Yurihonjo and Akashi, to Wuxi, Jiangsu province; Mito and Hiroshima, to Chongqing; Kawasaki, to Shenyang, Liaoning province; Hamamatsu, to Hangzhou, Zhejiang province, as well as Shenyang; Hikone, to Xiangtan, Hunan province; Kagoshima, to Changsha, Hunan province; and Satsumasendai, to Changsha. In addition, Hiroshima Prefecture has been providing aid to Sichuan province.

Fundraising activities were organized by the Chinese Chamber of Commerce in Japan, alumni associations of universities, scientific institutions, Ito-Yokado and Toyota, among others.

"It is the virus, not the people, that is bad," an official at Japan's Ministry of Health, Labour and Welfare said at a news conference in response to reports of discriminations abroad.

Public health crises can serve as an opportunity to improve relations. After the May 2008 Sichuan earthquake, Japan sent a rescue team to China and provided 1 billion yen in assistance.

When an earthquake struck Japan in March 2011, China sent a professional rescue team to the disaster zone and provided 30 million yuan ($4.3 million) in assistance. It also provided Japan with 10,000 tons of gasoline and 10,000 tons of diesel for free, and an additional 20 million yuan of assistance. China's total aid to Japan was estimated at more than 200 million yuan.

China-Japan relations will embrace a warm spring. Social governance, people's livelihoods, public health and global governance are expected to become new highlights of bilateral cooperation in the future.

Since China and Japan are close neighbors with growing common interests, the future of their relations lies in peaceful coexistence and win-win cooperation.

February 17, 2020

The author is director of the Institute of Japanese Studies at the Chinese Academy of Social Sciences.

Sacrifice, Toil and Tears — China and the World in the Fight against the Pandemic

Three neighbors must stand together

By Woo Jin-Hoon

Shi Yu/China Daily

During the severe acute respiratory syndrome outbreak in 2002-2003, China accounted for 4.3 percent of the world's GDP, which increased to 15.8 percent last year. While China's contribution to world economic development last year was 27.4 percent.

So if the novel coronavirus outbreak reduces China's growth, its impact will be greater than that of SARS, not only on China, but also Japan, the Republic of Korea and East Asia as a whole, indeed the entire international community. Since the epidemic outbreak, the Chinese government has taken unprecedented measures to prevent

International Coordination Essential to Deal with Global Risks

and control the disease, which while gradually yielding results have also temporarily frozen much of the domestic market and suspended the operation of many factories.

Thanks to the epidemic, global oil prices have fallen, global supply chains have been seriously hit, and many factories in China's neighboring countries have suspended production. And since Chinese tourists spent $130 billion on overseas trips in 2018, the sudden drop in the number of Chinese traveling abroad will deal a serious blow to the global tourism industry and related sectors.

Epidemic will have big impact on ROK economy

The service sector now accounts for 54 percent of China's GDP, up from 42 percent in 2003, and consumption contributes more than 70 percent of the country's growth. This means that China's economy is much more dependent on services and consumption than it was at the time of the SARS outbreak. And given that consumer demand reaches its peak during Spring Festival, the epidemic outbreak just before the Spring Festival holiday has hit the Chinese economy hard.

As 25 percent of the ROK's exports are destined for China, the ROK is likely to bear much of the impact of the epidemic in China. With consumption shrinking and industrial production taking time to recover in China, the ROK's exports of intermediate and consumer materials to China will decline. As such, the businesses of ROK enterprises in China are expected to be severely hit.

The ROK's industrial chain is closely linked to the Chinese economy, and once the supply of intermediate materials from China stops, the production of finished goods in the ROK too will be interrupted. And since China's share of the ROK's tourism revenue has increased from 14 percent in 2003 to 48 percent in 2019, a drastic reduction in the number of Chinese tourists to the ROK due to the epidemic will surely reduce the ROK's tourism sector revenue.

Japan may face a tough test ahead

If the outbreak in Japan worsens, the country's exports to China will decline, which will hurt the Japanese companies operating in China, because about 1,900 Japanese enterprises operating in China are mainly engaged in manufacturing, and China is the destination of 37 percent of the global exports of auto parts. And with Chinese tourists accounting for 40 percent of all foreign visitors to Japan, the Japanese government is closely watching the impact of the epidemic on its own economy.

Considering that the East Asian value chain is now centered on China, it will greatly benefit Japan and the ROK if China contains the epidemic sooner rather than later. If the epidemic continues longer because of a lack of coordination among China, Japan and the ROK, it could have a huge impact on the manufacturing plants of the three countries and suppress their consumption.

The countries that account for a large percentage of the supply of intermediate materials to China are the United States, the ROK, Japan and Germany, and these five have been hit by the virus. In other words, if something goes terribly wrong with China's intermediate material supply capacity, it will affect the global economy.

Post-outbreak development policies being worked out

While focusing on epidemic prevention and control, China, Japan and the ROK are also preparing policies to stabilize their economies after the epidemic is contained. The Chinese government is mulling interest rate cuts and tax cuts to expand liquidity supply and infrastructure investment, while the ROK is providing small and medium-sized enterprises with liquidity relief assistance and working out macroeconomic policies to deal with its economic woes.

Japan, on its part, is extending financial relief to its tourism enterprises, as well as small and medium-sized enterprises, which are facing great difficulties. Such measures will not only help the three countries overcome the impact of the epidemic but also play a crucial role in promoting their and the global economy's recovery.

After the epidemic is contained, it is necessary for the three countries to strengthen their cooperation mechanisms so as to prevent the spread of infectious diseases. Through cooperation and joint research on epidemics and other emergencies, the three countries can also reduce international concern about their economic capabilities and social stability. This will not only strengthen exchanges and cooperation between the three countries and the international community, but also minimize the negative impact on their economic cooperation, business exchanges and tourism.

Beijing, Tokyo and Seoul should deepen cooperation

Apart from establishing a joint anti-epidemic mechanism, the three countries can also strengthen international cooperation to prevent and respond to the outbreak of infectious diseases, such as advancing cooperation to help tackle infectious diseases in developing countries with weak health infrastructure, in order to contribute to the continued health of the global village.

By cooperating in the fight against the novel coronavirus, China, Japan and the ROK can further deepen their cooperation and mutual understanding, consolidate their mutual trust, and take a solid step toward common peace and prosperity.

March 6, 2020

The author is a guest professor at International Business School, Beijing Foreign Studies University.

Our role in the coronavirus outbreak

By Zamir Ahmed Awan

56-year-old Pakistani national Syed Zulfiqar Hussain Abbasi, who has lived in China for 37 years, volunteers to measure a child's temperature in Beijing on March 3, 2020. Abbasi volunteered to take the temperatures of the residents in his neighborhood as a precautionary health measure.

Zou Hong/China Daily

China and Pakistan, known as "Iron Brothers", have a very special relationship. The two countries enjoy harmony and understanding on all issues, whether national, regional or international. They have stood with each other in all difficult moments. China has helped Pakistan greatly, whether during an earthquake in 2005 or a devastating flood in 2010. Pakistan also showed its generosity during the Wenchuan earthquake in 2008 in China.

Currently, the novel coronavirus pneumonia outbreak is a major natural disaster in China, and Pakistan has not let China feel alone.

V
International Coordination Essential to Deal with Global Risks

The Pakistani government and the people of Pakistan have stood with China and demonstrated comprehensive solidarity.

The senate of Pakistan passed a strong resolution in favor of China and reaffirmed its full support to China in this moment of difficulty. Pakistan has donated medical materials and dispatched medical teams to work with Chinese brothers and sisters hand in hand to overcome the epidemic.

Pakistan is the first country to resume its flights with China just after the suspension of only three days. On the political front this sends a strong message that Pakistan stands with China under all circumstances. Although China and Pakistan are working under close coordination to control the spread of the coronavirus and keep monitoring the passengers for the incubation period, upon complete satisfaction and clearance, the passengers are allowed to travel. Airports in China and Pakistan are working in close liaison to monitor the passengers and screen them properly. But this gesture has signaled to the international community that they should not cut off ties with China or isolate China, but extend their all possible cooperation and join hands to fight against the coronavirus.

There is a huge community of more than 300,000 Pakistani students. Some of them are working with the Chinese as volunteers. In particular, one of the graduates from a Chinese institution, Doctor Usman, has traveled to Wuhan to serve with the Chinese medical teams. His sincerity and love for China are admired in both countries. In fact, he is a role model for many others to be followed.

Pakistani nationals are safe in China and the Chinese government is looking after them in a very special manner. The government of Pakistan is thankful to the Chinese government for special treatment and protection provided to Pakistani nationals. Pakistan's government has decided not to evacuate its nationals from China, indicating full trust in the Chinese government's capabilities. Actually, the Chinese government is taking all possible measures to overcome the epidemic and we believe that China will overcome soon.

Media has played a very constructive role at this crucial moment. In Pakistan, there is no panic and no Sinophobia, while in the Western world, there is panic and Sinophobia. The West has overreacted and shown bias against China. The Pakistani media has projected the real situation with a positive sense and educated the masses with preventive measures. There is no need to hate or discriminate.

We believe that it is a natural disaster like any other earthquake, fire, volcano or flood. Such epidemic outbreaks have also been witnessed in recent history, such as Ebola, SARS and MERS. Previous epidemics have also claimed human lives and after some time were suppressed or eliminated. China is working hard to address all concerns regarding the coronavirus. China has been fully utilizing all resources — human, financial or technical, and scientific — to overcome it.

Our role is to trust Chinese capabilities and their sincere efforts, and, if possible, extend a helping hand. Or at least, we should not criticize China, discriminate against Chinese or underestimate Chinese capabilities. We must avoid fake news and negative propaganda. If possible we should extend moral and political support, in addition to material support in the form of medical supplies, and medical staff and doctors. The developed nations may extend scientific assistance and help in developing a suitable vaccine.

The outbreak of the coronavirus has been declared a global threat by the World Health Organization (WHO). The international community must join hands to fight against the coronavirus globally. Humanity is at stake. All human beings have a responsibility, and should share in their part of the contribution. Trust that our collective efforts will achieve our goals of saving humanity soon.

February 14, 2020

The author is a Sinologist (ex-diplomat) and nonresident fellow of the Center for China and Globalization, National University of Sciences and Technology, Islamabad, Pakistan.

International Coordination Essential
to Deal with Global Risks

Biosafety challenge calls for greater cooperation

By Mostafa Mohammadi

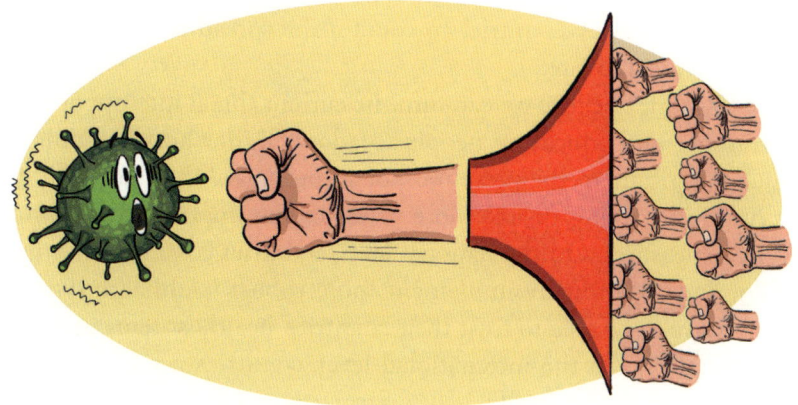

Jin Ding/China Daily

The world is experiencing a special situation due to outbreak of novel coronavirus. The virus has mostly affected China and its people, with individuals and businesses adversely influenced. However, the people are strong enough to fight and win the battle against the virus. The Chinese government responded swiftly and with great resolve to the public health emergency and mobilizing all its resources to overcome the critical situation in Hubei province where the outbreak has been the most severe. Iran, my country, has also been affected by the novel coronavirus and unfortunately 54 people have died by Sunday and many more have been infected.

This is not the first biological threat to humans and will not be the last. There have been several epidemics since the beginning of 21st century, although the West has mostly managed to avoid the worst, but it does not mean that an epidemic will never seriously trouble those parts of the world. Biological threats are every country's problem, not only those that are most badly challenged by the emergence of a serious public health threat.

Sacrifice, Toil and Tears — China and the World in the Fight against the Pandemic

In the case of the novel coronavirus, which is clearly a serious threat to people around the world considering how highly contagious it is, I think that there has been insufficient international coordination, and countries and airlines individually decided how to manage their relationships with China, which have obviously been ineffective. There has also been a lack of public awareness campaigns informing people of what they can do to minimize the risks of transmission. And concerted efforts by countries to counter the spread of the virus have been too little, too late.

However, I believe we can turn the current threat into opportunity by training and educating people to adopt higher health standards, which contribute to the prevention of an outbreak. The role of NGOs is crucial in making people more aware of the importance of simple hygiene measures. On the national level, countries have to collectively design and individually implement more robust healthcare systems. People have to be able to trust their countries' health systems in critical circumstances. On the international level, countries need to enhance their cooperation on health issues. Stronger public health ties among countries will facilitate collaboration in times of crisis. I think a new international coordination mechanism to specifically manage biological risks should be considered.

China and the world will definitely win the battle against the novel coronavirus. All people with any kind of humanity are supporting the people who are affected by the virus in any way. As Persian poet Sa'adi (1210-1291) wrote:

"The sons of Adam are limbs of each other, having been created of one essence. When the calamity of time affects one limb, the other limbs cannot remain at rest."

We all have to rethink our roles in human society so we are better prepared for the future public health challenges that are sure to emerge.

March 2, 2020

The author is visiting lecturer of management in Shahid Beheshti University of Iran, and Head of Youth Committee, Iran-China Friendship Association.

International Coordination Essential
to Deal with Global Risks   V

Adversity reveals true friends

By Wang Kejian

Li Min/China Daily

Lebanon is a small country located on the eastern coast of the Mediterranean. It has experienced few severe outbreaks of an infectious disease, and has limited experience in dealing with an epidemic. But Lebanon is on the arterial routes linking Asia and Europe and many Lebanese people live abroad or have business contacts with foreign countries. So the country does face a certain risk of importing a contagious disease. At the early stage of the outbreak of the novel coronavirus in China, I met with the Lebanese prime minister, foreign minister, and minister of health during Spring Festival to inform them of the development of the epidemic and the prevention and control measures China has implemented.

Sacrifice, Toil and Tears — China and the World in the Fight against the Pandemic

Lebanon confirmed a novel coronavirus infection on Feb 21 and people in Lebanon are paying more and more attention to the epidemic. Due to the lack of understanding of the virus, some people in Lebanon have panicked and even resisted Chinese goods or normal exchanges between the two countries.

The Chinese embassy has sought to ease people's anxieties about the plague by maintaining close communication with the Lebanese Ministry of Health, the Ministry of Foreign Affairs, the airport and medical institutions, keeping them updated with the latest information. Considering that China is Lebanon's largest trading partner and that Lebanon is facing an intensifying economic crisis, the Chinese embassy has passed on four important messages to the Lebanese businesses and media.

First, China is confident and is capable of defeating the epidemic. The Chinese government and people have spared no effort in fighting the novel coronavirus, and have adopted the strictest and most comprehensive prevention and control measures. Data show that the measures are effective, and the epidemic is being controlled. At present, the Chinese side is in full swing in its battle against the epidemic, and work is starting to be resumed in an orderly manner. Under the strong leadership of the Communist Party of China Central Committee with President Xi Jinping as the core, China is fully confident of winning the battle by giving full play of the advantages of the socialist system with Chinese characteristics and the dedicated efforts of people throughout the country.

Second, the epidemic will not hinder the Chinese economy in the long term. As the Chinese government has adopted the strictest epidemic prevention measures and some countries have canceled flights and issued travel bans on people traveling to and from China with disregard for the World Health Organization's recommendations, China's domestic tourism, consumption, logistics, and manufacturing and the economy have all been affected. The epidemic has also impacted international shipping, tourism and the production chain. In 2003, the outbreak of the severe acute respiratory syndrome (SARS) hit China's economy, but the economy soon resumed rapid growth. Now China's economy is stronger, so is the government's leadership.

With the strong government mobilization capabilities and closer foreign cooperation, we have every reason to believe that China's economy will be able to maintain its long-term sound development.

Third, it is safe to do business with China and buy Chinese products. The World Health Organization has said that the virus can only survive for a few hours on the surface of dry objects, and that normal trade will not increase the risk of transmitting the virus. The WHO has also repeatedly emphasized that it has not recommended countries adopt travel and trade restrictions on China. We hope that all countries will respect its recommendations, do not overreact and avoid unnecessary panic or put pressure on normal personnel exchanges and pragmatic cooperation in various fields.

Fourth, we look forward to further strengthening economic and trade cooperation with Lebanon. Lebanese domestic parties and sects have complicated contradictions, and external forces have deeply intervened in Lebanese affairs. Faced with the question of which side China would choose, we have made it clear that China does not look for a proxy in the Middle East, does not seek any sphere of influence and does not attempt to fill the "vacuum". In Lebanon, we will never be partial to any party in the conflict, and we are willing to coordinate and cooperate with all parties on the basis of mutual respect and win-win cooperation.

All sectors in Lebanon fully recognize and appreciate China's approach and express their willingness to strengthen cooperation with China and jointly respond to the current epidemic. Lebanese President Michel Aoun, Parliament Speaker Nabih Berri and leaders of major parties have expressed their support to China through letters and videos. When some countries adopted restrictions on the normal exchanges with China, the Lebanese government has maintained communication with China in light of the principle of mutual trust, insisted on not taking excessive prevention measures and have not restricted people-to-people exchanges between China and Lebanon.

The world today has become indivisible, and the fate of people has long been closely linked. Local issues and global issues can be mutually transformed. The outbreak of the epidemic reminds us that no country can stand alone in the face of global challenges. In the fight against the epidemic, China has made great efforts and sacrifice in prevention and control, and many countries have extended their assistance and expressed their support to China. This fully demonstrates the strength of international cooperation and reflects the idea of a community of shared future for humanity.

We really appreciate the trust given by the Lebanese government and that they are willing to overcome the difficulties with us. We are grateful to the Lebanese people for their support. We hope that China can emerge from the shadow of the epidemic as soon as possible, and hope that Lebanon can emerge from its economic crisis soon. In the future, we are willing to work with Lebanon to promote the relations between the two countries and bilateral cooperation.

February 26, 2020

The author is Chinese ambassador to Lebanon. The author contributed this article to China Watch, a think tank powered by China Daily.

UAE stands resolutely with China during coronavirus challenge

By Ali Obaid Al Dhaheri

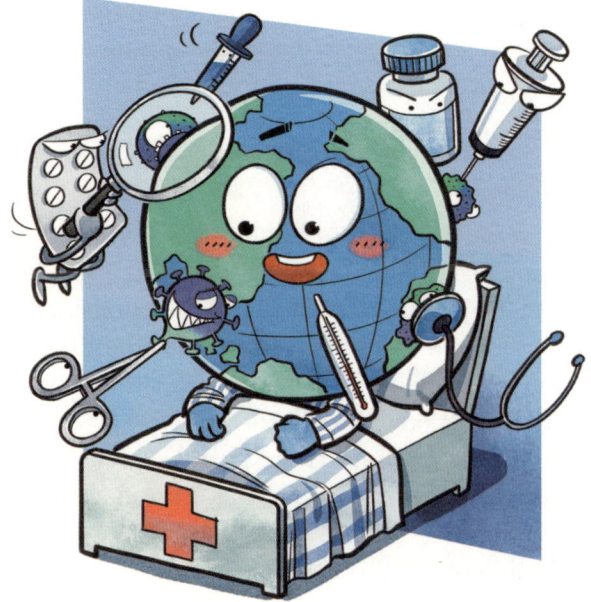

Song Chen/China Daily

China has faced the coronavirus challenge with a great degree of strength and resilience. In the UAE, we are left amazed at the remarkable response of the Chinese government and of the Chinese people.

The government and people of the United Arab Emirates would like to offer their support during this challenging time for China. We stand resolute in solidarity with China to support the country in its hour of need.

Sacrifice, Toil and Tears — China and the World in the Fight against the Pandemic

Indeed, we have great confidence that China will get past this quickly. In fact, there are positive signs such as the International Monetary Fund (IMF) expressing their support to China's efforts to tackle the novel coronavirus outbreak and expressing confidence that China's economy "remains resilient".

This dilemma is unquestionably vast, however this has come at a time when China has never been so well-prepared for such a challenge. China's approach to dealing with this situation is admirable and it is truly astounding that they have managed, for example, to rapidly build two hospitals in Wuhan with a combined capacity of 2,500 capacity, including Huoshenshan Hospital completed in around 10 days and which is already operational.

This demonstrates the characteristic strength of the Chinese in the face of adversity.

In its 70 years the People's Republic of China as a nation has faced great challenges, and the country has successfully dealt with poverty reduction within a short period — the number of poor people in China has declined from 100 million in late 2012 to just 16.6 million by the end of 2018. This means that in just six short years, there has been a reduction of 80 percent.

This illustrates an important point — when the Chinese government focuses its efforts on challenges, it can achieve remarkable results.

The leadership of the People's Republic of China have been swift and responsive in their efforts to contain the virus to a restricted region within Wuhan and have redoubled medical support. I would echo the Director-General of the World Health Organisation who said, "If it weren't for China's efforts, the number of cases outside China would have been very much higher."

The UAE leadership stands resolutely with the Chinese government in support of their commendable efforts to deal with the coronavirus and have great faith in their significant capabilities to overcome this challenge. The strength and fortitude of the Chinese nation is shining through and we can see a collective pulling together across many layers of Chinese society.

Our nation intends to support China as best it can by deepening healthcare cooperation and providing medical equipment where possible. Our country's AI and Cloud Computing sector has already launched a humanitarian initiative to support healthcare personnel in China trying to contain the coronavirus outbreak, through its pioneering AI-focused healthcare practice. Hundreds of thousands of units of essential goods such as surgical masks, medical gloves, goggles and protective clothing are also being relayed from the UAE to support the medical effort in the affected areas.

The positive efforts by the Chinese government to tackle the coronavirus are gradually bearing fruit and we encourage the Chinese people to stay strong and pull through this crisis. I am confident that this issue will be successfully dealt with China's characteristic strength of will to rise to any challenge.

February 6, 2020

The author is ambassador of the United Arab Emirates to China.

Sacrifice, Toil and Tears — China and the World in the Fight against the Pandemic

Responsibility, support, confidence and tolerance

By Yao Fei

Ma Xuejing/China Daily

At the beginning of 2020, an outbreak of a new type of coronavirus rapidly spread throughout Hubei province. The 1.4 billion Chinese people have started a massive war against the epidemic. At the same time, in the face of this common enemy to humanity, the World Health Organization and many countries, including Spain, have shown their support to China, by providing technical, material and other assistance.

At present, the prevention and control efforts can be summarized in four key words: responsibility, support, confidence and tolerance.

International Coordination Essential to Deal with Global Risks

China has taken comprehensive and stringent measures to establish a nationwide joint prevention and control system, and as part of this system resolutely decided to suspend public transportation in Wuhan and other cities in Hubei province. All the 31 provincial-level regions on the Chinese mainland have initiated the first-level response to a public health emergency. Many have gone well beyond the International Health Regulations and the WHO recommendations.

Bearing in mind the overall situation, the Chinese government is coordinating and allocating the country's human and material resources, organizing and dispatching medical personnel to assist Wuhan and other cities in Hubei. Within 10 days each, Wuhan had completed the building of two special hospitals, adding more than 2,000 beds for treating patients. The first batch of mobile cabin hospitals in Wuhan with a capacity of 4,400 beds, mainly for mild cases, was officially opened and will help control the epidemic at the source. Medical researchers are working around the clock to develop a vaccine. Enterprises are producing medical supplies at full capacity. People from all walks of life and overseas Chinese are actively contributing to the fight against the virus.

In an open, transparent and highly responsible manner, China has established a daily reporting mechanism for the outbreaks, released timely information on the epidemic both at home and to other countries. It notified the WHO of the outbreak as soon as possible, identified the pathogen in record time and shared its genetic sequences with the WHO and other countries.

At present, the confirmed cases outside China account for less than 1 percent of all cases, which indicates that China has done its utmost to control the outbreak and protect the health of people worldwide. As WHO Director-General Tedros Adhanom Ghebreyesus pointed out, China has set a new benchmark for responding to the outbreak.

In a globalized world, human destiny is closely linked. In the face of global public health events, no country can detach itself from the international community. Only through cooperation, can we defend ourselves from the virus.

The fact that many countries, including Spain, have followed WHO recommendations and not taken hasty measures to restrict travel and trade is also of great support to China's response to the outbreak, for which we are grateful and deeply appreciate.

But at the same time, some countries are taking the opposite approach, taking the opportunity to shout, even gloat, and take extreme measures to "ban China". They will not help curb the spread of the epidemic, but will instead create panic and cause huge losses to the global economy.

Our confidence comes from the strength of the socialist system which enables the country to rally resources to deal with daunting tasks, and from the Chinese people who have shown solidarity confronting the epidemic.

Our confidence comes from a growing awareness of prevention, more effective diagnosis, tighter controls on the spread of coronavirus, and the worldwide efforts to develop vaccines and drugs. Spain has an advanced health system, advanced medical technology and rich experience in emergency response. We are ready to tackle the epidemic. The virus should not be used for politically motivated attacks. Unfortunately, we have seen discrimination against Chinese people in some countries because of the epidemic.

But at the same time, we are even happier to see the full understanding, firm support and sincere wishes of the Spanish government and people. King Felipe VI, the President Pedro Sánchez and the relevant Spanish government departments have all emphasized that there is no reason to treat Asian residents as suspected carriers of the new coronavirus. Every day, we receive letters from all over Spain. People are all cheering for China, paying tribute to the Chinese people and fighting against the discrimination shown toward the Chinese.

We in turn would like to reassure the Spanish people that most recent arrivals from China have taken proper precautions. When you see Chinese people wearing masks in public places, please don't be nervous. This is a sign of responsibility on the part of the Chinese people, who are not only protecting themselves but others.

People with the same determination can overcome all challenges. We sincerely thank our Spanish friends for their selfless help and sincere encouragement to China. We firmly believe that with the concerted efforts of the international community, we will be able to beat the epidemic and win victory.

February 17, 2020

The author is charge d'affaires of the Chinese embassy in Spain. The author contributed this article to China Watch, a think tank powered by China Daily.

Sacrifice, Toil and Tears China and the World in the Fight against the Pandemic

Victory will be won

By Gui Congyou

After the novel coronavirus outbreak, I went to the Swedish Ministry of Foreign Affairs to meet the Ambassador for Global Public Health. As soon as he was seated, he said to me that the epidemic itself could occur in any country or region at any time. China has taken timely measures to detect, isolate and treat the infected, and it has shown firm confidence and acted in an open and transparent manner. He was sure that with all of these efforts, China would be able to defeat the virus.

This was a vote of confidence from the international community on China's epidemic control work. Since the start of the outbreak, under the strong leadership of the Communist Party of China Central Committee with Comrade Xi Jinping as the core, the country has given full play to its institutional advantages and the Chinese people have united as one to help each other fight the epidemic. Up till now, we have achieved significant results, curbed the spread of the epidemic and won the recognition of the World Health Organization and the international community.

As President Xi Jinping has emphasized, public health security is a common challenge for humankind, and countries need to work together to overcome any threat. China's resolute fight against the epidemic is not only related to the health and wellbeing of the Chinese people, but also a major contribution to global public health. The Chinese embassy in Sweden has actively interacted with the Swedish government and people to contribute to the public health security of the world and the region.

We are communicating closely and sharing information with the Swedish government. I visited the European Center for Disease Control and Prevention in Stockholm and attended a briefing hosted by the center for the Sweden's mission to introduce China's progress in its epidemic prevention and control work and to promote cooperation between the two sides. The person in charge of the center sincerely thanked China for its close cooperation with the European

V International Coordination Essential to Deal with Global Risks

Union in adhering to the principle of openness and transparency, and emphasized that all EU countries stand with China in the fight against the virus. Several envoys in Sweden appreciated China's efforts and the sacrifices its people were making to control the epidemic and prevent the spread of the virus. We have established hotline contacts and actively coordinated with the Swedish Ministry of Foreign Affairs, the Public Health Agency and other relevant departments. The Swedish Public Health Agency has repeatedly called on the public to take a rational view and take the advised protection measures to avoid panic and overreaction. It also refrained from taking unnecessary measures such as closing the border.

Sweden has world-class medical research institutes, and many Swedish medical experts have provided suggestions for China's epidemic defense and control work. An expert from the Karolinska Institute, one of the world's leading medical universities, provided a plan to use existing drugs to treat critically ill patients. We immediately reported back to China and the idea was approved by the joint prevention and control mechanism of the State Council for clinical treatment. A well-known professor of infectious diseases at Uppsala University said to me that in the past 10 years, humans have been attacked by coronaviruses many times. This epidemic is not the first, nor will it be the last. The growing global population and globalization will undoubtedly increase the risk of pathogen transmission. China has responded in a textbook style and set a good example for other countries.

Protecting the health, safety and rights and interests of Chinese citizens and overseas Chinese in Sweden is our top priority in response to the epidemic. We lost no time in issuing consular reminders, suggesting that Chinese citizens in Sweden pay close attention to the official Chinese and Swedish information updates, correctly understand the epidemic situation and strengthen their protection awareness. The consular officer of the embassy provided timely assistance to a Chinese citizen in Sweden, and contacted the hospital for medical treatment at midnight. It was quickly determined that the person did not have the novel coronavirus. After a few cases of discrimination against Chinese people were reported in Sweden, I made representations to the Swedish Ministry of Foreign Affairs and accepted an interview with TT News Agency. I called on the Swedish people to oppose racial discrimination. To protect the legitimate rights

Sacrifice, Toil and Tears — China and the World in the Fight against the Pandemic

and interests of Chinese citizens and Chinese in Sweden, I demanded that the Swedish side take effective measures to prevent discrimination against Chinese from happening in Sweden. I am pleased to see that the Swedish mainstream society generally believes that the epidemic is by no means an excuse for discrimination and discrimination is contrary to Sweden's basic values.

The Chinese citizens as well as overseas Chinese in Sweden and Chinese companies in Sweden care about the epidemic situation. While doing their best to protect themselves, they are taking active steps to fully support domestic anti-epidemic actions. The Swedish Chinese Chamber of Commerce, Geely CEVT, and major Swedish overseas Chinese communities have actively donated money and materials to support Hubei province and other places to help them overcome the difficulties they face.

By standing together through the storm, we will see the rainbow after the rain. When I met with the Speaker of Sweden Parliament Andreas Norlén not long ago, he expressed condolences to the Chinese people on the outbreak of the epidemic. Many Swedish companies in China have donated money to Hubei and other places. Some Swedish friends have written articles and recorded videos in praise of China's prevention and control efforts and expressed condolences and support to the Chinese people. Their chants of "Come on Wuhan, come on China" are really moving. Recently, several cases of novel coronavirus pneumonia have also been confirmed in Sweden. China empathizes with the Sweden's difficulties, and all affected countries. In the face of the epidemic, all countries should realize they are members of a community with a shared future. I fully believe that as long as the international community is united, we will be able to prevail over the virus. Victory is ahead.

March 4, 2020

The author is the Chinese ambassador to Sweden. The author contributed this article to China Watch, a think tank powered by China Daily.

International Coordination Essential to Deal with Global Risks

United in solidarity

By Cao Zhongming

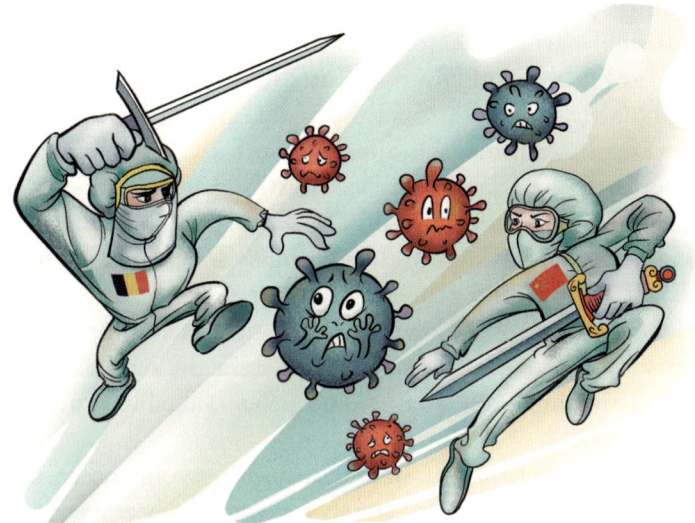

Ma Xuejing/China Daily

The recent pneumonia outbreak caused by the novel coronavirus in Wuhan, Hubei province, presents a common and serious challenge to China and the international community. The Chinese government has taken a series of decisive and stringent prevention and control measures from the outset to protect the safety and health of the Chinese people and to contain the further spread of the virus. Many of these measures go far beyond the requirements of the International Health Regulation. A nationwide inter-agency emergency response mechanism has been activated. Medical staff and supplies have been congregated and rushed to the aid of Wuhan and Hubei province.

The Chinese government has been updating information about the epidemic, and imparting to the public knowledge on how to stay healthy and avoid infection, so that everyone is consciously taking actions conducive to prevention and control. In the meantime, China

Sacrifice, Toil and Tears — China and the World in the Fight against the Pandemic

has worked to pool the efforts of leading specialists at home and abroad to focus on research and development of vaccines and medicines.

Throughout the process, acting with openness, transparency and in a responsible manner, China has maintained timely communication and close collaboration with other members of the international community, providing timely updates and working together with international partners to jointly confront the spread of the virus. China's prevention and control efforts have been widely acclaimed. World Health Organization Director-General Tedros Adhanom Ghebreyesus has affirmed his appreciation for China's unprecedented response to the new coronavirus. The strong political commitment, quick action and effective measures taken by the Chinese government to contain the outbreak are truly admirable. President Xi Jinping has issued instructions and provided guidance for the response efforts himself, showing strong leadership. The unparalleled speed, scale and efficiency of the mobilization efforts to stem the outbreak speaks to China's institutional advantages, and offers valuable experiences to other countries.

The Chinese Embassy in Belgium, following the principle of "diplomacy for the people", has closely followed the health conditions of Chinese in Belgium. The embassy has offered health tips, responded to people's concerns, advised them on measures to protect themselves, and provided assistance where needed, all the while advocating for calmness over panic. Overseas Chinese, Chinese businesses and Chinese students in Belgium, caring deeply for their motherland, have provided funds and in-kind donations, contributing their share to the fight against the virus. The first batch of protective suits, goggles and masks along with other much-needed medical supplies donated by the Association of Chinese Professionals in Belgium and overseas Chinese students have been shipped to China through Hainan Airlines' green channel.

The Belgian government has made positive remarks of the Chinese government's response to the epidemic outbreak. Major government officials have sent letters to express their sympathy. Elio Di Rupo, former Belgian prime minister, now serving as minister-president of the Wallonia region, the Francophone south of Belgium that enjoys friendship relations with Hubei province, has voiced his support for China. He said that China and Belgium will maintain sound cooperation and he is convinced that China will be able to stem the spread of the new coronavirus outbreak. Willy Borsus, vice minister-president of Wallonia, wrote to express the region's solicitude and firm support for Chinese friends and Hubei province in this difficult time.

Some local governments have assisted in opening up green channels for medical aid. The Belgian-Chinese Chamber of Commerce, the Wallonia Export-Investment Agency and the Flanders-China Chamber of Commerce have called on Belgian companies to make donations to the areas most affected by the outbreak. All of these bear witness to Belgian people's friendly feelings toward China.

In the meantime, however, there have been some European media outlets publishing cartoons insulting the national flag of China. We expressed strong indignation and condemnation of such acts, which breach the bottom line of civilized society, trespass the moral boundary of free speech, and deeply hurt the feelings of the Chinese people. But we believe these media organizations do not represent the views of the majority. Their indifference and malice are disdained by all righteous people. Many Belgians have left messages on the embassy's social media accounts voicing their firm support for China's fight against the outbreak, and denouncing the abominable drawing. This is an example to show the meaning of the Chinese adage "a just cause gains wide support, while an unjust one enjoys none".

We are convinced that as Chinese at home and abroad are united in solidarity, as all countries join hands together, we will succeed in defeating the epidemic at an early date. The epidemic, which will be brought under control, will not undermine the long-term and steady growth of the Chinese economy. This year China will complete the building of a moderately prosperous society in all aspects, continue to deepen all-round reform and expand opening-up. I believe all of these will inject fresh impetus into China-Belgium relations and further take forward China-Belgium pragmatic cooperation across all areas.

February 12, 2020

The author is the Chinese ambassador to Sweden. The author contributed this article to China Watch, a think tank powered by China Daily.

Two or three words about my China

By Faruk Borić

I have spent a good part of my career in the media, and my current job is closely related to journalism. So, I spend hours every day reading all that comes to my mind.

Starting with my first morning coffee until the last blink before bedtime I check what is new on the relevant domestic and international media as well as social platforms.

It often seems to me that this relationship is rather unnatural, and that we exaggerate, both myself and the media, which bombards me with all sorts of sensations, quite unnecessary for individual functioning, business success or progress of the society in which I live and operate.

For the past 15 days, the focus of the world public has been on China and the developments regarding the coronavirus epidemic.

Different media publishes information from different angles. Words of support come from all over the world, including Bosnia and Herzegovina (BiH).

The accident, on the other hand, has helped some media to grow canines and smell blood, and to show China once again in as negative a light as possible. As usual, what is happening in China, good or bad, has an impact on the whole world, and so has our reflection on our corner of Europe.

The coronavirus epidemic that has plagued China, the media and the public in BiH has been most intriguing when someone sensationally discovered that a bus with tourists from Wuhan was in neighboring Croatia and was "moving to BiH".

A sea of texts and "research" followed: where the tourists were, whether they crossed the border, where they would stay, how long they would stay on their journey through BiH to another neighbor, Serbia, what the bus looked like and more.

It was not in the public interest but raised tensions. Bolder and less savvy media outlets have been developing blatant conspiracy theories as to why Chinese tourists have bypassed a city that, by the way, is not on the tourist route.

Those most prone to sensationalism and clickbait-editorialism have openly advocated forbidding the Chinese entry into BiH, using hate speech to sow fear and generate general panic and, to be precise, xenophobia.

Fortunately, these kinds of media are minor in appearance, but that doesn't mean they can't do harm.

The damage was seen in some comments on social networks popular in BiH, especially Facebook. Here, individuals went beyond the media and wrote such nonsense and untruths about China and Chinese culture that one wondered if it was realistic for people in the 21st century to be so blinded by irrational hatred.

Either way, the Chinese tourists and their buses have left and most BiH citizens have a bitter taste and a sense of shame. In this case, and in some others, Bosnia and Herzegovina has shown that it is not immune to Sinophobia.

In addition to this vocal minority, Bosnia and Herzegovina spoke in a friendly, reasonable voice about the accident.

BiH Ambassador to China Tarik Bukvic responded correctly in the first days after the outbreak of the epidemic, saying he should not pay attention to sensationalist news and spread panic.

In an interview with BiH media, Chinese Ambassador to BiH Ji Ping shared two very important pieces of data: That the death rate from the coronavirus is only 2 percent, which is much lower than similar epidemics in the past, and that the number infected outside China is only 1 percent which indicates that China has found the right strategy and kept the situation under control.

In addition, public figures sent words of support to Chinese President Xi Jinping and the Chinese people.

Responsible media, such as the majority in BiH, are professionally reporting on an epidemic whose peak, experts say, has already passed.

It's been over five years since my first stay in China, which I fell in love with, strongly, passionately and at first glance.

I was last there late last year, visiting Beijing, Shenyang and Jinzhou.

I have seen numerous old friends who are in business or privately related to Bosnia and Herzegovina, and I have met new people, equally numerous.

With many delicacies in Chinese dining, we talked for hours and nights about various projects of common interest to both countries, arranging visits to BiH, laughing and singing.

I went through what is said to be "half the world", but nowhere was I greeted with such honor, kindness and hospitality as in my China.

These days I interact with many of them, inquiring about where they are, what they are and how they are.

I see the seriousness of them all when talking about the problem, but also the absolute belief that the epidemic will be resolved as soon as possible.

I can't wait to see them in BiH and show you the best that BiH has to offer, including beautiful nature and friendly people.

I share the belief in the Chinese authorities' ability and commitment of the Chinese people to solve this problem as well. And when all this is over, China will emerge stronger than ever.

February 13, 2020

The author is president of the China-BiH Friendship Association.

International Coordination Essential to Deal with Global Risks

V

Old friend stands firm

By Zhu Liying

Li Min/China Daily

At the beginning of the new year, an epidemic caused by a new type of coronavirus swept across China, causing great concern around the world. In the face of the epidemic, the international community has given precious assistance and firm support to the Chinese people.

Sacrifice, Toil and Tears
China and the World in the Fight against the Pandemic

As an old saying goes, although we're oceans apart, a shared moon connects hearts. We, as Chinese living abroad, have deeply felt the friendship of our foreign friends.

Mali, located in West Africa, is one of China's old friends. After learning about China's efforts to combat the epidemic, Mali has shown great understanding and support to China. Malian Prime Minister Boubou Cissé sent a special letter to Chinese Premier Li Keqiang, expressing his condolences to the Chinese government and people and his appreciation of China's determination and professionalism in fighting against the epidemic. He said that he believed that under the leadership of Chinese President Xi Jinping, China is fully capable of overcoming the challenge. The Malian government also issued an announcement offering its full support to China in combating the epidemic. Michel Sidibe, Mali's health minister, also expressed support for the powerful and effective actions taken by the Chinese government.

Major Malian websites and media outlets have published reports on China's actions to combat the epidemic. Many Malian friends have left messages to cheer up Chinese friends in difficult times. Friends from all walks of life have expressed their condolences and support to China through different methods such as letters, emails, telephones and short messages. On my social media platform, I have received a lot of encouragement and praise every day such as "Blessing China" and "Love China", some in Chinese and some in French. This year marks the 60th anniversary of the establishment of diplomatic relations between China and Mali. Over the past 60 years, helping and supporting each other has been a distinguishing feature of the relationship between the two countries and bears testimony to our traditional friendship. As an old Chinese saying goes, it is in the winter that we know pines and cypress can remain evergreen. We really appreciate all the support that Mali has given to us during the difficult times and we will remember this genuine friendship.

In the face of the epidemic, the Chinese Embassy and Chinese compatriots in Mali responded immediately. The embassy has kept in close contact with the Malian authorities, including the Prime Minister's Office, the Ministry of Foreign Affairs, the Ministry of Health, the Immigration Bureau and the airports. The embassy also timely released consular reminders and epidemic prevention notices through the embassy website, the WeChat official account and SMS platforms, and issued an entry reminder at the arrival hall of Bamako Airport. We have timely informed the Mali media and the Mali government of our response measures to ensure that normal personnel and economic and trade exchanges between China and Mali are not affected. Chinese compatriots and staff of Chinese-funded organizations actively organized donations. The Chinese community in Mali is also sending masks to China, and cooperated with the embassy to disseminate consular reminders and epidemic prevention notices. Compatriots in Mali are living a normal life, which is a big support to the domestic fight against the epidemic, and a contribution to the embassy's public diplomacy.

At this time, China, as a major country in the world, has shown its sense of responsibility to the world. President Xi Jinping has personally directed and deployed the prevention work, and Premier Li Keqiang visited Wuhan, Hubei province, to inspect the epidemic prevention work first hand, which show that the Chinese government puts priority on safeguarding the lives and health of the people. With firm confidence and scientific prevention policies, China has mobilized the nation in a very short period of time, and has adopted the comprehensive and rigorous prevention and control measures at all levels. The full coverage reflects the Chinese government's efficiency and ability, and the Chinese people fully understand the government's deployment and are actively cooperating with the government. Based on the principles of openness, transparency and accountability, the Chinese government has timely updated epidemic information, actively responded to the concerns of all parties, strengthened cooperation with the international community, and received affirmation and high evaluation from the World Health Organization and most countries. All of this support has become a weapon in the fight against the new coronavirus.

To control the spread of the epidemic, the Chinese government has adopted unprecedented quarantine measures. Wuhan Huoshenshan Hospital was completed within 10 days. It has demonstrated China's efficiency, and created a miracle showing China's will to combat the epidemic. Governments at all levels gave priority to people's welfare,

Sacrifice, Toil and Tears
China and the World in the Fight against the Pandemic

comprehensively coordinated medical supplies and living materials to areas with severe epidemics to ensure the local people's treatment and living conditions. The Chinese government also picked up Hubei tourists stranded in Thailand, Malaysia, Japan and other places by chartered planes.

The Director-General of the World Health Organization Tedros Adhanom Ghebreyesus has expressed his appreciation for the decisive measures taken by the Chinese government. He believes that they have not only protected the Chinese people, but also the people of the world. He emphasized that this is the advantage of the Chinese system and is worth learning. In response to some countries over-reacting to the outbreak by suspending flights, the International Civil Aviation Organization also issued an announcement strongly urging countries to follow WHO recommendations.

This is a war without the smoke of gunpowder. This is a test for the Chinese people. In 2020, what we feel is not only the brutality of the virus, but also the positive energy of the Chinese people to overcome all difficulties. The country has come through hardships before and it will this time. China is using practical actions to prove to the world that under the leadership of the Communist Party of China and with the unique advantages of the socialist system with Chinese characteristics, we have the confidence, ability and solidarity to win this epidemic prevention and control fight.

February 17, 2020

The author is Chinese ambassador to Mali. The author contributed this article to China Watch, a think tank powered by China Daily.

Peru is far away, but its friendship with China is close

By Juan Diego Zamudio

China's connection with Peru goes back 170 years. Chinese investments in Peru's mining, banking and telecommunications sectors have been increasing, especially after Peru joined the Belt and Road Initiative in 2019.

For Peru, China is its largest trading partner, so if the Chinese economy suffers, the Peruvian economy too will suffer because of the relationship the two countries have. China is the destination of 29 percent of Peru's total exports; it is also the source of 24 percent of Peru's total imports, according to 2019 data from the National Superintendence of Customs and Tax Administration of Peru. And by accounting for 24 percent of the total donations received by Peru in 2019, China is also the highest donor country for Peru.

Therefore, the novel coronavirus outbreak in China, as well as rising confirmed cases in many other countries, is a source of great concern for Peru. But the ambassador of China to Peru has emphasized that merchandise exported from China to Peru have no risk of containing the virus.

Reports say that the number of Chinese visitors to Peru will fall in the coming months, but since this is a lean tourism season in Peru, it will not seriously affect the Peruvian tourism industry.

Chinese policies and measures to fight the disease have surprised people across the world, including Peruvians, not least because China built a huge hospital in less than two weeks and its measures to control the spread of the virus are yielding results. Peru, and the rest of the world, should learn from China how to fight an epidemic and take care of its people.

Peru is far away from China in terms of distance, but not in friendship. With China, we have 170 years of relations, and about 10 percent of the Peruvian population today has Chinese origins. No wonder there have been discussions on how to take advantage of Peruvian culture, which is as old as Chinese culture. Peru has a history of more than 6,000 years. The oldest city in the Americas is Caral, where you can study how the residents survived natural disasters in a desert and seismic zone.

Unlike the pessimistic projections some people have made — because they believe the situation in China will not improve — we know that the impact of the novel coronavirus will be short term. There are many reasons to believe that the Chinese economy will not suffer in the long run, especially because China thinks as a united whole, not as individuals, and can use emergency measures to put the economy and society back on the normal track. It has strong mobilization capabilities, fast strategies, and different countries are working with China, in a variety of economic sectors, as well as, mining, infrastructure, logistic, telecommunication, and so on.

Peru believes China can control the epidemic sooner rather than later. Historically, China has emerged from many crises and come up with policies and decisions that benefit not only the Chinese society but also the international community. Every crisis can be turned into an opportunity, and China knows best how to do that, by creating opportunities in the short, medium and long term.

As for Peru, despite not being advanced in telecommunications development, it can learn from the transfer of technology. Students of National University of San Marcos have joined Huawei's global competition in cloud computing and artificial intelligence, in a program I was in charge of.

I believe that the coronavirus outbreak will make China much stronger, because of the prevention policies it has adopted, and the collaborative work, technology transfer, best practices, risk diversification and scientific collaboration it has established with other countries, including Peru.

When it comes to cooperation and collaboration with China

to tackle global problems such as the coronavirus outbreak, China believes in the Chinese proverb, "If you want to walk fast, walk alone; if you want to walk far, walk together."

March 6, 2020

The author is head of the Office of International Technical Cooperation and a professor at the School of Economics, National University of San Marcos, Lima, Peru, and a visiting scholar at Fudan Development Institute, Fudan University.

Sacrifice, Toil and Tears — China and the World in the Fight against the Pandemic

Global cooperation more vital in fighting viruses

By Julie Sunderland

Every few years, humanity succumbs to mass hysteria at the prospect of a global pandemic. In this century alone, SARS, H1N1, Ebola, MERS, Zika, and now the novel coronavirus have all generated reactions that, in retrospect, seem disproportionate to the actual impact of the disease. The 2002-03 SARS outbreak in China (also a coronavirus, likely transmitted from bats to human) infected 8,000 people and caused fewer than 800 deaths. Nonetheless, it resulted in an estimated $40 billion in lost economic activity, owing to closed borders, travel stoppages, business disruptions, and emergency healthcare costs.

Such reactions are understandable. The prospect of an infectious disease killing our children triggers ancient survival instincts. And modern medicine and health systems have created the illusion that we have complete biological control over our collective fate, even though the interconnectedness of the modern world has actually accelerated the rate at which new pathogens emerge and spread. And there are good reasons to fear new infectious diseases: the Coalition for Epidemic Preparedness Innovations (CEPI) estimates that a highly contagious, lethal, airborne pathogen similar to the 1918 Spanish flu could kill nearly 33 million people worldwide in just six months.

Nonetheless, the fear-mongering and draconian responses to each outbreak are unproductive. We are a biological species living among other organisms that sometimes pose a danger to us, and that have evolutionary advantages over us of sheer numbers and rapid mutational rates. Our most powerful weapon against that threat is our intelligence. Owing to modern science and technology, and our capacity for collective action, we already have the tools to prevent, manage, and contain global pandemics. Rather than thrashing around

International Coordination Essential to Deal with Global Risks

every time a new pathogen surprises us, we should simply deploy the same resources, organization, and ingenuity that we apply to building and managing our military assets.

Specifically, we need a three-pronged approach. First, we must invest in science and technology. Our current military capabilities are the result of trillions of dollars of investment in research and development. Yet we deploy only a fraction of those resources to the rapid development of vaccines, antibiotics, and diagnostics to fight dangerous pathogens.

Advances in biology allow us to understand a new pathogen's genetic code and mutational capabilities. We can now manipulate the immune system to fight disease, and rapidly develop more effective therapeutics and diagnostics. New RNA vaccines, for example, can program our own cells to deliver proteins that alert the immune system to develop antibodies against a disease, essentially turning our bodies into "vaccine factories".

Looking ahead, the mandates of research organizations such as the US Defense Advanced Research Projects Agency and the Biomedical Advanced Research and Development Authority, which are already funding programs to counter bioterrorism and other biological threats, should be broadened to support much more research into pandemic response.

The second prong is strategic preparedness. We in modern societies put a lot of faith in our militaries, because we value committed public servants and soldiers who vigilantly guard against threats to national security. But while our public health and scientific research institutions are stocked with similar levels of talent, they receive far less government support.

In 2018, President Donald Trump's administration shut down the US National Security Council's unit for coordinating responses to pandemics. It has also defunded the arm of the Centers for Disease Control (CDC) that monitors and prepares for epidemics. But even more corrosive has been the administration's public denigration of science, which erodes the public's trust in scientific and medical expertise.

Consider a scenario in which the US is attacked by another country. We would not expect the defense secretary suddenly to announce that, in response, the government will quickly build new stealth bombers from scratch while it plans a counter-offensive. The idea is ridiculous, yet it accurately reflects our current response to biological threats.

A better approach would be to recognize health workers and scientists for their service, create the infrastructure to develop and deploy emergency health technologies, and proactively fund the organizations tasked with pandemic response. As a first step, the US government should reestablish the shuttered NSC unit with a dedicated "pandemic czar," and fully fund the agencies responsible for managing the threat, including the CDC, the Department of Homeland Security, and the National Institutes of Health.

The third prong is a coordinated global response. Although it is antithetical to Trump's idea of "America First," a multilateral response to pandemics is obviously in America's national interest. The US needs to lead on issues where cooperation clearly has advantages over national-level policies. The US should support global mechanisms to identify and monitor emerging pathogens; coordinate a special force of health workers that can immediately deploy to epidemic sites; create new financing facilities (such as global epidemic insurance) that can quickly mobilize resources for emergency response; and develop and stockpile vaccines.

Here, the first step is for governments to increase funding for CEPI, which was created after the 2014 Ebola epidemic to develop and deploy vaccines. The agency's initial funding, provided by a coalition of governments and foundations, totaled only $500 million, or about half the cost of a single stealth bomber. Its budget should be far, far larger.

In the arms race with pathogens, there can be no final peace. The only question is whether we fight well or poorly. Fighting poorly means allowing pathogens to cause massive periodic disruptions and impose huge burdens in the form of lost economic productivity. Fighting well means investing appropriately in science and technology, funding the right people and infrastructure to optimize strategic preparedness, and assuming leadership over coordinated global responses.

It is only a matter of time before we are confronted with a truly lethal pathogen capable of taking many more lives than even the worst of our human wars. We are intelligent enough as a species to avoid that fate. But we need to use the best of our knowledge, talent, and organizational capacity to save ourselves. And we need to focus on responsible preparation now.

February 13, 2020

The author is, a former director of the Gates Foundation's Strategic Investment Fund, is a co-founder and Managing Director of Biomatics Capital Partners. /Project Syndicate

Sacrifice, Toil and Tears — China and the World in the Fight against the Pandemic

Strong public health response key to containing virus

By Tom Frieden

The outbreak of the novel coronavirus in China and its spread around the world show how fragile public health systems can be, and how urgently all countries must step up to address infectious diseases and other health threats. Every country can save lives and money, and better support families and communities, by strengthening their capacity to find, stop, and prevent health threats of all types.

The United States and China have engaged in a productive and mutually beneficial collaboration on a wide range of public health issues for the past 30 years. In 2002, China created the Chinese Center for Disease Control and Prevention. In my eight years as director of the US Centers for Disease Control and Prevention, I had the honor of participating in a strategic partnership with the Chinese CDC and meeting at least annually with my Chinese colleagues. I have seen first-hand the dedication of the Chinese CDC leadership and staff.

Five key elements to address health issues

During my more than 30-year career in public health, I've learned that the most effective public health units at local, city, state/provincial, national, and global levels have five key components that enable them to address a wide range of health threats:

• Sufficient funding. Stable and assured funding is necessary. The US CDC is funded at $12 billion per year — approximately $40 per person, supporting more than 23,000 staff, more than a hundred world-class laboratories, programs in dozens of countries and extensive grants for public health programs in the US.

• Sufficient number and quality of staff to detect, investigate, stop, and prevent health threats.

State and local health departments in the US have more than

200,000 members of staff, and public health workers are experts in nearly every aspect of health promotion and disease prevention, from infectious diseases and environmental health to non-communicable diseases and injuries. Salary scales for top experts at the US CDC are above the usual allowed by the government.

• Close connections with other public health and healthcare entities. The essential importance of a national public health institute is not just providing reference laboratories and technical leadership, but also upgrading skills and capacities of subnational public health agencies. The US CDC does this by directly funding state and city health departments, and sending them embedded staff on long-term assignment. The US CDC is highly regarded by leading specialists and works closely with them in areas such as infection prevention in hospitals and establishment of clinical guidelines.

• Technical independence in the context of political support. As director of the US CDC, I briefed former president Barack Obama whenever needed, and had much freedom to act independently. The CDC's technical expertise is respected both within and outside of government, both in the US and globally. Direct access to the highest levels of government gives US CDC authority and ensures that public health is prioritized at a national level.

• Effective communication. The US CDC communicates frequently and effectively with the public, doctors, the media and policymakers. It produces the Morbidity and Mortality Weekly Report, a weekly epidemiological digest widely respected as a definitive resource worldwide. In times of crisis, it follows the risk communication principle: "Be first, be right, be credible."

Two important Sino-US programs

In my time as US CDC director, we and the Chinese CDC identified two joint priorities: increasing the number of top-level Chinese epidemiologists completing a rigorous training program from 15 to 80 per year, and addressing the heavy burden of heart attacks and strokes through a sodium reduction program.

The Chinese CDC's two-year China Epidemiology Training Program prepares public health staff to better find and respond to health emergencies — including epidemics — and serve as future public health leaders. Increasing the number of trainees to 80 in each year's class would have made the Chinese program the same size as the US Epidemic Intelligence Service, the US CDC's flagship training program. After increasing to 30 new trainees a year, progress stalled, preventing China from benefiting from a larger group of trained public health professionals who could help identify and respond to health threats.

Reducing salt intake prevents hypertension, heart attacks, and strokes. The sodium reduction initiative in Shandong province, started in 2011, has been the largest comprehensive salt reduction project in China. With strong support from the Chinese CDC and the Shandong government, and with collaboration from the salt industry, sodium consumption was reduced and hypertension prevalence dropped within five years. Unfortunately, complications on data policies have prevented this information from being published internationally in ways that could expand this progress to other areas in China and globally.

In my current position with Vital Strategies, we are honored to be registered as an International NGO in Shandong and to partner with groups in many parts of China on prevention of cardiovascular disease. Non-communicable disease now accounts for 9 out of 10 deaths in China, with nearly half of those caused by cardiovascular disease. High blood pressure is the world's leading modifiable risk factor for preventable mortality; less than 1 in 6 people with hypertension in China and worldwide have it under control. China's rate of strokes is many times higher than the US rate; strokes can be prevented by control of blood pressure.

Strength in collectivity

My team and I have been following the progress of the response to the novel coronavirus epidemic closely and working to support our Chinese partners. I'm impressed that China has taken extensive measures to control the virus, and this appears to have slowed its spread. Reports that this effort is negatively affecting the health system's ability to provide standard healthcare are concerning. For comparison, during the 2014-16 Ebola outbreak in Africa, more people died from interruptions in day-to-day health services than from Ebola itself.

SARS, Ebola, and now the novel coronavirus show that we don't have the luxury of time. We need systems in place in advance to quickly find and aggressively fight disease. Our biggest vulnerability is transmission in countries with weak health systems. It is encouraging that China has joined the global effort to support lower-income countries in Africa and Asia so that public health systems in those countries can find, stop, and prevent epidemics.

One thing is clear: China and the world will be safer as we collectively learn more about how this coronavirus spreads and the effectiveness of different control measures in healthcare facilities and in the community. We are all connected in the fight against a common enemy: dangerous microbes. When any country strengthens its public health system's capacity to find, stop, and prevent health threats, it protects families and communities, contributes to health and economic progress of that country and makes the world healthier and more productive.

February 28, 2020

The author, former director of the US Centers for Disease Control and Prevention, and commissioner of the New York City Health Department, is currently president and CEO of Resolve to Save Lives, a global non-profit initiative of Vital Strategies, working with countries to make the world safer from epidemics.

Sacrifice, Toil and Tears — China and the World in the Fight against the Pandemic

Fight against virus will be uncertain without cooperation of China, US

By Jasna Plevnik

This is a very special moment for China and the world. The novel coronavirus has stopped travel, soccer and business, but America's intertwined economic and geopolitical competition with China has continued.

At the Munich Security Conference held a few weeks ago, US Secretary of State Mike Pompeo and Secretary of Defense Mark Esper were deeply aware of the delicate situation in China due to the epidemic, but despite this, they roughly attacked China and arrogantly threatened Europe with interruption of security cooperation if it continues its 5G relations with China.

The speech on geopolitics, because of economic reasons, overshadowed human sympathy at the conference whose main idea was to discuss peace and cooperation.

The pragmatic attitude of the US administration to the virus, that is, the benefits that America could receive from the health disaster in China, was confirmed by Commerce Secretary Wilbur Ross, who looks at the virus like a partner that could help in accelerating the return of jobs from China to America, which is one of the goals of the US administration in economic relations with China. Since 2017, the United States has been promoting decoupling of the US economy from China, as well as from other countries, even from its strategic ally Germany. Big American business does not support the tearing of the tissue of economic dependency in the world economic order and back to protectionism.

Human sacrifices

China, though in a situation when its leadership, at all levels, has put a lot of energy into fighting the epidemic, has begun to meet the conditions of the first phase of the trade deal with the US. Some US analysts doubt China's ability to buy from the US $200 billion worth of goods over the next two years.

It is good for China, and the world, that America's offensive realism has not become a mainstream in international relations. China does not seek sympathy from America but a fair approach to its economy and foreign policy and role in the world.

Japan has proven itself a good neighbour, not only because of its donations to China, but also as an investor with an understanding of the uncertainty that has plagued China's economy, setting aside regional economic and strategic rivalries that shape relations in Asia.

The United Kingdom has recently decided to include Huawei in the construction of its 5G network, although America has lobbied against such a decision.

The interest of the new British government is not to follow a policy of decoupling from the Chinese economy, but to reach a favourable trade agreement with the world's first trading power, though the virus has slowed down negotiations on a Sino-British trade agreement.

Covid-19, of course, cannot weaken China's position as a global power, but China's diplomatic agenda for 2020 has been hit hard. Many international meetings and conferences had to be postponed.

This year is important for China-Europe relations that have been developing in the direction of economic partnership and friendship, regardless of their differences in political systems. An annual China-EU summit is scheduled to take place in Beijing, followed by a summit of China and 17 countries in Central, Eastern, Southeast and Southern Europe.

The preparations are underway for the China-EU flagship meeting in 2020, scheduled for September in Leipzig. All preparations should be completed by the end of June, which means that Croatia that now chairing the Council of the European Union, is also involved in some way in those preparations.

The general warns

It is in the interest of China and the European Union to sign a bilateral investment agreement in Leipzig as progress has been made on many issues, but the key issues of industrial subsidies and "forced technology transfer" have not yet been addressed.

Germany's policy toward China has been friendly even before the outbreak of the virus corona, and Berlin did not accept the US

Sacrifice, Toil and Tears — China and the World in the Fight against the Pandemic

administration's strong pressure to lead economic cooperation with China by favouring a military alliance with America at the expense of market decisions.

German Chancellor Angela Merkel, who is due to travel to China later this year, has invested a lot of diplomatic zeal and efforts to reach an agreement in Leipzig that is also important for the advancement of the global economy. The agreement would be the crown not only of the EU-China cooperation but of Merkel's China diplomacy. The Chancellor believes now it is the right time for the agreement. Especially as politician Norbert Röttgen appeared in the contest for the next president of the ruling Christian Democratic Union party, who is widely known as a keen critic of current Chinese-German ties.

In fact, Covid-19 has strengthened China's position as a global power in a certain way, as China has shown that it is well prepared for global leadership in crisis situations. That was recognized to it by the World Health Organization. The whole world has been amazed with China's high mobilization capacity: a large hospital was made in two weeks! President Xi Jinping has repeatedly emphasized that the Chinese are not only responsible for the health of the Chinese people, but also for the health of the people of the world.

John R. Allen, president of the Brookings Institution, a retired four-star Marine Corps general and former commander of NATO International Security (ISAF) and US forces in Afghanistan, thinks US donations to China are a great thing, but not enough. Global spread of the coronavirus requires, said the General, a joint global leadership of America and China in the fight against virus corona and the binding of significant scientific resources for the benefit of all mankind.

It would be development of international relations in the right direction because there is no stability in the global world without the cooperation of America and China.

March 4, 2020

The author is president of Geoeconomic Forum Croatia. The article first appeared in the Daily Newspaper Vecernji list, Croatia.

China-US relations during coronavirus outbreak

By Pan Yixuan

Editor's Note: The outbreak of the novel coronavirus has prompted some to claim that it will accelerate the "decoupling" of China and the United States. Two experts shared their views on the epidemic's impact on bilateral ties with China Daily's Pan Yixuan. Excerpts follow:

China and the US not able to decouple

The novel coronavirus outbreak has restricted the movement of people and created a temporary shortage of production capacity that may lead to the outflow of manufacturing chains from China.

But with tens of billions of yuan spent on medical facilities and supplies, resolute measures such as quarantining cities, nationwide mobilization and international cooperation, China is gradually bringing the epidemic under control, which will promote the resumption of stalled production chains.

The electronic manufacturing giant Foxconn, which is one of Apple's suppliers, has built production lines for protective face masks that China is in short supply of due to the epidemic. If it has adequate production, the company can even supply such masks beyond its own needs.

Worries about the epidemic should not be exaggerated. The foundation of the Sino-US relationship that is based on close economic ties cannot be easily shifted.

China has halved tariffs on $75 billion US products as a reciprocal measure to the cut in US tariffs on Chinese goods scheduled to come into effect on Feb 14.

On Feb 7, the Chinese and US presidents talked over the phone about the implementation of the "phase one" agreement signed on Jan

15, with the US leader expressing his confidence in China's ability to win the battle against the virus.

Instead of decoupling, the series of talks have put Sino-US trade and economic relations back on track.

It is true that there is the potential for technology decoupling, as their competition in 5G and artificial intelligence is heating up, but international cooperation on global health security challenges because of the coronavirus have reinforced their common interests in the application and development of technology.

There is no need to exaggerate worries about Sino-US relations during the epidemic.

Li Zheng, an assistant research fellow at the China Institutes of Contemporary International Relations

Just a short-term "decoupling"

Due to the novel coronavirus outbreak, the US has introduced entry restrictions on foreigners who have been to China within the past 14 days and quarantined US citizens and permanent residents returning from China.

Such restrictions constitute a kind of quarantining of China that could result in a short-term decoupling of China-US relations.

During the period of economic stagnation in China brought about by the epidemic, companies will seek replaceable market and manufacturing places outside China.

But leaving China's huge market and trained labor force will cost a lot and may be a bad idea if the epidemic ends in a few months. Meanwhile, for similar reasons, there might not be an acceleration in the return of jobs to the US during the outbreak as US Commerce Secretary Wilbur Ross claimed that there would be.

The US has made entry limits so strict that China-US and the world's trade and economic ties will suffer uncalled-for restrictions. It's not important to debate whether Washington has overreacted to the epidemic and acted beyond the suggestions of the World Health

Organization. It's more essential that Beijing and Washington should negotiate to reach a reasonable agreement and strengthen cooperation to fight the epidemic.

Although the "China threat" theory remains in the US given the recent remarks by US Secretary of State Mike Pompeo, the epidemic should not be an excuse to justify the "permanent decoupling" of China and the US.

The duration of the coronavirus epidemic plays an important role in the newly signed Phase-one Sino-US trade deal. The longer the epidemic lasts, the more the implementation is impacted and so delays its realization.

Luckily the recent talks between Chinese and US presidents showed confidence in the further development of bilateral relations.

Chen Qi, professor of international studies at Tsinghua University

February 14, 2020

Sacrifice, Toil and Tears — China and the World in the Fight against the Pandemic

Global cooperation vital to fight against COVID-19

By Priyanka Pandit

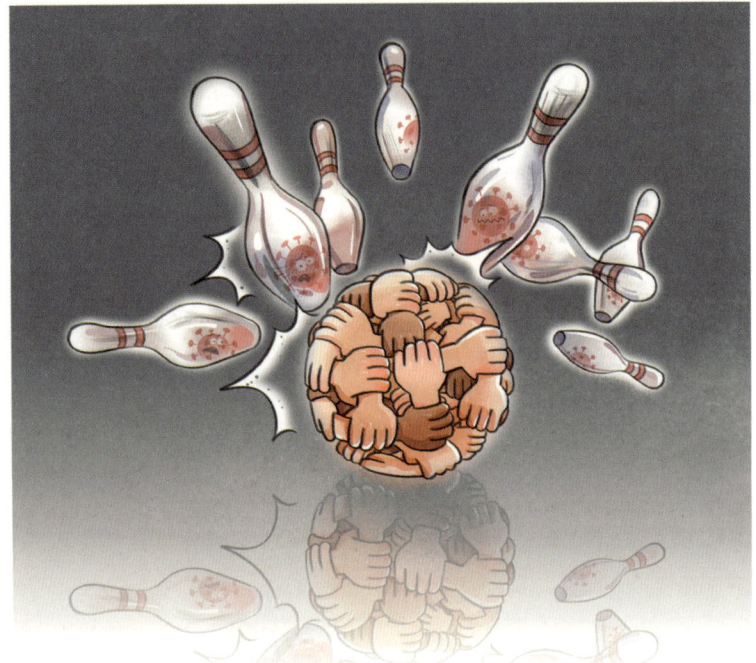

Li Min/China Daily

The Chinese economy has been severely hit by the novel coronavirus outbreak. And although the Chinese government has taken comprehensive measures to treat the virus-infected patients and contain the epidemic, the spread of the coronavirus to other countries seems to have created a global panic. Adding to this is the frustration caused by the "no known cure" for the coronavirus, which has claimed more than 2,600 lives in China.

V
International Coordination Essential to Deal with Global Risks

The World Health Organisation declared the COVID-19 outbreak a public health emergency of international concern on Jan 31, but it did so not because it was dissatisfied with the Chinese government's measures to control the epidemic but to help poorer countries to deal with the coronavirus. The declaration will strengthen WHO's disease surveillance on countries with relatively weak healthcare systems, prepare them to deal with the virus, and create awareness to contain the epidemic.

The coronavirus outbreak has put huge pressure on Beijing, especially because it has occurred at a time when the China is close to achieving the goals set in the 13th Five-Year Plan (2016-20). While the Chinese people pin their hopes on the government containing the epidemic, the international community is closely watching China's response to the outbreak. All these have made the task of controlling the outbreak even more difficult for the Chinese authorities.

The Chinese government has responded decisively to the outbreak, which marks a departure from its public health policy during the severe acute respiratory syndrome epidemic in 2002-03. The government has also acted swiftly to close all sea food and live animal markets in the country along with imposing travel restrictions on people within China.

The International Health Regulations Emergency Committee has taken note of the Chinese leadership's commitment to investigate and contain the outbreak. It has praised the government for communicating daily updates about the epidemic to WHO and for adopting a comprehensive multi-sectoral approach to prevent the further spread of the virus.

But given the uncertainty over the virus's transmission, stepping up international collaboration is the need of the hour. Though the novel coronavirus was detected in China, it cannot be argued that the onus of finding medical solutions and preventing its spread lies with Beijing alone. It's time the international community supported the countless Chinese medical personnel who have put their own safety in risk to work round the clock to treat the virus-infected patients.

An outbreak of such a magnitude often acts as a litmus test for humanity and compassion. Even the most powerful country becomes vulnerable and requires the support and cooperation of the other countries to contain such an outbreak. As such, countries with advanced public healthcare systems should actively chart out strategies of cooperation with WHO and China to contain the epidemic and find a vaccine for COVID-19.

For instance, such countries could send medical supplies to China to assist the Chinese government's virus control efforts, generate global awareness about the symptoms of the virus, conduct joint research to find a cure for the virus, and prevent the spread of anti-China sentiments abroad.

With the rising cases in South Korea and Japan, it's clear that no country alone can control an epidemic like COVID-19. Complicating the situation further is the multiple side effects of the virus. Apart from its potentially deadly pathogenic character, the virus leads to social exclusion and exacerbates the already existing differences on biomedical approaches to epidemic control and global health standards. So collective efforts are needed to end the differences in the battle against COVID-19, control its spread and find a cure for it.

February 26, 2020

The author is the research fellow at the Indian Council of World Affairs, New Delhi, and a visiting fellow at Chongyang Institute for Financial Studies, Renmin University of China.

International Coordination Essential
to Deal with Global Risks

V

Only coordinated response can control outbreak

By Amitendu Palit

Song Chen/China Daily

The novel coronavirus, or COVID-19, has now spread to about 50 countries affecting about 90,000 people. Although the overwhelming number of COVID-19 patients is in China, more and more cases are being detected in other countries. Since many of the people who have tested positive for COVID-19 in other countries

Sacrifice, Toil and Tears

China and the World in the Fight against the Pandemic

do not have a recent travel history to China, COVID-19 is gradually becoming a global pandemic. The World Health Organization has accordingly raised the alert level to "very high".

The COVID-19 outbreak is causing damage to both humans and economies across the world. The first aspect is already visible. As of now, human casualties have been the highest in China. But the number of infected is rising rapidly in the Republic of Korea, Japan, Italy and Iran. From its earlier concentration in Asian countries, particularly North and Southeast Asia, COVID-19 has begun spreading to other parts of Asia, and Europe. It is probably only a matter of time before the virus is detected in practically all parts of the world. Such an eventuality will have significant impacts on global public health.

Not all countries equally equipped to fight outbreak

But all countries are not equally prepared to handle the outbreak. Countries such as Japan, the ROK, Singapore, the United States, Italy — and China — have the financial capacity for implementing most stringent precautionary measures. They also have modern public health facilities comprising good doctors, capable nurses and efficient pathology laboratories. Right from the advanced level of mechanical screening put in place at various airports of many countries to the high degree of isolation in quarantines, these countries are using their top and best facilities and practices.

However, the same cannot be expected from all countries. As the virus spreads to less-developed countries and regions, the ability of the latter to detect the virus will decrease. This would be due to a combination of limited detection facilities, insufficient healthcare infrastructure and low knowledge about prevention practices.

The problems faced by the relatively poor countries would be aggravated by the lack of medical supplies. Across the world, there is a shortage of medical accessories for tackling COVID-19. These include face masks and alcohol-based hand sanitizers to be used as precaution and disinfectant. The shortage was visible even before the epidemic assumed its current proportions. It is expected to get worse because China — one of the major global producers of such products along with Southeast Asian countries — has been forced to cut back production due to the outbreak.

Global economic damage could be substantive

The shortage of medical accessories is only a small part of the collateral economic damage COVID-19 is likely to inflict on the global economy. The scale of economic damage would be substantive. They could include massive disruptions in various supply chains — semiconductors, automobiles, smartphones, pharmaceuticals, chemicals and garments — that depend critically on China, as the country is a major producer of parts, components and raw materials used upstream in these chains.

At the same time, China has also, over the years, developed as an important final market for many consumer products thanks to the steady increase in the country's per capita income. Both segments of the supply chains are going to be affected, particularly upstream supplies would be affected due to reduced production in China.

It is already reported that containers leaving Chinese ports with supplies are getting stuck in other countries' ports as necessary documents for unloading are taking a long time to reach from China, because offices in the country have not been functioning normally with many employees working from home. At the downstream end, COVID-19 would lead to a reduction in overall economic activity and lower incomes across most of China. This would reduce the purchasing power of households and individuals and their ability to maintain, let alone increase, the current consumption level.

Slowdown in China will impact rest of the world

As China's economic growth rate is expected to reduce, at least in the next couple of quarters, the impact will be felt on the rest of the world. China is very significant for the global tourism industry, both in terms of foreign tourists visiting China and Chinese tourists travelling across the rest of the world. Travel advisories issued by various countries have already blocked the flow of tourists. At the next level, the tourism and aviation industries are bracing to tackle the large number of cancellations and low number of new bookings, as more and more countries report new COVID-19 cases.

The scale of the outbreak has definitely caught people by surprise. The rise in the number of new cases, and WHO's warning on the unpreparedness of the world for tackling a pandemic, needs to be taken seriously. Affected countries need to collaborate among themselves by sharing information on the number of cases, travel histories of people and precautionary and control measures. In the absence of such policies, the COVID-19 outbreak could acquire even more fearful dimensions.

Also, countries that detected coronavirus cases in the initial stages, and therefore have gained some experience in tackling the virus, must share their knowledge of containing the disease with those countries that are less prepared to tackle COVID-19. Otherwise, poor countries would be fatally hit.

March 4, 2020

The author is a senior research fellow and research lead (trade and economic policy) at the Institute of South Asian Studies, National University of Singapore.

Preventing global food security crisis

By Fan Shenggen

Ma Xuejing/China Daily

The COVID-19 outbreak is showing a new trend. While the situation in China has improved dramatically, several countries, especially the Republic of Korea, Japan, Italy and Iran, have been reporting more new cases. In fact, these countries have reported more new confirmed cases than China.

That the first case was reported from Nigeria on Feb 28, the day when the World Health Organization raised its alert level against the epidemic to "very high", is particularly worrying as the continent is also fighting another threat from the desert locusts that could affect food security of millions in the region.

Global food security already faces challenges

COVID-19 is a health crisis. But it could also lead to a food security crisis if proper measures are not taken. The world is already facing food and nutrition security challenges. According to the United Nations Food and Agriculture Organization, more than 820 million people across the globe are already suffering from hunger, although the Chinese number reported by FAO is grossly overestimated.

Close to 150 million children in countries around the world are stunted because of lack of proper nutrition. And in many countries, hunger and malnutrition have been on the rise for the past three years due to conflicts and the refugee crisis, climate change and worsening inequality, with the Middle East and Sub-Saharan regions being particularly vulnerable.

Epidemics like HIV/AIDS, Ebola and the Middle East respiratory syndrome (MERS) have had negative impacts on food and nutrition security — particularly for vulnerable populations including children, women, the elderly and the poor. For example, when the Ebola epidemic hit Guinea, Liberia and Sierra Leone in 2014, rice prices in those countries increased by more than 30 percent and the price of cassava, a staple in Liberia, skyrocketed by 150 percent.

In China, however, despite the severe acute respiratory syndrome (SARS) outbreak in 2002-03 delaying the winter wheat harvest by two weeks and triggering panic in Guangdong and Zhejiang provinces, the epidemic didn't affect production and prices on a large scale in the rest of the country.

Need to learn from previous epidemics

The SARS and MERS outbreaks had relatively little impact on the economy and food and nutrition security of China, largely due to the country's resilience and ability to cope with emergencies. Countries such as Singapore, Vietnam and Canada, too, showed such resilience, because they have enough food reserves and boast of vibrant value chains linking the domestic and international markets.

But Ebola had a huge impact on some African countries' agricultural production, marketing and trade. On the production side, due to road blockages, farmers had limited access to inputs such as seeds, fertilizers and insecticides. And many of the regions faced acute labor shortage.

All this resulted in more than 40 percent of the agricultural land not being cultivated. As for marketing, farmers could not transport fresh produce to local and urban markets. In addition, day meal programs in schools were disrupted because food aid could not be delivered to the schools. And trade was disrupted as international shipping services were either delayed or cancelled because crew members of cargo vessels refused to travel to those countries for fear of being infected.

Food prices will shoot up if nations panic again

The 2008 food price crisis, too, taught us a valuable lesson. The crisis was caused by droughts in Australia and Argentina, increasing oil prices, rising use of food grains for biofuel production and trade policy failures. These prompted many countries to impose various export policies to restrict the export of food products.

For example, there was no shortage of rice supply, but due to panic behavior, many countries imposed higher taxes on rice exports or banned rice exports altogether. Rice prices doubled in the global market in six months, causing severe disruptions in rice trade and leading to a food price crisis. If countries become panic this time too, food trade and markets could be disrupted, albeit on a much larger scale.

Act now to prevent food security crisis

The novel coronavirus is still spreading and it is difficult to say when it would be contained. So to ensure food security for all, we need to take urgent actions at the global and country levels.

First, there is a need to closely monitor food prices and markets. Transparent dissemination of information will strengthen government management over the food market, prevent people from panicking, and guide farmers to make rational production decisions. And to nip market speculation over supply in the bud, the government should strengthen market regulation.

Second, it is necessary to ensure international and national agricultural and food supply chains function normally. China has set a good example of how to ensure food security during the current epidemic by, for instance, opening a "green channel" for fresh agricultural products, and banning unauthorized roadblocks.

Innovative methods to keep sales growing

E-commerce and delivery companies can also play a key logistical role. For example, as lockdown measures have increased the demand for home delivery of groceries, e-commerce companies have come up with an in-app feature for contactless delivery, allowing the couriers to leave a parcel at a convenient spot for the customers to pick up, which rules out person-to-person interaction.

Third, social safety nets are needed to protect those who are the worst affected and most vulnerable. These safety nets, which could be in the form of cash or in-kind transfers (context-specificity is important here), should be accompanied by intervention by health and nutrition officials, because investing in the health and nutrition of vulnerable populations could lower the mortality rate of diseases such as COVID-19 — as nutritional level and mortality rates are intricately linked. Social safety nets are also crucial in the post-epidemic period to drive "reconstruction" efforts.

Fourth, more investment is needed to build an even more resilient food system. Such investment must come from national governments as well as the international community, as enhancing the capacity of developing countries to prevent or contain a food security crisis is a collective effort. In today's highly interconnected world, contagious diseases such as SARS, Ebola, avian flu and COVID-19 could easily travel across borders.

Vital to have safeguards against zoonotic diseases

There is also a need to build safeguards for the prevention and control of zoonotic diseases. The international community needs to do more to prevent future outbreaks of zoonotic diseases such as Ebola, SARS and avian flu, including regulating meat, seafood and wildlife markets. Many zoonotic diseases originate in wildlife. HIV, Ebola, MERS, SARS, and possibly COVID-19 too, all originated in wildlife and jumped to humans.

Moreover, it is important to ensure the smooth flow of global trade and make full use of the international market as a vital tool to secure food supply. And global institutions such as the World Trade Organization, FAO, World Bank and the International Monetary Fund must ask countries to not use COVID-19 as an excuse to issue trade protectionist policies.

March 9, 2020

The author is chair professor at Beijing-based China Agricultural University and former director-general of Washington-headquartered International Food Policy Research Institute.

Outbreak to impact EU-US-China ties

By Fraser Cameron

The novel coronavirus outbreak will have a major impact on relations between the European Union, China and the United States, the world's three biggest economic actors responsible for more than 50 percent of global wealth.

Some US politicians have sought to blame China and the EU for failing to tackle the outbreak, thereby showing zero understanding of the need for global cooperation to combat the worst pandemic in decades. Trust in US leadership is certain to take a further tumble after the US administration's erratic handling of the crisis.

US-EU ties frayed even before travel ban

Relations between the EU and the US were already frayed before the US banned passenger flights from Europe (initially excluding the United Kingdom). The move came as a huge shock to the EU and prompted a strong protest from EU leaders who were neither consulted nor informed in advance. European Council President Charles Michel and European Commission President Ursula von der Leyen, in a joint statement, said the coronavirus outbreak is "a global crisis, not limited to any continent and required cooperation rather than unilateral action". This was an unusually blunt critique of the US' action and revealed the lack of trust between Brussels and Washington.

For the first time since the creation of the EU, there is an occupant in the White House opposed to European integration, and who has gone so far as to describe the EU as a "foe" actively seeking to take advantage of the US by its trade surplus and not paying enough for its defense. The US administration also sought to weaken the EU by supporting Brexit and suggesting the US leader's "friend", Boris Johnson, should be prime minister even when Theresa May was still in office.

Transatlantic relations have also been poisoned by the US leader's disavowal of the Paris climate change agreement and the Iran nuclear deal, two major feats of European diplomacy. The US' withdrawal from the Intermediate-Range Nuclear Forces Treaty and unilateral support for Israel's expansionist policies in the West Bank have left the US leader at odds with European leaders. The US has also imposed tariffs on European steel and aluminum on the spurious grounds of national security, and has pushed the EU to open up its agricultural market and threatened to impose tariffs on European cars if it does not.

The US administration's mishandling of the coronavirus crisis and its economic impact, especially on global stock markets, could influence the US presidential election and throw up a surprise result. Certainly, this would be welcomed in Europe but it would be illusionary to think that all transatlantic problems would be resolved if, say, Joe Biden were in the White House. Transatlantic cooperation would improve on climate change and Iran, but tensions would remain over defense, trade and China, because these reflect a more structural and longer-term divergence of EU and US interests.

Conspiracy theories add to poor US-China relations

The novel coronavirus pandemic has increased mistrust between the US and China with conspiracy theories being aired, and each side blaming the other, which has hampered efforts at global coordination to tackle the crisis. Before the pandemic, US-China relations were characterized by Washington's trade war with Beijing. And only after months of wrangling did the two sides agree an interim trade deal in January.

Both parties have an interest in the "phase one" trade deal being implemented, but the extent of the impact the coronavirus outbreak will have on trade is not clear. The US administration wants to portray the deal as a success before the November election. Beijing, too, wishes to keep the deal in place to avoid a return to previous tariff levels and increased uncertainties, especially amid efforts to jumpstart the Chinese economy. A prolonged crisis will mean further disruption to the Chinese economy and to the country's pivotal role in global supply chains.

There are already calls in the US Congress and elsewhere for the

US to decouple from China. So far few companies have done so, but that could change. The incumbent US administration has overseen a transition from the Barack Obama administration's position of regarding China as partner in some areas such as climate change to a potential enemy that must be contained. And trade rivalry has now transformed into technology rivalry as is evident from the US's pressure on European countries to ban Huawei.

EU, China are partners and competitors

The EU and China have cooperated closely in the fight against the coronavirus outbreak, exchanging information and sending medical supplies and experts to the worst affected regions including Wuhan in China's Hubei province and Lombardy in Italy.

Regrettably, the pandemic has led to the postponement of the EU-China summit scheduled for the end of March in Beijing. That would have been an ideal opportunity for the new EU leaders to get to know their Chinese counterparts. The pandemic has led to a lockdown of EU institutions and thus slowed the important negotiations on an EU-China investment treaty. Last year the EU made clear that there would have to be measured progress toward this agreement, otherwise a raft of defensive trade measures would take effect.

The EU and China are partners in several areas, from climate change and ocean governance to the Iran nuclear deal and promoting security in Afghanistan. But they are also competitors in some areas. But interestingly, European governments have not followed the US' "diktat" on banning Huawei, with several EU member states allowing the Chinese tech giant to participate in their 5G infrastructure construction. Trade between the EU and China will inevitably slow this year as a result of the pandemic, but unlike in the US there is little talk of decoupling the two economies.

The pandemic is thus having a major impact on EU-US-China relations. It has disrupted trade and travel, and sparked a national rather than an international response. In an ideal world, there would be no talk of a "foreign virus"; instead, there would be acknowledgement that a pathogen knows no borders and has no political loyalties. The pandemic is a common threat that requires a coordinated global response. But that is not the way the US administration thinks and thus the US' relations with both the EU and China may continue to suffer.

March 18, 2020

The author is director of the EU-Asia Centre.

We will get through the pandemic together

By António Guterres

Song Chen/China Daily

The upheaval caused by the novel coronavirus — COVID-19 — is all around us. And I know many are anxious, worried and confused. That's absolutely natural.

We are facing a health threat unlike any other in our lifetimes. The virus is spreading, the danger is growing, and our health systems, economies and day-to-day lives are being severely tested.

The most vulnerable are the most affected — particularly our elderly and those with pre-existing medical conditions, those without

International Coordination Essential to Deal with Global Risks

access to reliable healthcare, and those in poverty or living on the edge.

The social and economic fallout from the combination of the pandemic and slowing economies will affect most of us for some months.

But the spread of the virus will peak. Our economies will recover. Until then, we must act together to slow the spread of the virus and look after each other.

This is a time for prudence, not panic. Science, not stigma. Facts, not fear.

Even though the situation has been declared a pandemic, it is one we can control. We can slow down transmissions, prevent infections and save lives. But that will take unprecedented personal, national and international action.

COVID-19 is our common enemy. We must declare war on this virus. That means countries have a responsibility to gear up, step up and scale up.

How? By implementing effective containment strategies, by activating and enhancing emergency response systems, by dramatically increasing the testing capacity and care for patients, by readying hospitals, ensuring they have the space, supplies and needed personnel, and by developing life-saving medical interventions.

All of us have a responsibility, too — to follow medical advice and take simple, practical steps recommended by health authorities.

In addition to being a public health crisis, the virus is also infecting the global economy.

Financial markets have been hard hit by the uncertainty. Global supply chains have been disrupted. Investment and consumer demand have plunged — with a real and rising risk of a global recession.

United Nations economists estimate the virus could cost the global economy at least $1 trillion this year, perhaps far more.

No country can do it alone. More than ever, governments must cooperate to revitalize economies, expand public investment, boost trade, and ensure targeted support for the people and communities most affected by the disease or more vulnerable to the negative economic impacts — including women who often shoulder a disproportionate burden of care work.

A pandemic drives home the essential interconnectedness of our human family. Preventing the further spread of COVID-19 is a shared responsibility for us all.

The United Nations — including the World Health Organization — is fully mobilized. As part of our human family, we are working 24×7 with governments, providing international guidance, helping the world take on this threat.

We are in this together — and we will get through this, together.

March 17, 2020

The author is secretary-general of the United Nations.

Policy action for a healthy global economy

By Kristalina Georgieva

While quarantining and social distancing is the right prescription to combat COVID-19's public health impact, the exact opposite is needed when it comes to securing the global economy.

Constant contact and close coordination are the best medicine to ensure that the economic pain inflicted by the virus is relatively short-lived.

Many governments have already taken significant steps, with major measures being announced on a daily basis — including the bold, coordinated moves on monetary policy.

But clearly, even more needs to be done. As the virus spreads, increased coordinated action will be key to boosting confidence and providing stability to the global economy.

The IMF has published a set of policy recommendations that can help guide countries in the difficult days ahead.

What more needs to be done?

Three action areas for the global economy

First, fiscal. Additional fiscal stimulus will be necessary to prevent long-lasting economic damage.

Fiscal measures already announced are being deployed on a range of policies that immediately prioritize health spending and those in need. We know that comprehensive containment measures — combined with early monitoring — will slow the rate of infection and the spread of the virus.

Governments should continue and expand these efforts to reach the most-affected people and businesses — with policies including increased paid sick leave and targeted tax relief.

Beyond these positive individual country actions, as the virus spreads, the case for a coordinated and synchronized global fiscal stimulus is becoming stronger by the hour.

During the Global Financial Crisis (GFC), for example, fiscal stimulus by the G20 amounted to about 2 percent of GDP, or over $900 billion in today's money, in 2009 alone. So, there is a lot more work to do.

Second, monetary policy. In advanced economies, central banks should continue to support demand and boost confidence by easing financial conditions and ensuring the flow of credit to the real economy. For example, the US Federal Reserve just announced further interest rate cuts, asset purchases, forward guidance and a drop in reserve requirements.

Policy steps that we know have worked before — including during the GFC — are on the table. Major central banks have taken decisive coordinated action to ease swap lines and thus lessen global financial market stresses.

Going forward, there may be a need for swap lines to emerging market economies.

As the Institute for International Finance said, investors have removed nearly $42 billion from emerging markets since the beginning of the crisis. This is the largest outflow they have ever recorded.

So central banks' policy action in emerging-market and developing economies will need to balance the especially difficult challenge of addressing capital flow reversals and commodity shocks. In times of crisis such as at present, foreign exchange interventions and capital flow management measures can usefully complement interest rate and other monetary policy actions.

Third, the regulatory response. Financial system supervisors should aim to maintain the balance between preserving financial stability, maintaining banking system soundness and sustaining economic activity.

This crisis will stress test whether the changes made in the wake of the financial crisis will serve their purpose.

Banks should be encouraged to use flexibility in existing regulations, for example by using their capital and liquidity buffers, and undertake renegotiation of loan terms for stressed borrowers. Risk disclosure and clear communication of supervisory expectations will also be essential for markets to function properly in the period ahead.

All this work — from monetary to fiscal to regulatory — is most effective when done cooperatively.

Indeed, IMF staff research shows that changes in spending, for example, have a multiplier effect when countries act together.

What the IMF can do

The IMF stands ready to mobilize its $1 trillion lending capacity to help our membership. As a first line of defense, the Fund can deploy its flexible and rapid-disbursing emergency response toolkit to help countries with urgent balance-of-payment needs.

These instruments could provide in the order of $50 billion to emerging and developing economies. Up to $10 billion could be made available to our low-income members through our concessional financing facilities, which carry zero interest rates.

The Fund already has 40 ongoing arrangements — both disbursing and precautionary — with combined commitments of about $200 billion. In many cases, these arrangements can provide another vehicle for the rapid disbursement of crisis financing. We also have received interest from about 20 countries and will be following up with them in the coming days.

In addition, the Fund's Catastrophe Containment and Relief Trust (CCRT) can help the poorest countries with immediate debt relief, which will free up vital resources for health spending, containment, and mitigation. In this regard, I commend United Kingdom's recent pledge of $195 million, which means the CCRT now has about $400 million available for potential debt relief. Our aim, with the help of other donors, is to boost it to $1 billion.

In this way, the IMF can serve its 189 member countries and demonstrate the value of international cooperation. Because, in the end, our answers to this crisis will not come from one method, one region, or one country in isolation.

Only through sharing, coordination, and cooperation will we be able to stabilize the global economy and return it to full health.

March 25, 2020

The author is managing director of IMF. /IMF Blog

Sacrifice, Toil and Tears — China and the World in the Fight against the Pandemic

Protect workers from economic pandemic

By Guy Ryder

The human dimensions of the COVID-19 pandemic reach far beyond the critical health response. All aspects of our future will be affected — economic, social and developmental. Our response must be urgent, coordinated and on a global scale, and should immediately deliver help to those most in need.

From workplaces, to enterprises, to national and global economies, getting this right is predicated on social dialogue between governments and those on the front line — the employers and workers. So that the 2020s don't become a re-run of the 1930s.

ILO estimates are that as many as 25 million people could become unemployed, with a loss of workers' income of as much as $3.4 trillion.

However, it is already becoming clear that these numbers may underestimate the magnitude of the impact.

This pandemic has mercilessly exposed the deep faultlines in our labour markets. Enterprises of all sizes have already stopped operations, cut working hours and laid off staff. Many are teetering on the brink of collapse as shops and restaurants close, flights and hotel bookings are cancelled, and businesses shift to remote working. Often the first to lose their jobs are those whose employment was already precarious — sales clerks, waiters, kitchen staff, baggage handlers and cleaners.

In a world where only one in five people are eligible for unemployment benefits, layoffs spell catastrophe for millions of families. Because paid sick leave is not available to many carers and delivery workers — those we all now rely on — they are often under pressure to continue working even if they are ill. In the developing world, piece-rate workers, day labourers and informal traders may be similarly pressured by the need to put food on the table. We will all suffer because of this. It will not only increase the spread of the virus but in the longer-term dramatically amplify cycles of poverty and inequality.

We have a chance to save millions of jobs and enterprises, if governments act decisively to ensure business continuity, prevent layoffs and protect vulnerable workers. We should have no doubt that the decisions they take today will determine the health of our societies and economies for years to come.

Unprecedented, expansionary fiscal and monetary policies are essential to prevent the current headlong downturn from becoming a prolonged recession. We must make sure that people have enough money in their pockets to make it to the end of the week — and the next. This means ensuring that enterprises — the source of income for millions of workers — can remain afloat during the sharp downturn and so are positioned to restart as soon as conditions allow. In particular, tailored measures will be needed for the most vulnerable workers, including the self-employed, part-time workers and those in temporary employment, who may not qualify for unemployment or health insurance and who are harder to reach.

As governments try to flatten the upward curve of infection, we need special measures to protect the millions of health and care workers (most of them women) who risk their own health for us every day. Truckers and seafarers, who deliver medical equipment and other essentials, must be adequately protected. Teleworking offers new opportunities for workers to keep working, and employers to continue their businesses through the crisis. However, workers must be able to negotiate these arrangements so that they retain balance with other responsibilities, such as caring for children, the sick or the elderly, and of course themselves.

Many countries have already introduced unprecedented stimulus packages to protect their societies and economies and keep cash flowing to workers and businesses. To maximise the effectiveness of those measures it is essential for governments to work with employers' organizations and trade unions to come up with practical solutions, which keep people safe and to protect jobs.

These measures include income support, wage subsidies and temporary layoff grants for those in more formal jobs, tax credits for the self-employed, and financial support for businesses.

But as well as strong domestic measures, decisive multilateral action must be a key stone of a global response to a global enemy. The G20's virtual Extraordinary Summit on the Covid-19 response on March 26 is an opportunity to get this coordinated response going.

In these most difficult of times, I recall a principle set out in the ILO's Constitution: Poverty anywhere remains a threat to prosperity everywhere. It reminds us that, in years to come, the effectiveness of our response to this existential threat may be judged not just by the scale and speed of the cash injections, or whether the recovery curve is flat or steep, but by what we did for the most vulnerable among us.

March 26, 2020

The author is director-general of International Labour Organization.

Afterword

The Editorial/Opinion department of China Daily and its website dedicate this book to those who lost their loved ones to the novel coronavirus outbreak, and to the medical personnel who fought on the front line against the epidemic.

This book is indebted to the contributions of journalists from China Daily and other media organizations who rushed to Wuhan without caring for their own safety to report from the epicenter of the outbreak in China.

The book is a compilation of China Daily editorials, and commentaries by scholars and other experts which represent the authors' own views and don't necessarily reflect those of China Daily, from the initial stage of the outbreak to mid-March. From perspectives on China's governance and the impact of the outbreak on the Chinese and global economies to the emergence of a new social phenomenon in the wake of the outbreak and China's ties with other countries, the book presents broad analyses.

Needless to say, this book is the result of the hard work of the editors, writers, and the Editorial/Opinion department during the outbreak.

We also appreciate the help from our colleagues in the Art and Photography departments of China Daily. The thought-provoking illustrations and the telling photographs have enriched the content of the book, which is a testament to China's battle to overcome a crisis.

We also appreciate the valuable advice of the editors at China Intercontinental Press, which added value to the contents of the book.

This book represents the hope that, through cooperation and coordination, the world can and will win the fight against the novel coronavirus pandemic.

图书在版编目（CIP）数据

守望相助，携手抗疫：英文 / 中国日报社编 . -- 北京：五洲传播出版社 , 2020.4
ISBN 978-7-5085-4442-7

Ⅰ.①守… Ⅱ.①中… Ⅲ.①新闻—作品集—世界—现代—英文 Ⅳ.① I15

中国版本图书馆 CIP 数据核字 (2020) 第 075801 号

守望相助 携手抗疫

Sacrifice, Toil, and Tears: China and the World in the Fight against the Pandemic
—— A compilation of China Daily's commentaries on the novel coronavirus outbreak and its impacts

总 策 划：	周树春						
学术顾问：	王 浩	孙尚武					
主 编：	邢志刚						
副 主 编：	朱 萍	宋 平	李 洋	张春燕	宋 薇		
评 论 员：	朱 渊	王 慧	黄向阳				
编辑记者：	朱启文	胡 璇	章 婷	王漪清	刘建娜	姚宇馨	潘宜萱
	王 侃	吴义学	张周项	刘 毅	布英娜	刘 夏	王 哲
	赵若宏	单学英	邓京荆	孙晓宇	陈 钰	宋婧祎	

出 版 人： 荆孝敏
责任编辑： 苏 谦
助理编辑： 高倩倩
装帧设计： 李 璐　杨 平

出版发行： 五洲传播出版社
地　　址： 北京市海淀区北三环中路 31 号生产力大楼 B 座 6 层（100088）
发行电话： （010）82005927，82007837
网　　址： http://www.cicc.org.cn　http://www.thatsbooks.com
印　　刷： 中煤（北京）印务有限公司
开　　本： 787×1092　1/16
印　　张： 21
版　　次： 2020 年 5 月第 1 版第 1 次印刷
书　　号： ISBN 978-7-5085-4442-7
定　　价： 136.00 元

中宣部全国宣传文化系统文化名家暨"四个一批"人才项目

Cultural Master and "Four Batches of Talents" Program of the Publicity Department of the CPC Central Committee